PRAISE FOR VICTORIA DALPE

"Anne Rice for the post-Twilight age."

— GEMMA FILES, SHIRLEY JACKSON AND
SUNBURST AWARD-WINNING AUTHOR OF
EXPERIMENTAL FILM

"Hungry horror fans take note: like a box of poisoned petit fours, Dalpe's collection delights and sickens with every bite."

— MOLLY TANZER, AUTHOR OF *CREATURES OF WILL AND TEMPER*

"The sharp, pointedly-observed, disquieting stories in *Les Femmes Grotesques* live in our modern in-between spaces. After reading them, they'll take root and tendril within your own in-between spaces. There's nothing you can do about it."

— PAUL TREMBLAY, AUTHOR OF *A HEAD FULL OF GHOSTS* AND *THE PALLBEARERS*

"*Les Femmes Grotesques* is mystical, magical, and fey in the more savage sense of the word. Be it industrial-strength urban legends or cautionary occult tales, Dalpe tightly winds fresh dark skeins of weirdness around old school horror."

— LAIRD BARRON, AUTHOR OF *SWIFT TO CHASE*

"Each of the stories in this intriguing collection begins with seemingly familiar landscapes and characters, but things aren't what they seem. Dalpe's lyrical writing carries us through twists and turns that shift our assumptions of who the monsters and victims are on the journey to wonderful, unexpected endings."

— LINDA D. ADDISON, AWARD-WINNING AUTHOR, HWA LIFETIME ACHIEVEMENT AWARD RECIPIENT AND SFPA GRAND MASTER

"Women are indeed grotesque in Victoria Dalpe's astonishing debut collection, *Les Femmes Grotesques*—and they are beautiful, monstrous, strong. Equally beautiful is Dalpe's lush writing, leading her protagonists through transmutations as spectacular as the strange and beguiling worlds they move through. From the tragic to the triumphant, *Les Femmes Grotesques* is a dark and dazzling vision that may very well change you, too."

— LIVIA LLEWELLYN, AUTHOR OF *FURNACE*

"Victoria Dalpe's *Les Femmes Grotesques* is a fearsome work to behold. These dark and sensuous tales are filled with rich prose, intriguing characters and settings right out of your most gorgeous nightmares. This is an unforgettable collection you don't want to miss."

— GWENDOLYN KISTE, BRAM STOKER AWARD-WINNING AUTHOR OF *THE RUST MAIDENS* AND *RELUCTANT IMMORTALS*

"Victoria Dalpe's *Les Femmes Grotesques* is ferocious fun, a witty and bloody mixtape of folk magic and cosmic hazards set against a backdrop of modern decay."

"Victoria Dalpe's characters in *Les Femmes Grotesques* were living real lives long before being disrupted by the horrors she's dreamed up. Each is painted with prose that belies the dark oil flowing beneath their daily strifes, threatening to bubble up and consume even the towns and cities that surround them. These are not safe stories. A surprising and recommended short fiction collection."

"The modern gothic tales in Victoria Dalpe's *Les Femmes Grotesques* are steeped in shadow and ruin, her outsider protagonists reaching for a connection forever out of reach. These are old-fashioned scares elevated through deep explorations of character."

"Whether you're exploring the shadows beneath an impromptu loft apartment, attending a very unlikely support group, or venturing to an alternative take on *The Island of Dr. Moreau*, Victoria Dalpe's stories will take you down the rabbit hole. Follow them. You never know where you'll end up, but you'll also never regret the trip."

— ORRIN GREY, AUTHOR OF *HOW TO SEE GHOSTS & OTHER FIGMENTS*

LES FEMMES GROTESQUES

"The Bone Woman"- Victoria Dalpe

LES FEMMES GROTESQUES

Short Stories

VICTORIA DALPE

CL4SH

Copyright © 2022 by Victoria Dalpe

Cover by Matthew Revert

ISBN: 978-1955904230

CLASH Books

clashbooks.com

Troy, NY

For my Family

CONTENTS

🦋 I 🦋

A CREAK IN THE FLOOR,
A SLANT OF LIGHT

I f the world were sane and things in it generally existed in
some kind of sensical order, then the mammoth old door
would have been the entryway to a medieval monastery.
But the world is what it is and the imposing door was what it
was: the entry to a ramshackle old mill building. This much made
sense though: when it opened, it opened with a screech.

Out of the darkness a pale, pock-marked head with a peculiar haircut, long on one side, short in chunks on the other,
braided rat tail resting on one shoulder, peeped out. The man
squinted in the midday sun, shading his brow with his hand;
finally, he spotted the young man on the step.

"Yeah?" he asked indifferently.

The young man fidgeted, his army rucksack digging into his
shoulder. "Looking for Pete. He was supposed to meet me here?"

"Pete, huh?" The man with the haircut frowned and
scrubbed at his face, "Yeah, he was supposed to be back by now,
but he isn't. You the new guy, Charlie Hand or something?"

"Charlie Chan actually . . ." the young man said, glancing
around the cracked parking lot at the few cars, most on blocks or
half gutted. He turned to the doorway of the sprawling warehouse again. "He say when he'd be back?"

"Nope—but I can show you your room and get you settled in. C'mon." The doorway emptied and Charlie lugged his bag up the uneven granite steps and into the darkness. He was momentarily blind, for the hallway he now stood in was almost entirely black. No windows, no lights, no indication at all beside the open door and his stretched-out shadow along the floor, that it was day at all.

"This door is a bitch. C'mon this way, we're on the top floor."

He started walking, briskly, and Charlie had to hustle to keep up. Now that his eyes had adjusted, he could see a line of dim light bulbs lit along the soaring ceilings. They did little to illuminate the space though, being too small and too intermittent against the press of such persistent darkness.

The place smelled of dust and damp, of wood, and machine grease, a hundred years' worth soaked into the soft long planks the two walked along.

"So how you know Pete?" Haircut threw his hair back as he walked, the chain on his wallet swaying and clanking rhythmically.

"Went to high school together. I was looking for a change, he suggested coming down and crashing with him." Charlie looked at the occasional door, some had stenciled names, others were plastered with flyers, most were blank. They passed one with a patio set complete with an umbrella; an overflowing ashtray and a beer pyramid finished the tableau.

"We're on the third floor, but that elevator," Haircut pointed to a large industrial elevator at the end of the long hallway, that they had walked, "is unreliable, so unless you find a great couch on the street or something, I'd recommend using the stairs. Some kids got stuck in it at a party last year, but our slumlord landlord decided to try and get them out himself, 'stead of just calling 911, on accounts of this not being a residential building and all. Anyways, he tried to pry the door open, it was stuck mid-floor, and get the kids—three girls from art school—out through this tiny hole. Two got out but the last one was a bigger girl, and real claustrophobic." He paused for effect as he yanked the industrial door, revealing a much-graffitied stairwell.

"What happened to her?" Charlie asked, mouth a little dry. The stairwell was artificially bright, and the garish colors and overlapping images along the walls, combined with the sour smell of stale beer and piss, made him uncomfortable. He'd never much liked tight spaces. The fact that a huge ten-foot neon skull with *memento mori* written across it watched him from the landing the whole way up didn't help.

"Well, she got stuck, and she was freaking out, like losing her shit you know? She claimed there was *something* in there with them. Something biting her. And just as they were pulling her out . . . the janky-ass rig the landlord had used to pry the door open fell out and the doors slammed shut with her half in and half out."

"Oh, my God."

"Yeah, it was fucked, she broke her back, was screaming like nothing I have ever heard, saying something was biting at her legs inside the elevator. By the time that dickhead landlord called the cops, she'd died from internal bleeding. He made us all stay in our spaces, quiet as mice. Told the cops the girls were trespassing and the elevator had an out of order sign on it, but they used it anyway."

"But what bit her up?" Charlie asked, wishing he wasn't so curious. His guide shrugged and smirked, half his face hidden by hair, "Nothing man, nothing in there with her. She was just fucked up."

HAIRCUT WAS A LITTLE BREATHLESS, HAVING TOLD THE STORY while marching up three flights of stairs. Charlie had goosebumps, hating the feel of the hall, and the ugly paintings, hating that he had nowhere to go and that Pete was not his guide.

"Here we are, third floor." Haircut opened the door and they stepped into a slightly brighter hallway than the first floor. Along the ceiling were windows, so dusty and dingy they were impossible to see out of, but it did illuminate the space. The long hallway stretched on and on, and same as the first floor, there were many doors along each wall. Some had setups like front porches and one sported an ancient hibachi grill.

"Our space is the red door, last on right. All these spaces have names, ours is Love Canal."

"Love Canal? Like the toxic neighborhood?"

"Yup." He turned back and grinned. Charlie was trying to figure out how old his guide was, he was medium height and painfully thin, his white T-shirt hung on him, and the army pants he wore were tattered and cut off at mid-shin. His combat boots were held together with duct tape. He could have been seventeen or forty.

They reached the red door. "Home sweet home," Haircut said.

The door was indeed bright red, though a crappier paint job would be a challenge to find. There was a doormat that was very faded, but still clearly said FUCK OFF on it.

"Charming," he muttered to himself as he followed his guide in.

The smell was the first thing he noticed, heavy on animal piss and cigarettes, the second was how large the space was. The ceilings were easily twenty feet high, and the place stretched on and on, ending in huge floor to ceiling windows along the back wall. From those windows, dusty light streamed in, giving him a view of the snaking river below and the city outline in the distance.

The wooden floors were creaky and scarred. Paint splotches and deep gouges were so regular as to appear intentional. Homemade walls, most of questionable construction ability, created small rooms, more like little personal shacks or hovels, considering their appearance. One even had mismatched windows and flower boxes and a front door complete with mail slot.

"Okay so we got five people here, you'll be six. This is my

place, up there, call it the tree house." Charlie looked up following the pointed finger and was surprised to see a structure running atop another, it had a ladder on one side and a rope on the other, a bannister along the outside and it did look like a tree-house, something Swiss Family Robinson about it.

"You got Bernadette in the cottage, she's not a day person, or really a night person. Probably best to avoid her." Charlie noticed flower boxes were filled with fake flowers at her windows, and the curtains, lace in one, red gingham in another, were drawn.

"Ti lives in the workshop," Haircut pointed to a room with an open door. Inside Charlie could see a wall of assorted tools, and piles of sawdust. "He works construction so he's gone days."

"Mal is over there in the arcade. Mal, MAL!" The two men walked to the next door, which was little more than a big piece of plywood on some sort of makeshift hinge. He pushed it open and they stepped in. The room was a box, walls covered with paper, most of it stapled directly to the walls. A vintage pinball game was tucked in one corner, in another was a banged-up arcade Pac-Man. Along another wall was a TV with a video game going. The sounds were so low Charlie initially thought it was muted. In the middle of the room was a futon, covered in clothes and debris, and on it was a man playing the video game. Three cats lay on the bed with him. The room was thick with the stench of animal.

"Mal, this is Charlie, he's staying in Pete's."

Mal looked up; he was heavy, wearing pajama pants and a soiled T-shirt. His skin was very dark, his hair was bright pink, and he gave little more in way of greeting than a head nod.

"What are you playing?" Charlie asked, somewhat interested, somewhat desperate to find anyone normal in this place.

"Nothing special," Mal replied curtly. Haircut gestured they should leave.

"Welcome to Love Canal," Mal said to Charlie's back as he exited.

VICTORIA DALPE

"Pete's room is over here. The VIP lounge as we often call it."
Haircut opened the door. It was a traditional door built into a
more traditional wall, with sheetrock and an electrical outlet and
all that. The room had one of the tall windows, and it was open,
allowing fresh air in.

"I wouldn't worry too much about Mal," Haircut said once
the bedroom door was closed. "He's actually a big teddy bear
once you get to know him. But he's wary of new people, pretty
territorial about our space."

Charlie nodded and walked around the room. In one corner
was a loft bed, below it a desk and computer. Along the opposite
wall was a banged up, but still decent leather loveseat and a
wood coffee table. Another area held Pete's musical equipment.
The wall was papered with hundreds of songs and sheet music.

"Yeah, Mal's a good guy, he just doesn't leave the space, like,
ever."

Charlie turned back to his guide, eyebrows up, "Never?"

"Nope. He used to, but two years ago he got mugged bad.
Beat up, shredded up, and spent like a month in the hospital.
Don't bother asking him about it, he won't say a thing, even to
the cops. But after that, he never went outside. He orders his
food in, orders all his shit from Amazon, gets his money from a
grandma or something. I don't ask, not like he would say."

"I won't," Charlie said. He walked toward the big window
and another bed, this one a twin, with a small nightstand and
lamp. A paper dividing screen half folded up gave the austere
space a little privacy.

"That'd be your bed." Haircut pointed. Charlie went to it,
dropping his heavy bag and looking out the window.

"Great view," he said quietly, looking at the river. In the
room, on a rolling clothes rack, like drycleaners used, hung T-
shirts and jeans, a few blazers, and a much-loved leather jacket.
He'd recognize Pete's leather jacket anywhere. Below it a row of
shoes, lined up and shined like soldiers. Didn't look like Pete had
gone anywhere long term without his stuff.

6

"Pete say where he went? How long before he would be back?"

"Naw, man, he rushed out of here last night, just said that I should be here to let you in and show you around. He's been really out of sorts since he and Charla broke up; they shared the room. You know her?"

Charlie didn't like the swirl of emotions he felt at the mention of Charla. Once he was sure his voice sounded casual; he said, "No, he never mentioned her to me; he just told me he had a room for me."

"Probably for the best, she was a bitch. And she totally bounced mid-month and stiffed us on the rent. All her shit is still piled up near the door. Anyways, kitchen and bathroom are just outside your door. Think that's everything. Obviously don't eat food someone put their name on; and Bernadette is weird about toiletries so you may want to leave her toothpaste alone."

Haircut turned to go and Charlie called out to him, "you never told me your name."

"Dale, but everyone here calls me Dally."

"Thanks, Dally."

Dally closed the door after him, leaving Charlie alone in the large room. Outside the door, he could hear Dally's footsteps, then music piping in from above. *Must be in his treehouse*, Charlie thought.

After his long journey of planes, trains, and automobiles, and the sleepless night before, it felt strange to have arrived at his destination. He'd spent the last month imagining every version of his arrival, but they'd all centered on Pete: what he looked like now, how he acted. Was he different? Was he happy to see him? Did he remember that last summer?

But now Pete was gone, and Charlie sat in a room filled with his stuff instead. He tried to imagine Pete living with Dally, being friends with him, or the odiferous traumatized Mal in his soiled pajamas. Pete probably saw something Charlie didn't. It had always been that way, back when they were kids. Pete saw a lot of the good in people, even when it was hidden away and hard to find.

He looked at the music pinned to the wall. There were songs like "Hellhole," and "The Things Forgotten Remember You," and "Darkness Stares Back;" typical goth-y Pete. Charlie noticed a photo underneath some sheet music. It was the building's hallway, and at the end of it was an open elevator shaft, light glowing inside, creating a perfect white square. The longer Charlie looked at the photo, the less he liked it, the darkness too dark, the ominous maw of the elevator beckoning. He couldn't forget Dally's tale of the girl who died in that elevator. Could almost imagine her screaming that something was biting her.

Charlie turned around and took in the rest of the room. The loft-bed was made, the desk below was spotless, laptop folded up and plugged in. At least some things never change. Pete had always been fastidious. He imagined Pete sitting in his bed, with his dark mop of hair sticking up in all directions, shirtless, milky skin covered in tattoos, looking out at that great view.

He'd get to wake up with Pete every day.

CHARLIE WATCHED THE SUNSET FROM THE MASSIVE WINDOWS: thick purple clouds skating along apricot skies, cityscape below.

Then darkness, and still no Pete.

Charlie's curiosity and hunger finally dragged him from the room. He could smell cooking and followed his nose to the small ramshackle kitchen assembled from many other kitchens.

At the stove was a tall, honey-skinned man with muscled arms and only a pair of jeans on. His blond hair was pulled back in a low ponytail. He turned when Charlie came in, looked him up and down, then smiled. "Hey, new guy, name's Ti."

"Oh, hi I'm Charlie. You work construction, right?"

"I'm a carpenter actually. You hungry?" he asked gesturing with his spatula, "Making my mom's special ragout. Interested?"

The two men ate at the small scarred wooden table. Ti was handsome, he had an easy smile, and an utter lack of pretentiousness. He smelled of wood chips and sweat, and it wasn't an unpleasant smell.

"You know when Pete will be back?"

Ti shook his head, "Sorry, no, we're often on opposite schedules. I know he has a practice space down in the basement, maybe he's there? He's been there a lot lately, working on a new album. Been in the zone or whatever. Truth be told, I don't know where it is down there."

"Anyone in the space know where it is? His studio?" he asked Ti just as the door to Bernadette's cottage opened. Ti's face fell and he gestured toward her, "She'd know."

"She'd know what?" A hostile female voice asked. Charlie spun around, unsure what to expect. Bernadette was tiny, elfin both in scale and features: upturned nose, wide hazel eyes. Her hair was a shock of bleached white. She wore a kimono and flip-flops; her toenails were painted black.

"Oh hi, um my name's Charlie, I'm staying with Pete. But he wasn't here to meet me, thought maybe he was in his practice space. Maybe you could show me where that is?"

The small woman regarded him as if she'd stepped in something.

"He's not there," she finally replied.

"How do you know? Maybe he had band practice," Ti said, and she speared him with her gaze, eyes narrowed.

"I *know* he's not there, he was, but he's not now."

"So, do you know when he'll be back? I'm getting worried."

"I'd stay worried, because I don't think he *will* be back." With that, she slung on a leather jacket and marched out of the space. Charlie could only gape.

"She's crazy and she loves drama," Ti said. "She had a

thing for Pete that he never reciprocated, and she hated Charla. So, she won't be helpful."

"Do any of you guys get along?" Charlie asked, still watching the door in hopes she'd return.

Ti shrugged and opened another beer, "Bernadette, she's like a cat. You ignore her, she comes around, you pay attention to her and she swipes at you. But yeah, we're friends. We all are, really. Don't want you thinking we all hate each other. Charla was a piece of work though, a very divisive character around Love Canal. Pete was obsessed with her, he acted totally different once they started dating."

Two minutes later, a new girl came out of Dally's tree house and down the ladder. She was tall and whip thin with tight braids wound into a topknot. She nodded at Ti and Charlie, served herself and sat. Charlie watched her eat the pasta ravenously, sauce splattering the table and her cheeks. "I'm Charlie," he finally said.

"Hey, I'm Nasreen, Dally's girlfriend. You Pete's new roommate?"

"Yeah, though I haven't seen him yet. You?" After Bernadette's ominous statement about him not returning, Charlie was hoping someone in this space would be more helpful, or maybe less eccentric.

"Pete's been getting weird lately. I blame Charla," Nasreen said around a mouthful.

"It seems this ex-girlfriend was not popular," Charlie stated coolly.

"The *dead* girlfriend. They didn't break up. She was killed," Nasreen said.

"Killed?" Charlie asked, beside him Ti huffed and rolled his eyes, she glared at him.

"That was a rumor. I heard she hopped a train to Portland," Ti said.

"That was a lie, that's what they wanted people to think. That's what they always say. *Millbillies* just up and move: they have no jobs, no bank accounts, they hop from couch to couch, town to town. Charla is just one more kid that was here and is now gone, right?" Nasreen put down her fork and stared at Ti.

"Right," Ti said. This was clearly a game the two played often, they were fighting with the annoyance and affection of siblings. Charlie looked back and forth between them, finally interrupting. "Wait, who is the *they*? And what does this have to do with Pete?"

"They are what fucking killed Charla. And Pete knew. He was looking for them. But you know when you stare into the abyss, it stares back," Nasreen said, face serious.

Charlie was getting angry now. "You're just messing with me. Look I'm a little old for ghost stories, and honestly, it's pretty fucked up you're teasing me. I'm worried about my friend. If he is really in trouble we should call the cops, right?"

Ti put his hands up. "All right, all right. Nasreen stop talking nonsense. She's crazy y'know, pumped full of meds, can't even work she's so nuts. Used to start fires. And cut herself up."

"Fuck you, Ti."

"You love it, you love all the attention. You loved getting Pete all riled up and looking for ghouls and ghosts. I'm getting tired of this story that Charla didn't just dump his ass, but was murdered by monsters that live underneath the mill." Ti looked around the kitchen. "Where's Dally? He'll tell you the truth Charlie. Nasreen has a little too active an imagination."

"They are real! I've seen them. This isn't a joke and you all tease me like it is. Charla was killed; they killed her, and they ate her. What about the girl in the elevator, remember her screaming 'It's in here with me. It's biting me!' remember? There was something in there. I saw her legs when they pulled her out, and they were bit to shit. Big bites, bigger than my mouth." She pointed to her teeth, which were red with sauce, for emphasis.

"What do you think is down there, Nas?" Ti asked tiredly. Charlie was about to say that if people were going missing or possibly getting murdered then they should call the police or something. The very idea that Pete could be in danger chilled him to the core. At that moment, the corpulent Mal waddled in bringing with him the smell of cat pee and sour milk. He helped himself and eased into the chair between Charlie and Nasreen.

"You guys talking about that thing that killed Charla?"

"See! SEE?" roared Nasreen. "Tell them Mal, tell them *why* they killed her."

"She took a picture of them. Eating some club kid in an alley," Mal said matter of fact as he ate.

"Exactly. They come out at night to hunt. Some sewer drains out back. And Charla took their picture."

"You're telling me that Pete's ex-girlfriend had a photo of monsters eating someone and didn't show everyone?" Ti said doubtfully. "Did any of you guys see the actual picture — hmm? No. That is why this is all bullshit, Charlie. If any of these guys had real jobs, or real problems, they wouldn't be on this conspiracy bullshit train."

"Pete told me he had the negatives down in his practice space," Mal said as he rose and rinsed his plate and set it in sink. "I never asked to see them. I don't need to see them to know it's true." He raised his arm up and pulled back his T-shirt sleeve to reveal an armful of deep slashing scars.

"Mal! Come on, you gonna' tell this poor new guy that you were attacked by monsters that live under the Mill? Seriously, that is so fucked up." To Charlie Ti said, "He was *mugged* is all."

"He wasn't just mugged," Nasreen said, crossing her arms over her chest. "If you would just open your eyes and believe us, Ti."

"Not good enough guys, sorry. This hazing ritual is just messed up. He's fine, Charlie. These guys are just taking a joke too far." He gave Charlie's bicep a companionable squeeze.

Mal, strangely unfazed, looked at Charlie, "If Pete didn't come back maybe they got him too. There are things out there, and they don't like people knowing about them or talking about them." With that he walked out of the room.

Ti rose and sighed, "Charlie, Pete's probably just in his practice space." He turned to Nasreen, "Can you take Charlie down to see if he's there? I got to go, have that party to go to."

"Oh, *that* party. Tell Bonnie to pay me back that fifty dollars she owes me, or she can go fuck herself!" Nasreen hollered as Ti walked away. He spun half around and winked.

"You can tell her that yourself, now stop scaring the new guy." He smiled at Charlie.

"I'm not," she huffed and rested her head on her fist. Around this time Dally strode in, opened the fridge, and retrieved a beer. He chugged half of it, belched loudly, before taking in the scene.

"Still no Pete huh?" he said.

"Your girlfriend thinks he and Charla were eaten by monsters that live in the basement," Charlie replied.

Dally's face went stony and he sighed. "We've talked about this, Nasreen. It's a fun story, and plenty of weird stuff happens around here, but it's not ghouls or whatever you think it is."

"Stop just stop. We keep going around and around. That chick in the elevator last year, something bit her legs. Mal was ripped up, bitten, and scratched by a pack of them."

"When did he start talking about his attack?" Dally said incredulous, lighting a cigarette.

"When he thought someone would believe him. What about Quinn? Remember Pete's bandmate? He left all his stuff, even his wallet. Do you think he jumped a train without his wallet? Or what about the PitRats?"

Dally breathed out a plume of smoke, "Their van broke down, it was an ancient old thing."

Nasreen took Charlie's forearm, her hand hot, "Listen to this. A local band, the PitRats, were going on an East Coast tour— they left, but never showed at their first gig. Their van was found like three blocks from here in an alley, hood up, doors open, all their gear still inside, but they were nowhere to be found."

Charlie looked back and forth between the couple.

"It does sound like a lot of people have run into trouble," he said, trying not to freak out.

"Because it's a bad neighborhood! Not because there are monsters. Just assholes. There are a lot of junkies, homeless, illegal brothels. And the mental hospital, when its funding was cut, half those nutbags are out wandering around as well. There are plenty of human monsters Nas, you don't need to make more shit up." Dally pulled her up out of her chair. "We got to go anyways, got a show remember?"

"Fine. Yeah, you want to come, uh what was your name again?"

"Charlie," he and Dally said at the same time.

"You should come with us, should be some good bands. Meet some folks, get out of the space for a bit. Pete'll be back by the time you get back," Dally said, eyes sympathetic. Charlie shook his head.

"Can you just show me his practice space before you go?" Charlie asked.

"We're kind of late, but it's not hard to find. Down in the basement level, think its number one oh three or something. Got a screen print of a pink rat on the door. But you should just wait up here, best not to go wandering around down there at night." Dally rolled his eyes at Nasreen, "In case the ghoulies get you."

Charlie forced a laugh, "Thanks, guys, well, have fun."

They left, leaving Charlie with more questions than answers.

HE TRIED TO WATCH A MOVIE ON HIS LAPTOP, HE TRIED TO read, then he scoured his phone for anyone he could talk to about Pete but came up empty. He didn't really have a lot of friends—hell, he and Pete were barely friends. Not since high school had they really hung out together. He was spacing out, staring out the window when a light knocking on the door startled him. Bernadette peeped her head in, "I'll take you to Pete. If you want."

The hallways at night were not much different than during the day. The shadows felt like they had more weight to them. Occasionally, from behind a door, there would be music or voices. These small signs of life happening behind closed doors did little to alleviate Charlie's dread.

Bernadette still wore a kimono, it fluttered behind her. Though her legs were short, she moved at a breakneck pace and Charlie found himself nearly jogging to keep up.

"I've lived here the longest. Unlike all these art school faggots, I was born in this neighborhood. Oh—no offense."

"Offense?" Charlie said, feeling a trill of panic in his throat.

"About the faggot thing, I gotta watch my mouth."

"Why do you think I'm . . ."

"Pete. He said you were this little gay boy who'd *loved* him in high school. But that you were cool, and a talented writer. Whatever, either way, apologies." She sped ahead.

Little gay boy? Charlie's vision blurred for a second, anger and worry braided themselves in his chest. The idea that Pete thought he was a joke, that Pete had told them all about him. It hurt. When they reached the graffitied stairway and that glowing skull he felt the same anxious sensation as the first time.

"I don't like it in here," he said quietly as he gripped the bannister with sweat slicked hands. Opposite the skull, he noticed an oversized painted dragon watched him. It had a line of teats and at each a monkey thing suckled. Had he seen this image on the way up to the Love Canal? The paint looked much crisper as he passed it. Each individual scale seemed to glisten and move along the hundreds of tags and scribbles, like a tiger camouflaged by the jungle.

"Come on, keep up!"

They passed the first-floor entrance he'd come in earlier that day, what now felt like a hundred years ago, and down a grubbier flight of darker stairs. The miasma of buzzing fluorescent light, and swirling ugly imagery made Charlie nauseous. He stopped and squeezed his eyes shut, a pinwheel of vertigo nearly causing him to tumble down the last flight of stairs.

"Dizzy? They do that, to make people avoid it down here— too close to their nest. There are sigils hidden under the paint. To warn you away. The other guys claim it's just a fucking gas leak. A gas leak? Carbon monoxide? If that were true, why the fuck are we living three floors up and not running out screaming before we explode or die?" Bernadette motioned him on. "C'mon, not far now."

She pulled open a rough wooden door, covered in peeling paint. On the other side of the door Charlie's first thought was how dark it was, an absolute velvet black that caused his brain to misfire, projecting images of fireworks. The second thought, once Bernadette flicked the light switch on, was that it stank.

The concrete floors were slimy, and he saw little shallow puddles of standing water. The occasional bank of murky light showed moldy drywall, and a line of doors. At the end of the corridor was what appeared to be an elevator shaft.

Halfway down, Bernadette stopped at a door. It had a pink rat stenciled on it. Pete's.

She knocked, hollered, and kicked. When there was no answer from inside, she tried the door, it was locked. She fished around in her pocket and pulled out a set of keys. "For emergencies," she said.

The small damp room was little more than a cell. One wall was crumbling stone and cement with a shuttered window on rusty hinges. Everything inside was trashed. Sheet music littered the floor. The walls were bare, save strips of things that had been torn off and still clung, fluttering as they passed. Pete's speaker was smashed, his drum set overturned, a few of the drums punched through as if someone had stomped on them.

"You see," she said with a victorious smile, her eyes shining brightly, too bright. Charlie felt certain in that moment that this woman was mad. As if reading his mind, she said, "They got him."

He took in the destruction of his friend's space, feeling sick.

In the room along the back wall, there was a large metal storage locker. Both doors were wrenched open, the metal crumpled as if it were paper. But strangely, had been reclosed. He pried them open, and his stomach dropped as he stared into the ruin. There was a hole torn through the sheet metal back of the locker, revealing a crater in the crumbling wall that went down and down into the darkness.

"Holy shit." His mouth went dry. "Did something come in this way?"

"Yeah," Bernadette said, standing next to him and staring at the chasm, "looks like they found a way in. See, Pete was dumb, Charla was dumb. They had big mouths."

Charlie wanted to ignore the splash of red along the wall. It didn't look like paint. Worse still, when he looked down, was the footprint that didn't entirely look like a foot.

"They like people to talk about them, they love rumors, but they don't want stone-cold proof floating around."

"How do you know all this? I'm calling the cops. This is crazy, Pete could be hurt or in danger." Charlie's hands trembled as he pulled out his phone. No bars.

"They don't like to be seen," Bernadette said, arms crossed casually as she leaned against the closed door. The doorway to the hallway.

"How do you all seem to know so much?" he whispered.

"The others? They only think they know. Nasreen is just telling stories her old Persian Grandpappy passed down. I told you, I was *born* here, I'm from the neighborhood."

Charlie noticed she was blocking the doorway.

"And as much as I tease them, I like all these transient art school kids wandering around. Fresh meat."

Charlie glanced around him for some sort of weapon, he wasn't a big guy, but she was tiny.

"Truth be told," she continued, watching him, "I told Charla where to find them, on accounts of her being so curious, and because I fucking hated her. But, she was a fool to take pictures and give them to Pete. Pete was an idiot to store her negatives here, in that cabinet, just a few feet from their nests." She grinned, her hazel eyes bright. "And now you, the last loose end."

Charlie backed away from her, his back to the cabinet. That is, until a rustling from behind caused him to jump and turn, peering into the darkness. He could see nothing in the hole, but every sense screamed something watched him from the blackness. Then, before his eyes, the shadows turned into shapes — shapes with sharp teeth, and eyes only for him. Charlie heard the door open behind him, knew Bernadette was leaving him, but he couldn't pull his eyes away from the hole.

His last thought, as the creatures emerged: "Hey, at least I solved the mystery. I know where Pete went."

And then they were on him.

🦎 2 🦎

THE RIDER

She'd dreamt she'd died.

The details, like how exactly it happened, she couldn't remember. She just knew that it *had* happened.

And then, worse, in the morning, she wasn't certain that she'd ever woken up. In fact, from that morning on through the days and weeks that followed, she never felt that she had woken up. Strangely though, she adapted to this new dream-state and lived as if she was a ghost. She was seen but overlooked, heard but often misunderstood. Almost invisible. *Almost.* She could be touched, but the sensation never sunk past her outer clothes or skin. Numb and growing number all the time. And cold, always a little cold. She imagined the sensation was akin to freezing to death, a slow creep into the void. First devouring fingertips and toes, then up the limbs, till that chill got to the heart, freezing it mid-thump into a hard rock.

It wasn't until Andy, short for Andrea, was riding the bus to work one day, a few weeks into this dream-state, that something changed. She had headphones on, though what song played she couldn't say, she wasn't so much listening to music as she was not listening to anything else. She held a book in her lap and read the same line at the top of the page easily a hundred times. Since she'd "died" her morning routine had been like this. Waking as if still dreaming, tired no matter how much sleep she'd had the night before, her coffee barely denting the sensation of treading through water. She'd ride the bus, she'd get to work, she'd sit until it was time to go home. Then back on the bus, home, and bed. Over and over.

Suddenly, the bus lurched, the brakes squealed and everyone fell into each other. Those standing pitched forward, tripping over the seated passengers' legs and rolling into the narrow aisles. Bags toppled, purses emptied. Andy noticed a metallic tube of lipstick, resembling a bullet's casing, roll by her feet. When the bus stopped, there was a moment of confused silence. She was fine, having been packed in tight between two sizeable people. Other passengers were helping those on the floor, gathering their things, all had a dazed look about them. Outside the bus there was yelling and crying, a siren could be heard farther out. Andy took it all in, interested, mainly because it was something different than usual. She wasn't scared though and knew she should be. She gnawed her lip, trying to find some life inside of her, some fear of death or injury. *Was she suicidal then?* That was when she noticed the petite woman across the aisle was staring directly at her with wide crazy eyes and a funny quirk to her mouth. Not a smile, but close. The eye contact lasted long enough to be uncomfortable and Andy blinked first.

At that moment, the bus driver, who'd run outside, came back in with a police officer. The bus driver was ashen, his eyes red-rimmed. The cop called out, "Everyone okay here? Anyone need medical attention?" Someone toward the front waved and Andy could see an old woman cradling her arm. "Okay, folks stay put, I'll send EMTs in then we will get your statements and get you on your way. Call work, make your arrangements, this may take a little while. Thanks."

The bus driver mopped his face with a handkerchief and followed the cop back out the door. Through the bus's windshield, it took a moment for Andy to understand the smear of red on the ground. She watched an EMT tend to a woman on a stretcher, her body broken and her pale dress soaked with blood. Andy saw the moment they zipped up the body bag. She saw white dress and red blood turned to black vinyl. As if he could sense it, the medic looked up and met her eyes. His expression was stoic, but his eyes were sad. Then he turned away and began rolling the gurney. Movement beside her pulled her attention back into the bus. The strange woman from across the aisle was now sitting beside her, same intense stare, same quirked lip, now inches from her face.

"What?" Andy said, whispering, though she wasn't sure why she kept her voice low.

"I needed to get closer, to you, to tell for sure, but now I know."

"Know what?" Andy said, mouth going dry, this woman was clearly off, possibly deranged. Though her clothes looked clean and normal and in any other situation, she would be considered pretty, her eyes were crazy. They were large and a deep chocolate brown, almost black, the darkness of them swallowed the pupil and made her look like a shark, or a rodent.

"*You're like me*. I wasn't sure, but you are, I can tell." And then, without warning, she reached out and touched the skin on Andy's chest, above the neckline of her shirt and just below the clavicle. She used two fingers, like the blessing of a priest. It was the first touch Andy had felt, truly felt in a long time. The woman from across the aisle had cold fingers. Her touch was so cold it burned. But the sensation wasn't unpleasant, it was more startling than anything. As she'd *felt* so little of anything for so long. Andy came to her senses and knocked the woman's hand away, not hard, but forceful enough to show intent.

"I know how it is, to just exist. You're new to this aren't you?" the woman said.

"To what? What are you talking about?" Andy said. But a part of her knew what the woman referred to. That she was dead inside. All this time she thought of it as a deep depression, this persistent feeling of being dead. But a stranger had seen her and knew, not just knew but saw a shared affliction.

"I'll tell you, but not here, come on." The woman stood, slung her purse onto her shoulder and stuck her hand out to Andy. Outside it had started raining. The lights of the emergency vehicles lit the drops on the windows up like rubies.

Andy stood without taking her hand, "What about our statements? They aren't going to let us just leave an accident."

The woman turned back to Andy, piercing her through with those nearly-black eyes, "They aren't going to *let us* do anything. They don't even matter. You'll see." Before Andy could protest further the woman had grabbed Andy's wrist (that grip, solid and ice-fire like before) and marched past the other commuters, down the steps and out onto the rainy street.

Then without much ado, the woman just started walking away.

Andy took in the scene, the blood on the grille of the bus, a chunk of hair fluttering there. She saw a crushed stroller, looked for a baby. The bus driver wept on the curb. The crowd watched on the other side of the barrier, seemingly indifferent to the cold misting rain. Andy felt the twin sensations of wanting to see the horrors and not, like a child peeping through covered eyes. Then the yank at her sleeve by the woman and she was off down the street. The police officer finally noticed them, a small woman with dark skin who looked barely old enough to drink. She called out and came to them. "Ladies! We'll need your statements, please, stay on the bus."

All it took was the dark-eyed woman catching her eye and the policewoman's face fell, blank as a mannequin. The woman dragged Andy, still staring at the unresponsive cop, down the street, past the barricades, and away.

"How did you do that? She looked hypnotized," Andy said, breathless, confused and exhilarated. The accident, the stranger, and now the world, unfolding into an unfamiliar pattern. There was something exciting in the surreal quality her day had taken.

It felt good to feel excited, to feel anything frankly. "Where are we going?" Andy asked after they'd walked quite a few blocks and the rain had gone from sprinkle to deluge. The woman turned, her chin-length brown hair plastered to her wet face. Her lips had a blue tinge. The rain sluiced down Andy's collar, ice cold. Her feet were numb and squelched with each step. It had been some time since she'd been so uncomfortable and like the excitement, the novelty of it was most likely why she kept following.

"Not far now, Andy. Just a little further." She smiled. The woman had very white teeth, small and spaced apart like the milk teeth of a young child. A shiver snaked up Andy's spine, from the cold, from the woman's odd teeth, from the fact that she knew her name. A name she'd never given. Two or three blocks further and they reached an alleyway. The rain hadn't let up for a moment and the visibility was so poor Andy could barely see two steps in front of her, let alone orient herself and find a street sign or landmark to help her. She followed the woman into the alley, feeling both terrified and curious by the prospect of what came next. Even fantastical scenarios like organ harvesters and human trafficking held an illicit thrill, not that she wanted either of those horrible things to befall her, but she loved feeling something. She'd felt nothing for so long that even fear felt good.

The alley dead-ended in an overflowing dumpster and a graffitied wall. There was a door without a handle. The woman knocked on it. No special knock, just the standard knock, a few seconds later the door cracked and she whispered something into the sliver of darkness inside. Andy squinted but neither saw nor heard anything from inside, the rain was too loud. The door opened and the woman went in, swallowed up by the dark. Andy took the moment to debate running away, leaving the alley, getting to work, and continuing on the way she had been. Or option two, where she followed a stranger further down a rabbit hole out of her ordinary life and into something unknown.

She stepped through.

❧

THE HALLWAY SMELLED MUSTY. THE WALLS AND DOOR WERE thick and once closed, muted the rain to a mere whisper. The hall was dimly lit by an industrial bulb on an extension cord, the walls were cement. Andy reached out and ran her fingertips along them, they were rough and dirty. The woman did not speak and after a moment Andy realized there was no one she could see ahead of them. She'd never seen whoever opened the door and the fact that they were gone now sent a zing through her.

They rounded a sharp corner and came to three doors, all drab gray metal and identical. The woman went to the furthest and opened it, as she did she caught Andy's eyes and smiled. "Welcome home, Andy."

Home. Home, Andy realized when she stepped inside, looked to be a large and mostly empty storage room. Water stained ceilings overhead and flickering fluorescents looked down on scuffed linoleum, an unlit corner had stacks of old pallets, and the other side had a few foldout tables. A circle of unfolded metal chairs was arranged in a ring in the center of the room.

"Home?" Andy said her voice a mixture of disbelief and disappointment. The woman only smiled and removed her wet jacket. She gestured for Andy to do the same. She did, but it was like skinning a rabbit, her coat positively glued to her body from the rain. The woman draped their coats over the pallets and the *plup, plup, plup* of them dripping on the floor was one of the few sounds in the cold room.

"Have a seat, here. The others will be coming soon. You probably have a lot of questions." The two women sat in the circle of what, Andy counted, was twelve chairs. In the center, she noticed a black circle drawn on the floor in what appeared to be Sharpie. The circle was smaller than the circle of chairs so that her feet were just at its outer edge.

"What is this? Who are you? And how did you know my

name?" Andy said, her hunger for adventure curdling to annoyance the longer they sat quietly in the dingy space. The woman slicked her hair back and squeezed out the extra water on the floor beside her, a gesture more common at the beach than an abandoned warehouse or whatever this place was. She was clearly in no rush to answer Andy's questions, nor did she seem deliberately provocative. She just wasn't in a hurry. Andy got the impression that this woman, whoever she was, wasn't one to take orders. Only after she'd wrung out her hair and shucked off her low-heeled pumps and trouser socks, spreading pale pruned toes, did she answer.

"My name is Melora, and I'm like you. We are the same. All of us," and she nodded to the empty chairs, "We are the same. A tribe. Rare and valuable. I'm happy to have found you. As the others will be."

"And what are *we*? What is this lost tribe?" Andy asked, the words feeling ridiculous in her mouth. Was she merely indulging a delusional woman's fantasies? With a shock Andy realized she didn't care whether the adventure was real or in Melora's head. What did she have to lose? She'd felt more in one morning than the last few weeks combined.

Melora paused, chewing her lip, "It's different for all of us. But you probably experienced something, some moment, where you ceased to be the person you've always been. Like suddenly, someone turned the volume on your life all the way down."

"I dreamt I was dead, that I died in my sleep. That no one knew or noticed. And when I woke I still felt dead. I have ever since, it's like the dream never ended." Melora's eyes lit up and she smiled revealing those unsettling baby teeth again.

"Yes. That was the moment you left being one of them and became one of us."

"And what exactly are you? Since I thought it was called being 'clinically depressed' all this time." Andy's joke fell flat and she regretted even trying to make it.

"*You did die.* Or rather, a part of you died, let's call it your human soul, it died. And you've been living, or existing, as a husk ever since. Like you are a reverse ghost, a body but no spirit."

"A reverse ghost? And you are like that too? Your tribe are a bunch of. . . zombies?"

Melora shook her head the way a scolding mother would, "You aren't very funny, Andy. I think it better you just be honest and stop making jokes. No, we aren't zombies. We experienced a spirit death. Most stay in that state, the one you are in now, and can't transcend if there isn't a guide to take them through."

"Into what?" Andy asked.

"Into what comes next. You have a hole in you, your spirit died, and we need to fill that void with something else. Or rather, someone else." Melora reached out and took Andy's hand and the twin sensation of burning and freezing mingled on her skin. "I'm sure you want to ask the next question."

Andy swallowed, trying to wrap her head around it all, "Who?"

☙❧

IT WAS STRANGE EATING PIZZA AND DRINKING CHEAP WHITE wine out of a paper cup with the other members of the "tribe". As she and Melora chatted, the others slowly made their way in. They had brought the pizza and boxed wine. Andy had a hard time understanding this group or what it all meant. As absurd as it sounded, Andy did believe Melora that she'd died that night, or something in her had. She had felt the sensation of barely existing in all the time since. She wasn't even sad enough to be sad most of the time, or to care if she were in danger, or be suspicious of following a stranger out of a crime scene to parts unknown.

Now the others were there. The tribe. There was little to unify them as a group. They all looked different, various ages and backgrounds represented. There was even a child, which

Andy found a little shocking. The child was a small stout Asian boy with thick coke-bottle glasses who couldn't be older than ten. She knew she was staring, but she couldn't help it. He came up to her and stuck out a hand, fingers still chubby with baby fat.

"Name is Drake, or this body's name was Drake. *We* are Centurion."

"Centurion is our leader, or as close to one as we have, as there isn't much need for hierarchy here," Melora said as she sipped her wine.

The group had twelve members, one for each chair. They had to drag a thirteenth over because Andy was there. They ate and chatted quietly with each other, all sparing her their curious looks, and with time each individually or in pairs came to introduce themselves. Andy was not good with names normally, but this group she pressed into her mind like a stamp.

Centurion, the boy leader. Melora, small teeth and dark crazy eyes. Then there was Xavier who was round and milk-pale with a shaved head, and Neve who was his opposite, head shorn as well, but tall and whip-thin with the darkest skin Andy had ever seen. They held hands and seemed to be a couple. There was Thierry, who had a gray beard and only one eye, the other a cluster of scar tissue, and Mark, who was a lanky teen with long brown hair that hung in his face. Liz with copper skin and platinum hair, she wore a glinting septum piercing and a vampy Marilyn Monroe dress. Dolores was a stooped old woman with an elaborate bouffant wig. Damien, a classic goth type with dyed black hair and eyeliner, whose appearance she found most incongruous. Andy couldn't put her finger on why, but when he sat beside her, his talismans clanking, his patent boots creaking, he felt like someone wearing a costume.

"Welcome, Andy. It's so nice to meet another member of our tribe. I know how lonely it can be out there." Then he patted her hand and it was an almost fatherly, or even grandfatherly, gesture. She watched him walk toward the pizza, curious. Candy was next, she had huge boobs, an inch of makeup covering bad skin and tons of hair extensions. While she was dressed like a stripper and a cheap one at that, no one seemed to bat an eye. Candy reached out a hand with long sparkly blue nails and Andy shook it warily, but while garish, the woman was kind and soft spoken. The twins were next, Zora and Zoe. They were in their early twenties with straight brown hair, and they moved and acted like mirror reflections. And last, because he was late, was Darren. Darren was tall, dusky skin, muscular under his flannel and jeans, and had a mop of black hair. He was strikingly handsome and when he came to introduce himself, Andy felt a flutter in her gut she thought was long dead.

"Welcome fellow Rider."

"Rider?" Andy replied confused.

He brushed his damp hair back and smiled at her, like something out of a romance novel cover, "Guess we haven't covered that yet. Yes, we are all Riders. Empty vessels that can share our bodies with those who want to walk this earth but can't for one reason or another. Make sense?"

She laughed and it surprised her to do so, it had been so long, "No, that makes no sense I'm afraid." He patted her shoulder and she could feel his hand through the thin fabric of her blouse, ice cold and burning. "It will all make sense soon, Centurion is a good teacher and guide." The boy nodded, graciously, in thanks.

"Now that introductions have been done, let's finish eating and get down to it. I'm sure Andy has a thousand questions," Melora said. Andy looked at the group, trying to sense anything about them besides that they were all so different from one another. Did she feel any sort of kinship? If this was a scam, what was it? Was this all a much longer, stranger dream? She wasn't sure. She'd said earlier that she felt her dream had never ended, that she was still dreaming. Perhaps that was true.

Centurion stepped into the center of the circle. Everyone instantly stilled and turned to him. While he looked like a boy, when he spoke the idea that he was a child instantly vanished.

His body language and voice were that of someone quite dignified and much older. "Now that we've had introductions and some lunch I think we should start. Welcome Andy. I do mean that from the bottom of my heart, as Riders are a rare breed. Too often they go undiscovered and end up in institutions or taking their own lives before being brought to one of our enclaves. I'm happy that Melora found you." He and then the entire group bowed their heads in welcome. Andy sat ramrod straight, hands in her lap, unsure what it was that she was supposed to be doing in return. It was only when she caught Darren's eye and his welcoming smile, that she relaxed.

"Riders have the rare ability to take on another in their own bodies. Negative and misrepresented examples would be those who are possessed. You've seen *The Exorcist* I presume?" Centurion crooked one eyebrow up and waited for Andy's response. "Good. Yes, so if a Rider was unaware of their ability and left themselves open and unoccupied, entities can take advantage and come in, in a way that essentially hijacks the body. A possession. But I don't want to scare you. And that scenario is very rare. I just wanted to start on common ground. To show that you may be more familiar with Riders than you think. Moving on."

Centurion described a secret society that had existed for centuries, a group of individuals able to share their bodies and lives with other entities.

"These entities, that you are talking about, are they ghosts? Or demons?" Andy said.

"All kinds," he answered flatly, and Andy had to wonder about demons being real. But Centurion continued before she could ask more. "And many are entities from other worlds and planes of existence, travelers who cannot bring their physical bodies into this world. We allow them entrance into our bodies to learn and explore and we in turn learn from them. There is no more intimate coupling in the known universes, than to share your body with another, on the inside."

"It's like a marriage," Melora said with a smile.

"Do any of you have. . . someone with you right now?" A small ripple of laughter followed, causing Andy to frown. "We *all* have someone with us. All but you," Centurion said.

Andy looked quickly from face to face, trying to understand any of this, wondering again if this was an elaborate and bizarre hoax. To what end? No one was trying to get a credit card number from her. Centurion continued, "This boy, the body I inhabit, was a Rider nearly from birth. He was so empty that he was labeled severely disabled, unable to speak or walk. I'm an immortal entity, formless here in your world, and so I decided to move into the boy and settle in for his lifetime. There was so little soul inside him that my occupation caused his to vacate, besides the barest of whispers. I am the exception. All others here have a more balanced coupling."

"How can you expect me to believe any of this? It's absurd! That you are some immortal creature from another world?" Andy said. Centurion cocked his head to the side, his pose was decidedly unchildlike as he studied her. Andy squirmed under his attention.

"You think it's more likely that a ten-year-old boy hosts these meetings? That Melora just approaches strangers on buses and brings them here? We know who and what we are and we know what you are. That truth may take longer for you to reach." Centurion sat down, crossing his arms in a huffy fashion that Andy found a bit immature for a thousand-year-old alien or whatever he was. The group was silent, avoiding her eyes, and it was clear that Centurion was the one who set the tone for these meetings.

"I know this all sounds crazy, Andy," Melora finally said. "But believe me it's all true. I was alone and empty for so long. In and out of hospitals, look." She lifted her wrists and pulled back her sleeve revealing zigzags of old scars. "I wanted to die. I felt dead."

"You were dead." One of the twins said and she took her sister's hand. "We all were. But now we are something more.

Oliver and I have shared my body now for three years. We have the best conversations, he was a philosopher and poet. A magician, in his time. And we teach each other and care for each other."

"Melora isn't my name," Melora said, covering her wrists again. "I was so empty that when she entered me, I let her take the lead for the first year and I just rode in the back. I let her rename us. In time, through her coaching and friendship, I've found myself and come forward."

Andy stared at each face in the circle, her mind reeling. It was all so fantastical and so bizarre and yet a part of her, the lonely depressed part, yearned for it all to be true. But if it were true and she was a Rider, did she get to choose who went in or kick them out?

"How? How does this all work? How do you pick who you get, or do you? Or is it just whatever ghost is floating around?"

"You—" Centurion cleared his throat, interrupting handsome Darren, who closed his mouth and sat back in his chair.

"This circle here, is a basic summoning system that brings attention to a vessel looking for an inhabitant. Think of it like fishing, you are the worm, the hook, the spirits are the fish."

"Do I have to? Can I chose who it is?"

"In a way, this is a partnership between two beings. And, if you do not summon one, you have few options besides succumbing to the slow and cruel death of a body that has lost its spirit. Or an involuntary possession, which is like rape. You've been a shadow, living a lie, yes? Don't you want that to end?" Centurion pushed on, not allowing space for her to answer, "Step into the circle and become whole."

Andy stared at the circle, it was still just black marker on old linoleum tile. She could feel their eyes on her, anticipatory. The circle wasn't the issue as much as the reality that no one knew where she was, and these people clearly believed in magic circles. As silly as all seemed, she inched her feet back from the circle. Thinking back, she'd never even let so much as a toe into the circle, instead choosing to walk around it. She'd avoided it for reasons she couldn't name. And now they wanted her to just jump inside and let someone move into her body.

"It seems a little fast, no? Don't I get some time to think it over and decide?"

"Centurion, maybe Andy is right and we are rushing her. Can we at least give her a few minutes?" Darren said. "We all forget, but we've all been here. It's a lot. We are expecting a lot of trust." The group watched their small leader and although he clearly disagreed, he finally gave a curt nod. Andy released a breath she hadn't realized she'd been holding. Darren stood and walked over to her, crossing the circle on the floor without hesitation. Even seeing that, Andy kept her feet tucked tightly under the chair, as far from the line as possible.

"Take a walk with me, please?" He held his hand out, like a prince in a fairytale movie, and she let her hand slide in, cold skin against cold skin. Safe and secure. Andy could feel everyone's eyes on her back as he led her away from the circle and out the door. It was only once they were in the hallway that some of the tension bundled at the back of her neck released.

"He can be intense, but he's really a good guy. Well, for as much as he is a guy."

"What is he, really, an alien?" Darren glanced back at the door they came from and shrugged.

"I suppose you could say alien. A traveler of worlds. He's seen so much, experienced other planets, other creatures. He's truly amazing, if you give him a chance. If you give us a chance." Andy hugged herself, still cold and wet and wondering if she would ever be warm or whole again. She realized she hadn't been warm since the dream that she died.

"Are you cold and numb all the time too?" She asked.

"I was, before, when I was empty. I don't feel it now." He lifted her chin and met her eyes. His were almond shaped and a soft brown with long thick lashes. "I like you Andy. I feel a connection here, don't you?"

"It's like. . . we've met before." She wanted him to kiss her and wondered at the impulse. He was a stranger after all and a possibly delusional one. But when he leaned in she mirrored him and their lips touched. His mouth was cool, even on the inside, and she wondered if hers felt the same. As much as she wanted the contact and wanted to relish the feeling of his hands along her body, it was, like everything since she died, far away. It felt like it was happening to someone else. She could feel his mouth and hands but they didn't sink past the surface. Why would they? She was dead after all. She broke the kiss, sad.

"That bad?" He teased, but she sensed no malice or hurt pride. "This is why you must let them in, otherwise you're cursed to walk around living life in gray. Alone. Feeling nothing."

"Who is in there with you?" Andy said, her hand on his chest. He paused, looking away, as he chewed the inside of his cheek.

"We have a complicated relationship. As Centurion said though, without a host spirit you are basically dead on your feet."

"Does it hurt? When they come in?"

Darren thought for a moment, clearly weighing his words, "It doesn't, but it is strange. For me it felt like someone trying to fit inside a sweater I was already wearing. Uncomfortable. But then you merge, you meet, you talk, you bond. And then, you feel again." He brushed her lips with a fingertip.

"I don't have a choice, do I?" Andy stared at the closed door and could picture them waiting on the other side for her. All of them. She wasn't sure if she meant they would never let her leave, or if her life was over either way. It didn't matter.

"You want to continue on as you are? The living dead? You don't have a soul anymore Andy, only the memory of who you were in a body that forgot to die. And there are those who are only spirit, who need a body. Become complete." Darren's cool hand was on her arm, firm. She wanted to be more scared, but if she was honest, there was so little of anything in her. He was right after all, she was dead.

"Okay."

☙❧

THEN, SHE WAS OUTSIDE THE CIRCLE, THE TRIBE AROUND HER, watching eagerly. Centurion, in all his smallness and boyishness, stepped inside of the circle and beckoned her to follow. Andy felt fear, real fear, for a moment. She believed stepping inside would do something. She met each Rider's eyes and each nodded back, and none looked afraid for her. Melora nodded and put her hand to her heart. Darren smiled wide and how she wanted to kiss him again and to feel real desire. She wanted more. She wanted to be alive again. For food to taste good and hands to touch her, to laugh, to cry, to hope.

She stepped into the circle.

Inside, the pressure was different. There was the sensation of supercharged air, like during a lightning storm. Raging winds deafened her. She could feel the hairs on her body lift, feel her heart trip as her lungs begged for more air. The Riders standing in a circle were blurry as if through fogged glass. The pressure pressed on her and she felt as if at any moment, the wind could catch her and carry her up into the air, like riding a storm. Centurion took her hands and the contact grounded her. She tried to look at him, but was unable, there was a halo of blinding light around his head, and his eyes glowed an eerie blue. This must be the true Centurion, she thought, a creature of light and energy.

"Can you feel them? How hungry they are for you? They all want you," he said, his voice all the stranger in the circle, it was layered, one-part boy, one-part something else. "Can you feel them pressing in? Fighting to get to you?"

Andy nodded, the sensation of many feather light fingertips touching her all over was unsettling and exhilarating. Tears fell from her cheeks. "Give in, surrender yourself, and the right one will come. Much like a single sperm reaching an egg." She wanted to ask *how*, but as if he could read her mind, he continued. "You're a Rider, just let go, let them in. Your body knows what to do."

She closed her eyes, getting a welcome relief from the relentless pressure and Centurion's searing light. It was as if she'd stepped into a tornado. Only Centurion's hands kept her from flying away. *I want more*, she thought to herself, *I want to feel again, I want to live again. Help me.*

Ghost fingers grabbed and pulled at her body, her clothes, her hair. Rougher now and more urgent. They probed her eyes and ears and lips. Even with her jaw locked tight, those fingers were scratching at her teeth and gums. She shook her head, trying to keep them out, but Centurion was whispering to accept them. Heart in her throat and dripping with fear sweat she eased her lips and jaw. Suddenly forceful fingers, more than fingers, what felt like an entire choking arm was in her throat and she was gagging, drowning, and something was inside of her now. It inflated her ribs, scrabbled in her lungs, it was snaking around her guts. She wanted to scream but couldn't. No air, no room to gather air. Flailing, she fell to her knees. She wanted to pull it out, but there was no way, apart from turning inside out. It was *in*. It was running around beneath her skin, exploring her. She was aware of it flipping through her mind and memories. A violation.

"Who are you?" She said, aloud, or in her head, it didn't matter anymore. She was sprawled on the floor, limbs jerking, nails scratching. Voice swallowed by the deafening wind. Andy felt corrupted by the thing inside her, keenly aware of it settling into every cell. Alarm bells clanged all over her body, the sensation was like a burglar, a trespasser, a thief: *we've been invaded.*

"Not invaded. *Welcomed*," said a voice, whispery, sexless and chittering like an insect. Out of her own mouth. The sensation of being puppeted chilled her to the bone. "You welcomed me in. And here I am."

"Who are you? What are you?" Andy said, unnerved by the

sensation of hearing her voice inside and outside. All around them the wind raged on.

"Your friend, if you let me. Your master, if you fight me."

🙦🙤

TEN MINUTES LATER, ANDY OPENED HER EYES AND STOOD, she smoothed back her hair and clothes, then surveyed those watching outside the circle.

"Any issues?" Centurion said.

"Nothing major, she has a little fight left, but it won't be a problem." Andy's hands ran all over her body. "I like this one, young. Fertile." She looked at Darren and winked.

"It's nice to see you back in this reality. I missed you," he said with a smile.

"You too, all of you. It's a shame when a body dies, hell of a time getting back to you. Tell me all that I've missed." The thing that was Andy stepped out of the circle and Darren put his arm around her, pulled her in, and they kissed deeply. Then, the Riders talked and caught up, a lovely reunion with a lost member. And all the while, deep inside, behind the smiling face, like a stowaway on a ship, was the last remnants of Andy. Able to see and hear, but do nothing. The creature that had invaded her was remarkably strong, with a will like iron. Although the body was Andy's, the thing evicted her easily. What remained was little more than a shadow of the girl that had been.

Andy wondered if she'd been duped, or just lacked the strength of will to fight. Maybe whoever was stronger won the body and the other became the Rider. However, it worked, the creature wasn't saying.

Finally, she realized what this really meant: she was to be left little more than a ghost that had forgotten to die, cursed to watch someone else live her life.

❀ 3 ❀

THE GROVE

When I was seven, I asked my mother where we go when we die. The memory is quite vivid, even down to the details: the soft touch of her fingertips as her hand cupped my face; her smile, both sweet and sad, as I looked up. At the time, she'd been sick for a while. A wasting illness that had whittled her down to skin and bone. But still she was a glamorous woman, often wearing robes and luxurious silk kimonos. She kept her long curling hair loose and wild around her face.

"When I die, I will go into the ground. I will sleep forever and my dreams will become flowers and grass and mud and beetles. My breath will become the wind. My tears the rain. And my love will be the sun that warms your skin." I remembered smiling, liking the imagery. I went off to play, my question satisfied, and if she wept as she watched me through the window, if she felt sadness for leaving me, for loving me, it was hers and hers alone.

When, a few months later, she lay on her death bed, smelling of sweet sickness, her hair was all gone. Still glamorous, her bald pate was wrapped in shining scarves. I sat by her bedside and held her hand. I remember her hands so clearly because they were rough and crooked like a bird's claws. They were not the beautiful, soft hands bedecked with rings that I'd loved. But I held them all the same. I feared the future.

"When I die, will I go into the ground to sleep as well, with you?" I asked her, voice small. The realness of her impending death sinking in the more I looked at her and I was terrified to be left alone. Her skin was taut across her skull and her lips were pulled back, revealing rapidly yellowing teeth. She looked like a monster, a mummy.

"No, my dear, not you. You will never die. You are something else, something magical and mysterious. Something I found and took with me, to raise and love. Though I realize now how selfish that was, as I've had barely seven years with you. I wanted so many more."

"I will never die?" I asked then and I remember being relieved. I didn't want to waste away like my poor mother. It was clear that every moment she spent clinging to life was a painful one. Knowing she fought the grave to spend more time with her daughter was both beautiful and anxiety causing to one so young. I hated being the reason she suffered.

"No, my dear. Your body may break or be destroyed, but then you will wake, a few miles from here, in a beautiful grove. That's where I found you years ago. I was out walking and although I've lived in this house my whole life and walked the woods out back for just as long, I became lost. I wandered for hours, until I found a grove. I stepped over a circle of bluebells and then . . . I was there. The ground was emerald green moss, soft as velvet, the trees tall and unlike any I'd seen, and hanging off a branch, in the center, was a cocoon. Papery like a wasps' nest, only iridescent like a raven's wing. I touched it and when I did, it cracked open, and inside there you were. A perfect baby. You looked up at me and I knew you were to be my daughter."

Even to a child, who still believed in the magic of the world and the monsters beneath beds, this story seemed fanciful. I recall wanting to call for the nurse, who'd been in and out, cleaning and cooking. But she was outside, getting the mail, I could see her out the window, down the long driveway.

"When you were a toddler, I foolishly answered the phone when you were in the bath." She paused to lick her dry mouth with an equally dry tongue. "I was only gone a moment, mere minutes, but when I returned you were face down, drowned and dead. I was so sad, so horribly sad. I bundled your tiny body in an afghan and, for some reason, I carried you to the woods. In my grief, I found the grove, I know it was only because it allowed me to. In the grove, another pod, bigger this time. I laid your little form on the moss and ferns and went to the pod. It opened just as it had before, and there you were, exactly as you were that day. You said 'mama' and reached for me. I thanked the grove and promised to never let anything . . ." she trailed off, both from tiredness and sadness. "I can't keep that promise, my sweet girl. And for that I am eternally sorry."

She died that night. In the morning, I was alone, and an orphan. No father was ever named on my birth certificate, so I went to live with my mother's estranged older sister a few states away. She was kind enough, in her way, and raised me as best she could. I often wanted to ask about my mother and about the strange story she'd told me before she died, but I lacked the courage. As I grew older, the mystery of the grove, of me being born out of a cocoon, became a sad story a sick woman told her daughter, to protect her from death. I even tried to find the grove, when I was old enough to drive myself. The house had been bulldozed and a sign advertised a new housing development coming soon. I wandered the woods all day but never found a magical grove surrounded by bluebells.

I tried to move past it. But it would be a lie to say I don't wonder from time to time. A car cut me off once, could have been a bad accident. Would I have died? Could I? Or had I just absorbed my sick mother's delusions all those years ago?

At my adopted mother's funeral, it was impossible to wonder

if I would ever lie in a pine box and sleep in the earth, or if I would just wake up, restored and intact, in a magic grove somewhere.

And the chilling reality was that I wouldn't know until I died. Or didn't.

❧ 4 ☙

FOLDED INTO SHADOWS

"The Tremaine House was built in 1850 by eccentric engineer and designer Gerard Tremaine and his wife Elizabeth. At the time of its construction, it was the gem of the neighborhood and no expense was spared. Stained glass, high quality wood, plaster reliefs, elaborate hand painted murals, and imported tiles and wallpapers, all contributed to make this a beautiful, classic Victorian home. Unfortunately, time and tragedy left the old house empty, to fall into disrepair, its once fine appearance and reputation becoming more unsavory with each passing year." Agnes scrunched her face at the camera. Someone hollered *cut*.

"What's the problem, Agnes?" Cheryl, the show's producer, jogged up the sidewalk towards her.

"I'm not loving this intro. It's a little dry, considering what happened to me personally don't you think? It really lacks a hook."

"You want to lead with your dead brother?" Cheryl said, not even pretending to be sympathetic; she was a producer not a therapist. Agnes flinched but pushed on, Cheryl was all business, and they were making reality television. The only thing that mattered was how it played on TV. Just the ratings.

"Yeah, I agree. Honestly Agnes, I would love to bring that angle in more if you can handle it. Let's work on some rewrites for that." She raised her eyebrows. "You want to move on for now, talk about the original murders?"

Agnes felt an itch between her shoulder blades and looked back up at the old house. She had never liked having her back to it, and this time was no different. *Original murders*, not her brother, not yet.

"You okay?" Cheryl said, eyes narrowing, watchful. They had a lot of work to do and if Agnes went crazy, the show would fall apart. Agnes needed to be on the edge, emotional, fragile, but not step off the deep end.

"Yeah, just tired. I've been working hard to get this old place fixed up, I'm feeling burnt out."

"Well, *use it*. We'll slap on a little more makeup, get that runny mascara on you, and get you out there, the grieving sister, fighting ghosts and fixing houses." Cheryl went on, "Oh, did I tell you I set up a time for a local witch to come 'round with sage and shit to do a blessing? We have the Ouija board if you want to mess around with that at all. And of course, a priest."

Agnes started walking away from the other woman, back to her mark in front of the house at the gate. "Let's get these intros done, and go from there. I don't know how much paranormal stuff I want to bring in though, Cheryl. Don't want it to be too cheesy. It *is* mostly about the renovation."

"Of course, it will all be very tasteful. Trust me."

Agnes did not trust her producer. Cheryl had that hungry glint, looking for an opportunity to get out of what she called 'housewife and shut-in TV' and onto something bigger and better. She was young and driven, she had a natural instinct for good TV. Agnes knew what she herself was doing was crazy and probably unhealthy. She knew, as she too was made from the same fame-whoring stuff as Cheryl, that restoring the house her brother died in was good TV. It would elevate her show from the millions of other "lady flipper" house shows clogging up programming. The kind of aspirational programs that deluded the bored and uncreative into thinking they could get into real estate and design in their free time. Agnes at least learned the trade from her father and worked in it with him because they'd been poor. Being a pretty lady contractor had isolated her; from men who were threatened by her and women who found her an oddity. Not that any of that mattered now, it was just the back-story that got her to the front steps of the house that stole her childhood and ruined her family. She doubted new flooring and a coat of paint would heal those wounds.

THERE WERE THREE THINGS SHE KNEW ABOUT TREMAINE House before stepping into it. First, that it was bigger on the inside than the outside. Second, that people tended to go in and never come out. Third, and most important, was that her brother was one of the ones that never came out.

Agnes felt strange standing on the corner of Sparta Street staring up at the Tremaine House. It was a looming, boxy thing, under-maintained, and big enough to blot out the low hanging sun. She'd visited the house so many times in dreams over the years. Dreams where she tried to follow Jared in. She never got past the front door, even in her subconscious.

She hadn't actually seen the house since she'd lived on Sparta Street as a kid—two houses down. Her old house was still there; a tired split level with a bike dropped on the lawn and a drooping pot of mums on the step. She thought about knocking on the door, bringing in a camera crew, filming her old room and Jared's old room. Probably still would.

But it was the Tremaine House that was the real story. The scourge and siren of scores of children. A place filled with mysteries and fables. The house that was empty and abandoned when her parents moved onto the street and had been as long as anyone could remember.

Then Jared went in, and never came out. Her mother had a nervous breakdown. They moved far away, out of state, and the Tremaine House became a memory and a recurring bad dream. She could feel the creak of wood on the porch, feel the cold metal of the door handle. Hundreds of hours of sleep she'd banked, trying to get in.

Now, she owned it. The key felt hot in her hand. She could go in anytime she wanted.

It was getting dark, and while she was now the true owner, and had every right to open the rusty front gate and walk up the crumbling walkway, all the way to the big old front door, she couldn't. Not just yet. But she couldn't leave it either. So, she stood on the safe public sidewalk, under a circle of streetlight and watched the dark windows while the shadows stretched and elongated around her into night.

❦

"I THINK YOU'RE NUTS."

Daniel, her on again/off again boyfriend had said that a few months back. "This whole idea is like, looney bin crazy, Agnes. What are you gonna prove? That ghosts are *real*?"

"Maybe. Or maybe nothing, maybe I'll just fix up and repair a blighted old house, like I've done many times before. Improve the property values in my home community. Make the world a better place."

He rolled his eyes at her; on a good day he found her ridiculous, on a bad day, intolerable.

She knew what sort of day this would be from his sour expression.

"Closure," she said finally, chin up.

"Sensationalism, and frankly Agnes, it's tacky and disrespectful to your family."

"What family? My brother and dad are dead, my mother is in a nursing home and doesn't know the day of the week. Who exactly am I disrespecting? Myself?"

"Their memory, your lineage. All for some gross five minutes of fame. It's messed up."

She shrugged, not ready to admit her real reasons. In part because she knew Daniel was right. Buying the Tremaine House, the house where her brother died, or vanished, whatever you wanted to call it, was a bit strange. She knew that filming her home remodeling show inside the house and digging into her macabre history for ratings was a little tasteless.

Still, she thought it might bring some sort of healing, and it would be nice to see the scary old house made new again. It would connect her to Jared. This was for him, and for Sparta Street and for the town of Haven, so they could move on. She told herself that over and over, choosing to believe it whether Daniel did or not.

"If you can't handle it, then dump me. For the hundredth time, if I'm that gross, then just end this and go," she said.

He didn't, not *then*, but he did get up and walk out of the room, claiming to have a hard time looking at her.

He officially dumped her a week into pre-production.

⚜

AGNES WORSHIPPED HER OLDER BROTHER. SHE WAS SMALL and bookish, *mousy*, he was tall and golden. Cool. Jared was a cool guy. Even her parents clearly preferred her older brother, but why not? He was a good student, an athlete, adventurous. Maybe too adventurous.

It was almost cliché. A dare gone awry.

The Tremaine House was the classic spook house. The remaining relic of a bygone era left to grandly decompose while split levels and ranch houses popped up around it. When Agnes was a toddler, a young woman was found mutilated in the house.

Five years later, a homeless man set himself on fire and burned up along with the back portion of the house. When Agnes was in junior high, a boy fell from an upper window and was impaled on a fencepost. He survived but lost his leg. Local gossip said he would never talk about that night and what pushed him out the window.

But all of that could be explained: the mutilated woman's killer was later apprehended for committing a similar crime in another state. The homeless person fell asleep in a drug daze and his candle tipped over. The boy who fell out of the window was drunk, and his story, what little there was, was inconsistent.

It wasn't the bodies that were found in this house that earned it its reputation, it was the ones that *weren't.*

There were many people who went in on dares or to loot the place, and never came back out. That was what Tremaine House really got famous for, the vanishings. Police scoured the property hundreds of times looking for the people who'd gone in and never come out, leaving no trace, and no evidence of foul play. With each person it swallowed up, the Tremaine House grew more infamous.

"Good evening viewers, on tonight's episode we will explore the origins of the Tremaine House's ghastly reputation. It all started when Elizabeth Tremaine and her young daughter Elsa Tremaine, vanished one night. Gerard Tremaine, the husband, insisted it was a normal evening, everyone went to bed, and in the morning, he found they were gone. No clothes missing, no money taken, the carriages and horses left in the stables. His wife and daughter were just gone. The rumor mill in the town of Haven whispered that Gerard killed his wife and daughter, or that they were kidnapped, but no ransom notes ever came, and there was no evidence that a murder was committed. Police searched the house top to bottom. They never found any sign of Elizabeth or Elsa Tremaine. At the time, the police thought that because of its unique floorplan, there must be secret doors and passages in the house, where the bodies may have been hidden. But they never found them. Gerard Tremaine eventually killed himself. He hung himself from the house's grand front staircase, leaving a note that said he wished to be with his wife and daughter *but couldn't find the right door*. Was this a confession? We'll never know. I'm Agnes Tiller, and on tonight's episode we will be giving a much-needed facelift to that macabre foyer with fresh wallpaper, repair to the stained glass, and much more!"

SHE REMEMBERED HER MOTHER CRYING AND SCREAMING. IT was summer, the air already moist and sticky even that early in the morning. Agnes came downstairs in a rush, heart hammering. She couldn't remember ever hearing such anguish before. Unfortunately, with time, she would grow used to her mother's wailing.

She found her mother on her knees, wrapped in the spiral phone cord, rocking back and forth. She sobbed pitifully, and Agnes knelt next to her on the floor.

"He's gone. He's gone. He went in that fucking house and now he's gone." She looked into her daughter's eyes with eyes that were blood red and dark-circled, wild with grief. "Jared's gone."

Jared's gone.

Agnes recoiled. "No, you're wrong. It's just some stupid prank or something. You know he loves practical jokes. That's all this is."

Her mother shook her head no. "I wanted to believe that, but your father is down at the station now, he went with the police through that entire horrible house. The only thing they found was Jared's jacket, soaked in blood."

"A jacket isn't a body."

Her mother collapsed, howling.

Agnes was right, a jacket wasn't a body. The blood-tests

eventually came back from the lab, it was Jared's blood, but they never did find a body. So, if she were in a fanciful mood, she just told herself that he ran off, snuck himself out the back door, and started a new life.

"It was supposed to be a stupid joke," Tara Remming said. She was Jared's girlfriend. "A last hurrah before we all separated and went to college in the fall." Tara, and their other friend, Dale Eichman, were the last two people to see Jared alive. "We were at a house party and got dared to go into the Tremaine House. We had to go in, touch the bannister, and then we could leave. That's what they always dare you to do at the Tremaine House. That was it." Tara shuddered. "I didn't want to go, I told them that. I told them there was something wrong with the old house, something really creepy. But they made fun of me. Somehow, they got me to go in. A window on the front porch was unlocked and so we crawled in. Dale had a lighter, but that didn't do much, so we all huddled — Jared held my hand." Her voice caught and she was quiet for a moment.

"Things got weird after that. We crossed the living room, went into the front hall and touched the bannister. I remember it was dusty and you could see other fingerprints, from other kids who'd gone in. Dale grabbed this iron door stop that looked like a cat, to take with us. Then we turned to leave, go back the way we came. But we couldn't." Tara paused, as if she were trying to recreate the room in her mind. "It was the strangest thing, it was like the room shifted when our backs were turned. Like the doorway moved to the other wall. We had left the door to the living room open, but it was closed now, or rather the wall it should have been on was gone. There was just a blank wall with flowered wallpaper. The new door opposite was closed." Tara shook her head, her voice coming faster. "We were pretty freaked out and ran to that door, but it was locked. We tried the door on the other wall, also locked. The front door was locked as well. Jared and Dale tried to break it down, but, but, they couldn't." Tara was sobbing again. "We decided to go up the main stairs, they were the only thing that hadn't changed in the room, and crawl out a second-floor window, or call for help or something. Somewhere on the stairs, we lost Dale. He was in front of us, holding the iron cat as a weapon, and using the lighter to show us the way. I was behind them, holding onto Jared's jacket. Suddenly, Jared stopped, everything went dark. Dale had the lighter, but he was gone. Jared started calling Dale's name." Tara wiped her tears off on her sleeve, her face was a mess of smeared mascara and snot. "We ran up the rest of the stairs, freaking out, calling for Dale. It was really dark, dark enough that I could only see the outlines of doorways. I begged Jared to slow down, to calm down, to whisper. I didn't feel like it was safe to be yelling, to be letting anything know we were there. There *was* something there, I know it. Watching us, like it was playing a game."

"THE KITCHEN IS REALLY COMING ALONG," AGNES SAID, appraising the work the contractors had done that day. New marble countertops, retro reproduction lights, glass-doored cabinets. It was nice, high end, a little generic, but would show well in the before and afters.

"So, I'm thinking tomorrow we can have you putting up some of the subway tile backsplash while you talk about the kitchen reno; you know, have you in a tank top showing your guns and being butch. Heavy plug for the appliances, make our sponsors proud, then we'll have you walk out of the kitchen into the foyer. You stand at the bottom of the stairs, talk about the bannister and how kids were dared to touch it, and then look up the staircase, and say the next room to tackle is the master bedroom." Cheryl paused, waiting for Agnes to respond.

"Yup. The master bedroom. Then I will say: where my brother's blood was found. In the closet."

"I have some crime scene photos we can splice in during post.

We've got a backer who'll be designing custom storage for that closet, so we'll have to figure out a way to tastefully talk about their innovative design solutions and your brother's grisly demise in the same segment. That'll take a few tries I'm sure."

"Yeah." Agnes was tired, it was a long day and the rest of the crew had gone home. But Cheryl wanted to hammer out the schedule. Agnes didn't like to be in the house, even stripped and well-lit and filled with fresh paint smells. It was probably her imagination, but she agreed with Tara Remming, it did feel like something was always watching.

It was dusk, again, it always seemed to be dusk in the Tremaine House. Or perhaps it was just her fear about being in the house at night. She'd done an entire season of *Haunted Renovations*; buffed bloody floors, patched bullet holed walls and helped remove bones from basement foundations, giving face lifts to bad houses. Except for the occasional cold patch or mystery thump or creak, it had been surprisingly unscary work. Surrounded by swearing, spitting teamsters, and contractors helped too. Hard to be scared at seven am with Molly Hatchet blaring from a spackle covered boombox. But the Tremaine House was altogether different. She felt something inside it, even if it was just the palpable loss of Jared.

"Hey, do you believe in ghosts?" Cheryl asked. "We've been doing this shit for a year, and not one of these places feels haunted to me."

"Even this one?" Agnes asked, mouth gone dry, she feared the other woman's answer. Ten houses so far, and each had something horrible happen in it, but none felt so. . . watchful. "Maybe it's just cuz it's personal for you, Agnes. I mean it's pretty fucked, being in the house your brother went missing in. And this place does have a higher count of spooky stuff than any of the others we've done. Plus, the floor plan is super weird."

"But you don't feel anything in here? Like even a bad vibe?"

Cheryl shrugged and glanced around, "Not really. It is weird how I always feel a little disoriented though, the house isn't that big, but it's like I always went the wrong way, or in the wrong door."

Agnes nodded, knowing exactly what the other woman meant. "I can never get my bearings in here. I worry that I will set my drink down and it will be across the room when I go to get it, or the window behind me will be in front of me. I misplace my tools all the time, I lost my phone the other day, found it in a room I swear I didn't go in. All the teamsters say the same thing too."

"You made sure there isn't a gas leak or something, right?" Cheryl asked, semiserious.

WHILE TALKING THEY WENT UP TO THE MASTER BEDROOM. IT was two doors down the upstairs corridor on the left. The large room was ornate. Its plaster walls were cracked: it would all need to come down. The creaky pine floors were water damaged from a roof leak, but should be salvageable. The tiled fireplace needed to be repaired. Cheryl made notes in her clipboard as Agnes walked around pointing things out to her producer.

"It was just a puddle of your brother's blood they found, right?"

"Yes." Agnes opened the door, revealing a large empty closet with busy cabbage rose wallpaper. The wooden floor was bare, and in the center was a dark stain. "That's all they ever found of Jared."

"It's not like a house could just eat someone up, so where the hell is his body?"

"Where are all the bodies? The blood was the most they ever found of anyone who went in and didn't come out. Ten people have vanished in this house. Ten *reported* people that is, who knows how many actually have gone missing," Agnes continued, closing the closet door, not wanting to look at her brother's blood any longer than she had to. It would be doctored up tomorrow to look fresh and garish for TV. She'd get plenty of time with it then.

"I don't want to freak ourselves out, but what if there was some sort of serial killer that hid in the house and snatched people up? So, not a ghost, but just some freak. Maybe squatted in the attic or basement," Cheryl said, wrapping her arms around herself.

Agnes didn't like that idea any better, but at least it would make some sense. Imagined or not, she felt the house's watchfulness intensified then. She couldn't find a position in the room where she didn't feel both exposed and vulnerable. To stop herself spinning and glancing behind her she jammed her hands in her pockets and focused on Cheryl.

"Okay, so we will start removing wallpaper tomorrow, do the scraping for repaint. Get some cool light fixtures to switch out. You decide if you want to paint or put wallpaper in here?" Cheryl was trying to bring them back to reality, but Agnes barely listened.

"People can't disappear. Just like when something is lost. It doesn't just blink out of existence, it has to be somewhere, it's just where we can't find it, right?"

Cheryl sighed. "I have no idea what you are talking about."

"They come in here, and don't come out. That must mean one of two things." Agnes raised her pointer finger, "Either someone removed them—your serial killer theory—or they are still. . ." She paused to swallow, not to be dramatic, but the effect was the same, "they are still here somewhere, like the cops said way back when."

"You think your brother's body and those nine others are still here?"

Agnes ran a hand along the wall. "Things don't disappear, those people must be somewhere. Their remains that is."

"I dunno, Agnes. We've had inspectors over every inch of this house. You've been along every wall and door, you were in the crawl spaces and attics. How could you miss a secret room full of skeletons?" Cheryl blew out a breath, "Let's call it a night. We can discuss all this shit in the morning, in daylight cuz you, Agnes, not the house, are starting to freak me out."

৩৫৩

BILL, ONE OF THE TILERS, WAS GONE.

After some plumbing held up work, he and his assistant decided to pull an all-nighter so as not to lose a day of shooting.

His assistant, Troy, left the house at approximately nine pm to go pick up some takeout. When he returned, Bill was gone. Radio was on, his mud still wet in the bucket, tiles laid out as if he had stopped mid-project. Troy looked everywhere, but there was no sign of the other man. His car was parked out front, his cell phone propped up on a window sill out of the way of the mess. But there was no sign of Bill.

Cops came out the next day. Agnes and Cheryl were there, to give statements. Cheryl had a gleam in her eye, the gleam of a producer who could smell publicity. Agnes knew if this wasn't the Tremaine House, the house that ate her brother, if this was just another haunted house for the show, she would have had the gleam too. The gleam of ratings gold. The gleam of a supernatural themed reality show having something tangible and messed up happen on set—the vanishing house had vanished a crew member. This could make their career, this could get bigger tours, book deals, huge payouts.

Instead all Agnes felt was a sour feeling in her gut. The sensation, as she explored it, numbly sitting on the stoop of the house staring at the two cops, was guilt. This was her fault. She bought the crumbling old monster for pennies, she dragged a crew and cameras to dig around in the past. Not for answers, not for closure, but for ratings.

She leaned to the side and heaved all over the dead grass.

The cops both stared, as did everyone on the crew milling around.

"We understand this is hard for you, having experienced a loss in this very house, but I have to ask again: is there any way this is a stunt? Some sort of a hoax to create buzz around your program? We have a very upset wife and two little kids who don't think this is very funny."

"Officer, please, that is a little over the top, even for TV." Cheryl had her hand on her heart. "Though it would be a good idea. But no, no of course not. Or at least not with our knowledge. I can't speak for everyone here."

"He's local, are we sure they didn't do this as a prank?" Agnes said, voice small, wanting it to be true. Her hands squeezed tight together, slick with sweat.

"We'll keep interviewing everyone and be in touch," one of the cops said, and walked away.

"Jesus, I hope this doesn't get us shut down," Cheryl muttered as she fidgeted on her phone, "since I already leaked it to the press, figured why not drum up some publicity."

Agnes set her head between her knees, hating the feeling of the house at her back. She knew Bill wasn't hiding out for a publicity stunt, she knew the house had eaten him up, like so many others. She wanted to tell Cheryl they should shut down, she wanted to tell her she never wanted to step foot in that horrible house again. Then she wanted to burn it down.

But she said nothing, picturing instead her brother Jared, smiling and fearless, lovely in the glow of nostalgia, she imagined him opening a closet, teasing his girlfriend Tara. "See? Nothing there, probably a squirrel or something."

And then he was gone as if he'd never existed. The shadows folded over him, and he was gone. No scream, nothing.

"'*The shadows folded over him,*' you know that's what my brother's girlfriend said. When he went missing."

"What?" Cheryl said, her voice vaguely annoyed.

"The shadows folded over him. *Folded.* That's such a strange word to use to describe shadows, or stepping into a dark closet, don't you think?"

"Yeah, it's weird, maybe she imagined herself to be a poet or some shit. Anyways, I got to get the tilers caught up, don't want to lose another day's worth of labor if we can avoid it."

"You're serious?"

Cheryl sighed, "Agnes, don't give me that look. I can read your mind right now. I am not a monster, but this is my job, and we are doing this spooky home reno shit for a paycheck, and a real missing person on set? That is a bigger paycheck. It is harsh, I get it, but it's also our job. So, get it together okay."

"But aren't you scared?" Agnes whispered, not wanting the crew or the house to hear.

The other woman sighed and scratched at her scalp, "it's realer than any of the others. The house is hard to look at, hard to navigate, and people apparently keep disappearing. But do I believe in ghosts? In black holes? Or whatever? No. Bill will turn up."

৩৵৵

THREE WEEKS LATER, THE HOUSE RENOVATION WAS FINISHED. Bill never came back.

Agnes walked around the entire outside and had to admit the transformation was complete and dramatic. The decrepit old Victorian was like new again. Crisp white paint, freshly washed windows, and meticulously groomed landscaping. It was a great beauty again, far from the haunted house on the corner she had known. The house had been staged and they'd filmed the final walk throughs that morning.

There was a palpable sense of relief at the wrap party, the crew and workers all a little lighter, a little happier to not have to go back again. The house looked good and this renovation would be their best season yet. They could move on, never having to think of going inside that damned place again. All of them but Agnes.

They'd had witches walk through and burn sage, talk about

the strange energies. Priests splashed holy water and mediums channeled. All the same shit as usual. Off screen, all three did say that the Tremaine house, more than most, held a strange, watchful energy.

"Not bad or good," said the medium, "like it wants something, but what it wants is unclear. It also feels like a lie, like what I see, isn't what's real. I know that is a wall, but my mind wants it to be a door, y'know?"

Agnes did know, maddeningly well, that this house was hiding itself.

The weeks after Bill vanished, she'd searched the house, tore out floor boards, put holes in every wall and closet to peek behind. She never found a hidden crawlspace or false wall. There was no physical evidence that the house was anything but what you could see. But Agnes knew it was lying. The house always whispered that there were more: more spaces, hidden doors, a different floor plan, but she never found it. The unknowing, the relentless mystery of the place, of where everyone *went*, of where Jared went, was like a rat's persistent gnawing.

There were little accidents throughout the job and a lot of misplaced tools. The workers said there was a thief stealing equipment, but Agnes knew better. Night security never reported anyone coming to or from the damn house. The neighborhood knew better.

She did go to her childhood home, allowed herself on-screen tears as she walked the halls and went into the bedrooms. Everything looked totally different without the paneling and shag rugs of her childhood. Jared's room was some other kid's room now, with sports and band posters, dirty clothes on the floor, and a guitar in the corner. Jared was gone from that space, erased everywhere but from her memories it seemed.

"You okay?" This was Cheryl, holding out a red plastic Solo cup filled with wine. They sat together on the bottom step next to the famous bannister. A memorial to her brother, something that proved he existed once. Around them, the PA's and interns were cleaning up the party, hauling out garbage bags. Usually wrap parties were long and debauched affairs, but this one wrapped as soon as the last pizza slice was eaten; no one wanted to linger in the Tremaine House. Trina, one of the PA's said good-night and closed the door. Then, the two women were alone in the house.

"I thought doing this would bring me some answers, some closure. I bet my relationship with Daniel that it would."

"Daniel was a twat," Cheryl said, sipping her wine. Her lips and teeth were stained purple.

"Yeah, he was. But he had a point. Who was this for? Fixing this house up doesn't bring my brother back, hell, it didn't even give me any more answers than I had before."

"That may be the unfortunate punch line to all of this, Agnes, there is no answer. Some mysteries you can't solve."

"How do you move on then? Never knowing."

Cheryl shook her near-empty cup, "Alcohol? Anyways, come on, let's get out of here. It's late, we're wrapped, and while I still don't believe in ghosts, I'd like to get out of this fucking house."

Agnes insisted Cheryl go without her. She said she needed to have her final goodbyes, alone. The other woman insisted, but eventually she gave up because she was just a producer and the show was over.

With Cheryl gone, Agnes was all alone in the old house. It was the first time, ever. Everyone, including the security had gone home, and the house, which had been a hive of activity for weeks, was eerily quiet. The house was empty, except for bland staged furniture, and the smell of fresh paint and polyurethane.

She ran her hand along the door frames and walls as she walked room to room. She'd been everywhere in this old house, peeped in every keyhole, and yet she still felt a little lost. She was a little drunk, a little mad, and still yearned for the secrets of Tremaine House. Of Jared.

Agnes, standing in the dark rooms, with the only light street-light filtered in through the new curtains, could feel the old house holding its breath, hiding its secrets. Like a magician, always misdirecting the eye.

She recreated the path her brother had taken; up the grand staircase, and down the hall to the master bedroom. The room had come out quite nicely. It had a king-sized four poster bed in it now. She noticed her reflection, little more than a dark outline wavering in the dresser mirror, as she entered the room. She could see her childhood home out the front window. Did Jared see their home, had he looked out and thought of her as he was folded up into the shadows?

Facing the windows, she had the unmistakable sensation of being stared at. Turning quickly, she saw the closet door was now open a few inches, enough for someone inside to spy on her. She swallowed her fear and opened the door, not entirely surprised to see the walls covered again in cabbage rose wallpaper and a set of stairs ascending upwards instead of the custom built-in closet system they'd put in. She entered the closet and began climbing the stairs. She felt only a flicker of trepidation, but this was what she'd wanted all along. The house was finally willing to share.

Up the stairs, and then she was in a hallway that looked similar to the one downstairs, but still had the old wallpaper, the old carpets over old wood floors. The hallway had many doors running along its walls. All of them were closed, except one at the end.

She glanced back and saw that the stairs she'd come up were gone. The hallway ended now in a flat wall with that same busy cabbage rose paper. The same paper that she'd steamed off feet and feet of all over the house, but it just seemed to have crept back in, like weeds, or mold.

Had Jared come down this hall? Had Bill the tiler? She wondered if she was the first to be unsurprised by the hall, or that the house had more hidden within it than could be seen. Like a twist in a Rubik's Cube. Tremaine House had geometry that other spaces simply did not.

She finally reached the open door, and even though she was soaked through with sweat, and her heart punched against her chest, she knew there was no point resisting. The doors didn't open for everyone, and she'd been chosen.

She stepped through.

And was folded into the shadows.

5

UNRAVELLING

I hated to remember. But that's how memory works, of course, it's always there, waiting and threatening to wash across you like a drowning wave.

And this memory would not die. The house, consumed in flames, the feel of the heat against my skin. . .the smoke in the air. . .the hiss and the pop of a house devoured. . .the sound of the fire itself. A roar. And of course, the brutal, agonizing human screams. And the silence that followed them. What's worse: the sound of a scream or the chilling absence that follows it?

But like I said, I don't like to remember and I tried hard not to. There is only so much trauma a head can be filled with before one goes crazy. And I often felt I was at max capacity.

Though I'd be lying if every lighter flare, every fireplace pop, every tea kettle whistle, didn't put me on edge, cover my skin in goosebumps, or steal my train of thought. How could it not? I watched everyone and everything I ever knew burn, and that is not an easy burden to carry, especially when I was the one who struck the match.

THE MAN AT THE COFFEE SHOP REGARDED ME CURIOUSLY, over the top of his laptop, his eyeglasses reflecting the screen back and making it hard to see his eyes. But I didn't need to see them to know he was watching me. I could sense it. His intense focus had plucked me from my book and sent my head up and scanning the room. It's interesting how we've adapted to know when someone watches us. I've never been able to figure out exactly how we do it, fine hairs attuned to the subtlest shifts in air, some long buried sixth sense.

I wanted to believe he was just a man who looked across the room and saw a woman he found attractive. But the paranoid part of me, the *smart* part, or perhaps the jaded part, doubted it.

When he closed his laptop and approached, standing respectfully back, he held it in front of him like a shield. He cleared his throat, "Excuse me?" he said, voice soft, careful.

I tucked a finger in my book to save my place, and met his eyes. "I don't mean to bother you, but wondered if you wouldn't mind some company?" My eyebrows ticked up of their own accord, a little curious, a little tired of people like him. Subservient. Weak.

"Fine. Sit," I replied. He smiled and pulled a chair up, the table between us small enough we knocked knees.

"I'm Charlie, and I was just so captivated by you, from across the room. And I have to ask, and if it's disrespectful please accept my apology in advance." I waved my hand to rush him along, already knowing what he would ask, and knowing what would happen next.

"Are you *her*?" He said in an excited whisper, leaning in, both arms on the table.

"You a believer?" I replied coolly. Trying to hide my utter disgust. Wanting so badly for him to just be some man who thought I was pretty and wanted to take me out for a drink. Not another one of these clowns, meddling in things they had no right to. Bothering me in ways they had no right to. If any of them took the time to actually understand me, they would know to keep their distance, they would know to let a lady read her damn book.

He'd been talking, but I'd been wading in my own thoughts. I tuned back in, he was blathering on about his teen pilgrimage. And his parents, who were true believers from the old country.

"I never thought I would meet you, especially not like this, here in the daylight, so ordinary. Like regular people."

I smiled at him, making sure my eyes were cold as a shark's. "Yes, like regular people. And what did you really hope to gain by meeting me?"

He opened his mouth and closed it. Wanting to give a good answer, a wise and memorable answer. I waited. Impatiently. "I guess I would ask you, what are you waiting for? If there were certain things you wanted set in motion for you to complete your task? If there was anything I could do to help as a true believer."

You could leave me alone, is what I wanted to say. But the stupid monkey was looking at me, eyes round and glossy with admiration, waiting for my answer.

"You still have a group you meet with? You said your parents are true believers."

"Were," he interjected, "they were, but there was a fire. Like so many others. We are being hunted and persecuted, as you know. How can we be fruitful, how can we follow your words and teachings, when we are always being cut down?"

"But you are so resilient. Like weeds squeezing out through the cracked pavement in parking lots. Like cockroaches," I said barely above a whisper.

"Exactly! Exactly, Mistress, see you understand. They can hunt us, burn us, but we are stronger than that. The cause is bigger. You are worth it." He reached across the table, to touch me, but I pulled my hands away, tucked them in my lap well away. He seemed to realize the breach in etiquette and apologized.

"You didn't answer my question? Where is your group?" I pushed, glancing around the busy coffee shop, watching suited businessmen shout into cell phones, yoga moms wrangling strollers, and an army of office-less workers staring at screens. How I yearned for such ordinary moments.

"Yes, yes, Mistress. A small, but deeply devoted one, which I'm sure you already know, I'm sure you planned on me finding you today even. Your awareness does extend so much past my own."

I rolled my eyes and forced a smile, "Oh you flatter me, truly. Now if I wanted to meet your group, all of your group, could you arrange that?"

The man's face lit up, mouth a perfect O. "That would be amazing, that would be. . . it would prove our purpose in this world." He sniffled a little sob back, "Yes, yes Mistress. Tonight, I could get everyone together tonight. I'm sure of it, last minute be damned. Here, I will write an address, our secret spot, and you would meet us there yes? Oh my god, praise be, really, I can't even tell you what this means."

"I got it. Thanks Charlie, just give me the address."

MY MEMORIES ARE STRANGE, OFTEN FEELING LIKE SOMEONE else's, and not my own. Which would make sense because I've never entirely *been* myself. In this form at least. I often remember things as a child, about my parents, about school, about little elementary school boyfriends kissing me behind a stone wall. They aren't so much my memories, but hers. But since she and I are technically the same, I guess the memories are technically ours.

Does that make sense? Probably not.

I was walking down the street once, who knows where I was going, but I do remember it was a sticky hot summer day and the whole city stunk of spoiled milk and hot tar. I had on a little floral romper, and platform sandals, big movie star glasses, my hair in a hightopknot. And behind me someone called my name, "Joy? Oh my god, Joy is it you?!"

I turned, though no one had called me by that name, basically ever. And a man, burly, friendly smile, shaved head, bounded up to me, breathless. "I can't believe it, it's you. Joy."

And though I'd never met this man, my memories remembered him. Jamey. We'd worked together at a bar, he's been in school to be an EMT, and I (she) always thought he was a little too soft for the work. "Are you alright? I heard you went missing and no one had seen. . ."

"—Sorry I think you have the wrong person. My name isn't Joy." And his face, the sheer confusion, because he knew it was me, and that I was Joy, as much as my (her) memories knew him to be Jamey. This was the first time I'd been recognized as her, and it would be a lie if it didn't throw me. In part because I did remember him, and suddenly remembered dozens of shifts we'd shared, and an inside joke about Pink Squirrels, and the eccentric old lady who would always order them at our bar. Sometimes six in a night, and how we would have to run out to get the ice cream and other silliness to make them. Then, as a joke, we'd started ordering them in inappropriate bars and restaurants as well, just to piss off the bartenders.

"Sorry man, must have one of those faces, see you 'round," I said and spun, even as he called out to me and I couldn't bring myself to look back.

Since all my lives have been like this, it makes it hard to even know who I am. The sharing (stealing) of memories, of faces, of lives, perpetually keeps me wondering what on this earth is mine. Or ever was.

Besides of course, my oh so loyal followers who keep dragging me back.

AT THE RISK OF SOUNDING LIKE A PETULANT TEEN: I NEVER

asked to be born. I never asked to have a gaggle of sycophants who bring me back from whatever depths I slink back to when the body I inhabit dies. Who force me into these people shapes and force me to live in their world. The worst part? I honestly don't even know how many times it has happened. As long as there have been people. As soon as they could rub shit on walls in vague shapes, they've been summoning me. So, thousands, probably.

Before that, I existed, as much as there is actually a singular I, in a mostly formless state. Like a fog that floated along the plains, a natural element that was part of the world but not a participant. I looked at humans as little more than a curiosity, a notable mammal in that they fashioned tools and language, but little more. How they started to see and believe in me, that is something else entirely. And the more they believed, the realer I became. They killed in my name, over and over, and with each drop of blood I was pulled closer to their world.

How many stolen gods walked the streets with me? I often stop into churches and places of worship, looking for others like myself. But I've encountered very little, outside of my own strange existence, that could be deemed spiritual or magical.

Which is what always disappointed my devotees in the end. They want knowledge and power, and I have offered very little of either. They want the end times but I cannot give that to them. I don't want to.

CHARLIE'S GROUP MET IN AN OLD STORAGE LOCKER, YOU know those sad off the highway buildings where hoarders store their shit and never come back for it? The metal rolldown door entered into a 100 square foot windowless cell, essentially, which was one of the more pitiful "churches" devoted to me that I have come across in my long time on this earth. When I got there, the twenty-four-hour storage space was empty of any sort of security. I breezed right in, walking along identical hallways of labelled corrugated steel doors, until finally I reached mine. 608. Which was another bummer, they couldn't even get 666? Rapping upon the door, Charlie was quick to pull it open, his face positively filled with bliss and fervor as he welcomed me in.

It was depressing.

A lone bulb highlighted a dingy room of scuffed white walls and stained concrete floors. Folding chairs were laid out, with a folding table as some sort of altar to the back. The table was covered in a trash bag as tablecloth, no doubt for easy clean up.

"It's not much," Charlie said, pushing his glasses up his nose, "But it's private, and no hunters would think to flush us out here."

I walked the length of the small room in only a few paces, as I did that Charlie unrolled and hung a large mural. I recognized my sigil, similar to a broken ouroboros, crudely spray painted on what looked to be an old white sheet. I sniffed. These guys really were some of the lowest rent cultists I'd seen.

"There were times when my temples spanned acres and my sigil was mosaiced into the floor using rubies and diamonds," I said, and Charlie flinched, smoothing his hair back. "And now we cower in storage units."

"I'm so sorry for that, Mistress. But take comfort, what we lack in flashiness and grandstanding, we make up for in true devotion." He placed a hand on his heart and met my eyes. It was almost touching, but I was so very tired.

I was about to say more when a small group of devotees trickled in. Each in turn, silenced and humbled by the realization that I was already there. At some point I sat down on a metal folding chair, trying to ignore the wistful smiles and dreamy stares of my fan club.

"This is everyone, Mistress," Charlie said and pulled down the metal door, sealing us all inside. Already the air felt cloying and too close, I glanced at the small dusty vent in the corner, doubting it did much but let vermin in.

There were ten people in total, including Charlie. I sat in front of them, one elbow resting on the trash bag tablecloth. The group faced me in their folding chairs. Young and old. Fat and thin. Dark skinned and light. Say what you will, but at least I always got a diverse pool of worshippers. Once I realized they weren't going to say anything, and would probably wait indefinitely for my command, I decided to get started.

"Thanks for having me," I said, clearing my throat. They all sighed and covered their eyes, gasps and sobs. Thankful prayers.

"Thank you for appearing to Charlie." An older woman with pink hair and sparkly glasses said.

"You are a vision in the flesh, Mistress."

"Only say what you want of us, and we will do it," another said, an old bald man, with tears on his cheeks. "You are why we live."

"—Or die." Another woman chimed in, "Say the word and we will die for you."

"As so many of our tribe has done before us," Charlie said, meeting my eyes. "To the fallen of our tribe. Hunted and burned." He lowered his head, and the others followed suit.

The silence stretched, and I found myself getting bored with them already, as I had so many others. The problem with this type of devotion, this mindless slavering like a dog to his master, is that it becomes old fast. Supplicants are dull and empty headed. A gaggle of "yes-men." And with each incarnation and generation, I found myself growing more and more annoyed by them. These soft minded true believers, willing to throw themselves upon their swords because I commanded it. "Why do you all believe in me so much? What have I ever done to earn such devotion?" I asked finally.

They looked up, shocked, "You are the Mistress, the UnMaker, the Unraveller." I nodded at the litany of names, I've had hundreds after all, and it would take a long time if we had to go through them all.

"Why do you even want this world UnMade? Is it truly so

horrible?" I asked, looking around the dumpy space, admitting to myself yes, if everything looked like this, maybe I'd want to destroy it too. But I knew it didn't, and more than that, with each life I was squeezed into, with each lifetime of memories that became mine, the less I felt compelled to UnMake.

"Because the world is unfit, and the old gods should rule again. And you, the formless god of unmaking, is the first through the door." I leaned my head back and sighed, which confused the balding, paunchy true believer who had stood up to rattle off that recital of old text.

"But do you even know what that means? Do you really want to be UnMade? To cease existing? But more than that, do you want the world to be UnMade and returned to a primordial stage inhospitable to humans of any stripe? Why? Why keep bringing me back?" All ten sets of eyes were on me now, mouths open.

"Mistress, you are a cleansing storm, a way to start again. Made flesh by your believers to walk the world, to destroy it," Charlie said, somewhat petulantly as if I had forgotten.

I pinched the bridge of my nose, "Okay, last chance now, if I asked you all to turn your backs on your faith, forget me, and go off and find something meaningful, something *else* meaningful, would you?" They all shook their heads, a fat man in the back barking out a laugh.

"It's a test! Oh, I knew it. You are testing our allegiance to the cause! I understand now!" I scowled at him and rose.

"You dunderheads. You ever think about what I *want*? You think I want to keep being summoned up from the darkness and jammed into these bodies? Trapped in them until they rot off me? Forced over and over to live here as a person in your world? All the while you try to use me like some sort of tool. I'm a formless thing, you fools, in wanting to find a way to communicate with me, you have ultimately changed me! And in however many thousands of years, you have yet to convince me anything *but you still* need to be UnMade." I was yelling by the end and a few in the front cowered. I knew the room had grown hotter in my anger. The air smelled of ozone.

"But I am not a cruel Mistress, and if you want to be UnMade, then you shall be." I said, looking at each of them in turn.

"Mistress!" Charlie said, standing, hands up and placating. "We are sorry for displeasing you so."

I shrugged, "Yours is one of the last groups of true believers, Charlie. I'm nearly erased from this world. Every text I burn, every temple, every effigy I smash, every fucking *believer* gone, gets me closer to what I want."

"Which is what, Mistress?"

"To be left alone, you morons! I am a formless being and I want to break this cycle!" And with that I let out a pulse of heat and energy, it distorted the air, and upon reaching my tribe, it incinerated them, their bodies instantly consumed in flame. Screams tore from cooking throats as greasy black smoke coated the ceiling. My bedsheet sigil on the wall crumbled to ash and the metal chairs melted into puddles. The metal door bowed out, glowing orange, before tearing like paper, allowing the noxious smoke and myself out into the hall. The alarm sounded as the smoke billowed out black and toxic into the hall.

I strolled down the hall, feeling sooty, but lighter on my feet when a voice called out.

It was Charlie, burning, his flesh and visible bone gone white from the heat, "Why Mistress? Why?" He whispered, reaching out for me, his lips gone, his mouth little more than a skull with glowing white teeth.

"Because I never asked to be your fucking God. I quit, Charlie. *I quit.*"

And with that I turned on my heel and left them to burn.

"Can I buy you a drink?" I looked up from my book, at

the handsome olive-skinned man standing beside me. I squinted at him, trying to find ulterior motives, but came up, joyfully, pleasingly empty. He just thought I was cute.

"I'd like that."

"Wonderful. I'm Nick by the way, and you?"

I paused, rolling a hundred names around in my head, before smiling, "You can call me Caligo." Now that so few knew me, I could use one of my actual names.

"Interesting name, and what would you like to drink?"

I laughed, "As silly as it sounds, I would love a Pink Squirrel."

He chuckled, "If that's what the lady wants, that's what she'll get."

AND I COULDN'T AGREE MORE.

❧ 6 ❧

THE GUEST

It's hard to tell you exactly when the Guest arrived, which sounds strange I realize. How could you not remember when someone came into your home? I am fairly certain it was winter. I recall that nights had a way of crawling in early and the trees around our house were bare, the bark black and wet. Our house was set far back and high up from the road, the driveway a sloping serpent that wriggled over the hills and around the giant old elms. From the front windows, you could see down into the valley and the village below. It was very hard to sneak up on the old place, and because of that, the house felt a bit like a fortress. Its gray slate roof helped complete the castle-fortress image. The slick stone crawled with moss, bright green against all the gray. At dusk, that green moss positively glowed.

My brother had a penchant for spacemen and sci-fi and told me when I was very young that the moss was a sentient creature from another world. I, being a few years younger and of a trusting nature, believed him and would go out to talk to the moss. Worrying the poor space creature was bored to tears clinging to our old house, watching the woods and quiet street, I would tell it of my days, the small dramas of school, even what I ate that day for lunch. I would tell it about my dreams and I would read to it. In the harder years, when my smallness and strangeness set me apart, I think that moss was probably my only true friend.

What does the moss have to do with our Guest? It's related, but not all that important just yet. As an old woman now, I find myself the type to zig and zag in my thinking. It's like I'm a time traveler, one moment I am in the present, and in a flash, I am a scuff-kneed eight-year-old, blinded by summer sun and the wide-open grassy fields of my youth. I'm neither here nor there, or anywhere really. But you came to learn about our Guest and I will try my darndest to stay there.

I was seventeen when he came. In the house my mother and father, my older brother Darius, and my younger sister Felicia, which we all called Feenie. My father was an academic from a wealthy family and my memories of him are always squinting at me through thick reading glasses from behind towers of swaying books and specimens. He was a professor at the university, in the sciences. My mother was a social-climbing sort, she was a member of many clubs and organizations, volunteered often, and had a lot of lady friends. I always got the impression that she found my father dull and in turn myself, who'd taken after him as a quiet and bookish type. My brother Darius, the eldest and most lauded, was a golden boy; handsome and charming, an athlete and good student. What few saw, save me, was his mean streak. Feenie was like a doll, frilly and flouncy, she was the perfect daughter in that regard. A sweet little creature, pretty and preened, with big eyes and pink cheeks. I always flinched at the way she would flutter about a room, like a butterfly landing at each flower, for a little kiss. She would laugh behind her hand and how everyone followed her, how they wanted her. When our Guest arrived, she was only thirteen, but already the perfect coquette.

I think as much as I loved my family, I hated them, because I always felt so unnecessary. An extra child: one to never marry, to tend home, to grow stooped and ugly and old, caring for her parents like little more than a maid. An old maid. Darius and Feenie were too lovely, too coiffed, too rehearsed and I always felt crazy watching people believe them. Fall for them, fall in love with them. Everyone did. I was the only one who saw their truth, the cruelty of Darius and the callousness of Feenie. She thought it was all a big laugh, like the whole world was her puppet show to pull the strings.

So that was who lived in the home at the time. We also had a maid named Dori who did the cooking and cleaning, but she was often a silent and benign presence. Little more than background noise. But I'm getting ahead of myself again. It was cold, late fall or early winter, dark and stormy and barren. Skies gray and the air wet. That was how he arrived, on a storm, a wet thing come in from the wet world. And I remember thinking, as he entered the house, that the temperature dropped ten whole degrees. I was on the landing, coming down the stairs, and he looked up and our eyes met. And held. I couldn't remember his face, or strangely, the color of his eyes as much as the intensity of the stare. I'd never been looked at, or into, as I had at that moment. The focus caused my knees to weaken and something deep inside to clench in a way that was both pleasant and almost painful. The moment felt endless but in reality, was probably only a second or two, and then Dori was tutting and taking his coat. My father was coming down the hallway, arms open and welcoming. My mother was there, smiling and fashionable, inviting him into our home.

"Ah, that's my middle child up there, Angeline please come down and meet our guest."

And so, I did, legs unsteady as a lamb I made my way down without tumbling to meet the stranger. He was quite tall and I had to crane my head up to meet his face. Granted, I was small, both lean and short, and it always made people think I was younger and more fragile than I was. But the Guest regarded me differently. He met my eyes again, and up close I could see they were green, a vibrant wild green I'd never seen before. He had an angular face, pointed chin, and under his hat, a sweep of dark brown hair combed back neat as a pin. He smiled and his teeth were white and straight. He stuck his hand out and I took it, feeling as if I was in a dream, his hand was cold and wet, but I held it nonetheless.

"Angeline, it's a real pleasure," he said, and his voice, oh his voice, was rough and warm. It was intimate as if he only spoke to me and whispered in my ear. My whole body lit up with goose-bumps under the stress of his regard. "I'm Mr. Lich, a guest of the university, but please call me Ambrose. I do hope we will be good friends after all." I blew out the breath I was holding and liked the idea of the two of us becoming good friends. I licked my lips and noticed how he watched my mouth. I liked how he watched my mouth. "A pleasure," I said, quiet enough to nearly be a whisper.

"And here are my other two children, Mr. Lich, my son Darius here and the lovely Feenie." My siblings approached and I felt the subtle tug of my father's hand on my arm, pulling me back and pushing them forward. Darius stuck his hand out, all golden hair and gleaming teeth.

"A real pleasure Mr. Lich, my father has told me about your research, really interesting and out-there stuff. I look forward to picking your brain while you're a guest here." Mr. Lich chuckled and broke off their handshake.

"That will be most welcome, you will be attending the University next year I understand?" I watched the Guest and so badly wanted to see him less invested when he talked to my siblings, but he was just as interested and focused on each of them. And it broke my heart a little, I'm ashamed to admit. Feenie curtsied, actually curtsied, and looked up at him through golden lashes the way she'd been taught. I choked on my anger, watching her pose for him, I could smell the peony perfume and fumed as her pink-nailed hand reached up, palm down, and he leaned in and kissed it. She giggled, like the tinkling of a bell. Was he as charmed by her as everyone else was? Or would he, this mysterious stranger, who'd woken something expansive and wild inside of me, see Feenie for what she was? I was turning on my heel, heading toward the stairs when his voice called me back.

"Going so soon?" he said, and I couldn't make out whether the crooked smile on his face was mocking, flirtation, or something else entirely. "I hope I haven't offended," he finished.

Feenie took that moment to laugh behind her hand, "Don't pay any mind to Angeline, Mr. Lich, she is something of a bookworm, think this much human contact has positively exhausted her." If I could have yanked my sister back by the hair right then I would have. Instead, I settled for curling my hands into fists and smiling.

"Not at all Mr. Lich," my mother said, shooting me a quick look. "Forgive my daughter's rudeness. Welcome to our home, I am Regina, lady of the house. And now you've met all of my children, including my middle and least housebroken." I flinched when she spoke and I knew he'd seen it. My heart cracked with each little insult, knowing soon our Guest would see me much the way my family did, as an odd little outcast with her nose in a book. "I'm sure you are exhausted and soaked from your journey, Darius please go get the rest of Mr. Lich's things, and Angeline, show him to his room."

WHILE OUR HOUSE WAS LARGE, WE ALSO WERE A BIG FAMILY with four bedrooms taken up, my father had a study, there also was a library and so the guests were put up in the attic. This was not a punishment as the attic was of good size and normal ceiling height and had lovely views of the rolling fields and thick woods on all sides. There was a small heater and extra quilts on the old brass bed. I led Mr. Lich up the stairs, painfully aware of him behind me.

"Your family is most kind in hosting me," he said on the second floor as I gave him a rough tour of the rooms.

"My father enjoys having great minds under his roof. My mother loves reasons to plan elaborate meals."

"Do you mind me being here?" I turned to him then, hand on my chest to protest. Alone in the hallway I was suddenly aware of how close he was standing to me. I could smell him, or what was perhaps his cologne. It was spicy like pine and musk, but also crisp like sea air and fresh rain. A deep draught of Mr. Lich and I felt utterly transported to the outside world, lush and vast, wild. I shook my head to clear it and was sure my cheeks were pink. He looked down at me with his green eyes and the whole world seemed to fall away, his hands were on my arms, and I could feel them cool through the fabric of my top. I swooned then, like some Harlequin damsel, legs gone to jelly and the only reason I didn't fall was his hands steadying me.

"Are you well? Looked like you were about to faint." He smiled and I nearly toppled over a second time. I breathed in and out and squeezed my eyes shut until I saw little starbursts and only then did I step back and break his hold.

"Apologies, I mustn't have eaten enough today. I'm fine now, let me show you to your room, it's just up these stairs." After I gave the tour of his accommodations, I turned to head back down the stairs. I hated to leave Mr. Lich, that much I knew even then, there was some sort of pull that compelled me to be near him, to want him to touch me. I imagined I must look like quite the silly girl, seventeen and awkward, flitting about him like a pesky insect. I was at the top step heading down when called to me.

He'd opened his suitcase on top of the low chest of drawers, I could see everything was packed meticulously tidy and there was an assortment of books and glass vials as well. "I find, of everyone in your household so far, you to be the most interesting. Please tell me if I am stepping over any bounds, but I would very much like to spend more time with you while I am here. Just the two of us. Would that be alright?" Now I knew my face was as red as an apple. I'd probably blushed all the way to the bottom of my feet. I nodded, feeling faint and strange, the heady mixture of excitement and attraction clouding my mind.

"I too would like that, Mr. Lich."

"Please, if I am to call you Angeline, then you must call me Ambrose. And we will be friends, yes?" I nodded and fled down the stairs not wanting to embarrass myself and have him change his mind. Only once I was closed up in my room, with the door locked tight, did I allow myself a giddy squeal as I lay in my bed, tracing the plaster cracks in the ceiling, and imagining his bed nearly in the exact spot above mine. Thinking of him up there, taking his clothes off, lying in bed. I could close my eyes and summon his smell, feel those cool hands, and I could imagine them moving up my arms, touching me everywhere, leaving cool trails to mark where they had been. I was lost in my fantasy, my skin sweaty, when a knock on my door popped the bubble and brought me back down to earth. It was time to get cleaned up for dinner.

I CRIED OUT AS MY ENTIRE BODY RIPPLED IN PLEASURE ALMOST on the side of pain. Mr. Lich, Ambrose, rose from between my legs, face wet and shining. "I never get tired of that," he said, leaning over to kiss me. I tasted myself on his lips, enjoying the sensation.

"I don't think I will either, Ambrose," I said, and he rested his head on my chest, listening to my heart beat. The winter had been long and oppressive, endless snowstorms isolating us from the village and insulating us inside. It was hard to steal moments together, the family all being cooped up on top of each other. But we found the time, when I snuck up to the attic late in the night.

Though the first time, it was he who came to my room. I'd been dreaming, a strange dream where I sunk underwater, tangled in hair, or perhaps tentacles. The water was warm and murky. I struggled, but the more I did, the more tangled I became. When I finally woke, sweaty and wrapped up in my bed sheets, he was there, standing beside my bed, little more than a dark outline. I screamed out, but his hand came up and covered mine and he leaned in, eyes impossibly green in the gloom. His earthy, woodsy smell washed over me and calmed me. "I didn't mean to startle you. I heard you call out. I must admit I wasn't sleeping, I was up there thinking of you down here, below me. Are you, all right?"

He removed his hand and I took a deep breath in and out, "A dream, a bad dream, that's all. You shouldn't be in here. My father would lose his mind."

"He won't come in. No one will. I promise." He smiled, teeth shining in the scant light. Even then, his assurance should have alarmed me, but I was too smitten by a handsome and mysterious man in my room. I was suddenly aware of how thin my nightgown was, only the thinnest of layers between us. His hand on my shoulder was cool. "I want to kiss you Angeline. I want to touch you, I've wanted to since the day I arrived."

I know I said yes, or perhaps nodded, or maybe did none of those, but regardless he was on me. His mouth hungry, his hands voracious, and I leaned in, hungry as he, in my own way. I'd never imagined a man could truly lust after me. Too many years of being small, and odd, and mousy. I'd not even merited being the butt of jokes or bullying, instead being ignored and overlooked, even in my own family. For a man, and he was a man, a grown and accomplished man, handsome and worldly, to see me as something more, something worth his time, worth the risk of my father's wrath. Well, nothing could be more romantic.

And so, it went, after that night, that he would work all day with my father on their studies and formulas, buried behind beakers and stacks of swaying books. We'd all eat together and steal illicit touches and looks. I remember one particular meal, when we'd been sitting beside each other, that his hand, sneaky as an eel, made its way beneath my skirts where he teased and stroked me to the point of panting while carrying on an utterly benign conversation with my father about cell structure or some such. It was delightful to be so naughty under my own roof, delightful how indifferent Ambrose was to the charms of either of my other siblings, especially my beautiful and precocious younger sister. Feenie kept finding reasons to be half dressed around Ambrose, doors left ajar, mirrors angled just so.

I was lying beside him, naked save the coating of moonlight out the window, when I mentioned it, "My sister has a crush on you. I'm sure you've noticed."

"I have. Be hard not to. But don't be jealous, she is too young, too silly. And more importantly, regardless of her age, she'll never be you." And I felt my heart trill like a bird in a cage, a warmth spreading over my skin, his love filling me in ways I'd never known myself to be empty. "I came here for you."

OVER THAT LONG AND SNOWY WINTER, AMBROSE OFTEN SAID that. That he'd come to my family home for *me*. Whenever I pushed for him to explain what he meant, he would brush me off, choosing instead to distract with compliments or the administrations of his hands and mouth. I wondered, in darker private moments, if this was all just an act. That I was just an easy mark, a desperate young girl who was starved for attention that he could wrap right around his finger. I prayed that wasn't the case and that it was just years of finely-honed low self-esteem. But the inner voice was persistent as a toothache.

During these endless winter storms, an illness moved throughout the house as well, a wasting sort of sickness. My mother had it the worst. She was covered in rashes that leaked a strange green pus that almost smelled of pine needles. Dori, the maid, had it quite bad, vomiting a great bout of verdant vomit all over the tile floor she was scrubbing. I had to help her clean it, as she apologized over and over. Darius, Feenie and my father eventually also came down with the strange sickness, but as the storms raged on, it wasn't safe to take anyone to the doctor.

Only Ambrose and I remained well. I wondered if it was something in the food, because he barely ate, and what he did eat was entirely vegetarian. He drank lots of water but rarely anything else, declining coffee or bourbon with my father. I noticed his cups tended to be left nearly full, where he would only sip just enough to be polite. He often sat in sunny spots, eyes closed, and one day I asked him, playfully, "Are you sure you aren't part plant? The way you sun yourself, you look like one of mother's orchids." He found this question delightful and jumped from his chair to spin me and steal a forbidden kiss.

"I'm so glad I came here for you, Angeline. You are a perfect treasure. I'd always thought so, but now, I know so." I blushed, unable to meet those strange green eyes of his. Drunk on his love and attention. We'd gotten more brazen with our affections as each family member grew sicker.

"What's this?" A voice in the doorway, dripping with disgust. Darius. He had dark circles under his eyes, face sweaty with fever.

I tried to step back but Ambrose held my arms in his grip. Darius wrinkled his nose looking between the two of us. "I know this winter has been long and us, poor company, but I didn't think you'd be that desperate, Mr. Lich." Ambrose's hands tightened on my arm as he glared at my brother.

"I doubt my father will approve of any of this," he said, stepping into the room. "And she's a bit young for you."

"Shut your mouth, Darius. You don't know anything about anything," I said, but he merely smirked, arms crossed. The golden boy, cocky and untouchable. How I'd looked up to him as a small child, following everywhere, his foolish kid sister. He'd never see me as anything but.

Ambrose broke the hold on me and walked close to my brother, his posture rigid, aggressive even. It was the first time

I'd seen anything like that from him, as he was normally so gentle and loving. "You should rethink everything you've said, Darius."

"You threatening me? In my own house? Way I see it you are an adult and my sister is a star-crossed child. I doubt my father will appreciate his colleague diddling his daughter, you?" I remember opening my mouth to protest, but before I could, Ambrose had put his arms around my brother's neck and leaned in, his mouth to Darius' in a kiss. His screams were muffled by Ambrose's mouth. And I saw green, a bright frothy green liquid bubble up and out from between. Darius shook, seizing, and when Ambrose broke the hold, my brother fell hard to the floor, thrashing and shaking. I fell to my knees, crawling to him, and Darius held my eyes for a split second, they were bulging, capillaries bursting as his eyes bled red. His face was flushed, the corded veins standing out in his neck. And his mouth ran with green foam, quickly turning red as it ate into his skin, releasing a pungent smell that was a mixture of burning hair and stinking pond water. Darius was terrified and I was screaming, my hands fluttering uselessly around his body, until he stilled, the light dimmed in his eyes, and he died.

I couldn't believe it. It had all happened so horribly fast. "*What did you do!?*" I wailed, confused why no one had come running as I screamed. Ambrose looked composed, his mouth wiped clean, face ruddy, eyes bright. "I will protect you, us, as long as I walk the earth, Angeline. He meant to separate us, to hurt you, to hurt my career, to take it all away. This," he gestured between us, "means more to me than your brother. I know it's horrible to say, but it's true."

I THINK ABOUT THAT MOMENT OFTEN, WHEN DARIUS DIED. I wonder what would have happened if I'd fled, or called for help, or sent him away. The man was a killer. But I loved him and I loved being loved by him. And, as mad as it may seem, that was enough for me. Ambrose had woven himself into my heart and my spirit and the idea of losing him did scare me more than my brother dying. I'm sure I could say I was under some sort of spell, as Ambrose had a way of bending people to him, but I want to be honest. I'm old and have no need to lie. I was enough of a romantic that the love of someone so wonderful was worth more. I know how horrible that is. All I can say is that I'd been a sad and starved creature that, once fed, never wanted to go back to my old hungry life.

THE TONE OF THE HOUSEHOLD CHANGED AFTER DARIUS HAD died. But not as much as it would have had Ambrose not been there. He did something to them, my parents, they grieved, but the sadness was quiet and removed. In part because they were so sick. They rarely left their beds as rashes covered their bodies, their limbs growing green and fuzzy. Only Feenie still had some fire in her. She was devastated that Darius could die so randomly, of some sort of allergic reaction of all things. She did not believe, she wanted a doctor. So, Ambrose disconnected the phone. She was too sick to make her way through the snow, instead glaring at me as I brought her soup and bandages, filled with accusations and suspicions.

"I can't believe my sweet boy is gone," my mother said dreamily, she'd started walking around in her soiled nightgowns, holding his jacket, clutching it like it was a little dog. My father worked some in his lab, most curious by the secretions coming from his own body. Commenting on their unique and alien cell structure. And all the while there was Ambrose and I, together, flagrantly together now, dancing in the parlor, playing chasing games through the halls, making love wherever we pleased. Outside it snowed and snowed.

That winter it snowed so much it felt like we were trapped

inside a snow globe. Outside grew whiter and whiter and inside greener and greener. It started in the bedrooms, but soon came out of the sink and tubs, up the walls, and fogging over the windowpanes. The air took on the scent, not of a sick house, but of a greenhouse.

Surely, you must be wondering how I did not find it peculiar, how I did not go get help, how I just accepted it all. Frankly, I cannot answer, for love is a strange thing and I was drunk on it. Ambrose was the sun and I was like the vines that grew toward him, always reaching, always climbing.

When Dori died, crumpled on the floor, and soon became a lump of soft mossy green, I knew something was amiss. Then mother succumbed in much the same way, her bedroom a verdant jungle of swaying vines and blooming flowers, unnatural against the ice-covered window. My sister was little more than a breathing garden, my father the same down in his lab, his limbs having rooted themselves, lifting the floorboards and burrowing beneath.

"Ambrose. What have you done to them? What is happening to my home?" I finally asked one night after we'd made love on the blanket of moss and grasses that had grown across my living room floor. I'd taken to going barefoot, loving the spongy texture.

"Angeline, do you truly want the answer?"

"I do." Ambrose was quiet for a time.

"I came here for you. Or rather Ambrose Lich came here to work with your father, I came here for you."

I chilled, "So you aren't Ambrose Lich?" I noticed the ceiling above us now resembled a canopy of trees. He turned his body to face me, eyes luminous green in the darkness. Inhuman. The word popped into my head unbidden and chilled me. Even animals' eyes don't glow in the dark without light shined on them.

"Ask me," he said, licking his lips.

"If you aren't Ambrose, who are you?" He leaned forward

and kissed me, and as scary and strange as this all was, his kiss melted me, stripping me of my barriers, of my common sense. I did not fear him. I loved this man, whether I wanted to or not, whether it was smart or not. Whether he was a man or not. He tasted of forbidden springs and fog in the forest. He tasted green and lush.

"I've watched you and listened to you your whole life. You taught me how to love, you taught me there was more than just existing. You woke an identity in me. And when Ambrose came, I thought, here is the perfect vessel. I knew you would find him handsome and virile. You would be able to see me as something real, not just something that grows on the rocks."

I reeled, leaning away and putting my arms up, "You're crazy. How can that be true?"

Ambrose leaned closer, his green eyes brighter still, twin lanterns in a black night. And As I watched, his skin began to glow phosphorescent in the night, and the verdant smell of plants filled the room. "You told me many times I was your best friend, your only friend. What I couldn't tell you back was that you are also my best friend. I've been working towards being with you from the moment you stopped talking to me. When you grew out of believing."

"How can any of this be real? And why would you kill Darius, if you've known me, you've known him his whole life." Ambrose frowned.

"He was cruel to you, always. They all were in their way. No more. I came to be with you, to love you." He picked up my hands and pressed his lips to my knuckles. "You are worth transcending species and reality."

How could I argue against that? So very few of us experience real romance in our lives. And in Ambrose I had that. When one encounters the fantastical, one must go all in. Like Alice when she ventured through the looking glass. I stayed and he stayed, and the green ate and changed and reinterpreted our home and all who lived in it. Consumed the walls, the roof, and by spring, our old stone house was indistinguishable from the hill it sat upon. And over decades, the green spread and spread, my lover building me a kingdom. And while the body of Ambrose eventually succumbed back to the earth, he is still with me now. That bud over there, that leaf there, he is it and they are him. Everywhere and always. Like our love.

And that is our story.

7

THE GIRL IN THE STAIRWELL

Her body lay crumpled in the alley stairwell, limbs akimbo. She reminded me of a contortionist at rest, or a spider in wait. Of course, she was in fact just a woman who had been pushed or fallen, or some combination of the two, down two flights of unyieldingly cruel concrete steps. The fall had sent her careening, arms windmilling, "ass over teakettle" as my grandmother would have said, and finally, landing in a heap, limbs broken, body shattered, and very dead.

Her head was cocked at an odd angle, looking up at those who looked down the stairs at her. There was a strange defiance in the jut of her chin and her unblinking stare gazing up at us as if to say, "So what?"

I was the first to venture down, cautious on my own teetering heels until finally, on the fifth step, I just slid them off and ran barefoot down to the fallen woman. The cement was icy under my feet, making them ache. *She must be so cold*, the thought skittered through my mind as I reached her, crouched down, and touched her arm. She was not yet cool, but cooling. There was something strange about a lukewarm dead girl.

I felt her pulse, as if it would make one bit of difference—she was rearranged like a half-completed Rubik's Cube. This close to

89

her, I noted how lovely she was; her skin fair with a delicate sprinkling of freckles. The freckles made me think of her as girl-ish. She probably hated those freckles and daily wished them gone. But to me, at that moment, they made her much more real. Her hair was long and brown with a sheen of coppery red to it. Her eyes were hazel green, surrounded by thick lashes coated in heavy black mascara. They stared ahead, unseeing.

I took her hand, feeling an intimacy bloom with the dead girl. I would now be the one who found her body, who stayed with her. She was a stranger to me, but being so near her stillness, feeling her soft skin cooling in my hands, made me feel closer to her than anyone I had ever known. I wondered then if her soul floated nearby, or if I even believed in souls. Was she bobbing just above us like a tethered balloon, watching me, another girl from the club, a stranger who came out to have a smoke, and instead found *her*? Bent and broken, all alone in her deathly glory. Would she appreciate my hand in hers, or would it mean nothing to her because she wasn't there anymore?

A jackal-eyed crowd formed above us at the top of the stairs, and someone hollered down that the police had been called. I nodded and resumed my vigil, kneeling and shivering barefoot next to her, holding her hand. I knew everyone watching would assume I was her friend. Was I lying by omission, stealing her tragedy? Co-opting her demise? Did holding this girl's hand make me like the women who poison their children for the atten-tion? Guilt and shame cascaded through me as I crouched there in that cold stairwell. Still, I never let go of her hand. Never told the people watching from above that she was a stranger to me. The fact that I could be revealed as a sham at any moment by a friend or date looking for her made it all the more exciting.

I only let go of her hand when I noticed her small clutch purse glinting between her torso and the ground. Miraculously, the little spangly purse had not been torn off in the tumble; the chain, slung across her body had held firm.

Inside I found her license and stared at the smiling photo.

Melinda Johnson, twenty-five years old.

Melinda? The name did not fit her at all. It felt dated, like something from my mother's yearbook. Old and out of style.

My heart was beating fast, my body was covered in nervous cold sweat as I glanced up at the crowd milling above. Before I knew what I was doing, I slipped the ID into my own purse as well as the single key on a ribbon beside it. I resumed holding her hand, noting it growing colder and less pliant.

"Move aside people. Police. Break it up." I heard a deep voice call out before I saw the man, but soon he was standing at the top of the stairs looking down at us. He was an older man with dark skin and a square face. When he saw me, cowering and shoeless, holding Melinda, his expression softened.

"Miss? I'm going to come down now."

Was I the miss? Of course, I must be since Melinda was in no position to respond.

"I'm Officer Bennett. Could you please step aside so I can check on your—ah—friend?" He was treating me so delicately, like I was made of the finest glass. A thrill of excitement burbled up, and I had to bite my cheek to not smile at him. Instead, I lowered my eyes and let go of her hand.

As soon as I moved, he leaned in, his size and warmth crowding the small landing. Above, on the street the ambulance had arrived. Two EMTs waited at the top of the stairwell with a stretcher.

Officer Bennett felt for a pulse and carefully looked at Melinda. He sighed and turned to me.

"I am so sorry Miss, she's gone. Let's get out of the way and let the EMTs do their job. I can take a statement while you warm up."

He led me up and out of the stairwell where I slid my heels back on and teetered my way to his cruiser. I looked at all the staring faces, painted red and blue from the car's flickering lights. They watched me with such bare curiosity. So hungry for answers: What happened? Who was she? Who was I to her? I swelled with the attention, reveling in this new position of power.

The EMTs brought Melinda up and out in a slick black bag. Officer Bennett, ever the pro, tactfully distracted me from the body being removed. It was such a smooth maneuver that I knew he must have done it many times in his life. I felt a twinge between my legs at that. A wave of excitement brought on by the drama of death, caught up in the chaos of violence and loss broke in me.

Holding a small notebook and pen, his eyes were for me and me alone.

"What happened?"

"She fell. She was not very steady on her heels and she just. . . fell."

"I see. Had she been drinking?"

Had she been? It was a club, she was dressed to go out and it was late. It would be strange if she wasn't drinking.

"She was. I'm afraid I don't know how much though."

"You came together?"

Did we? A balloon was filling inside of me, making me giddy.

"No, we came separately. I think she planned on taking a cab home."

"And what is your friend's name?"

"Melinda."

"How did you meet?"

"Oh. It's a funny story really. I work at a clothing store and she came in. We were both wearing the same dress—one that store didn't even sell! We were so like that—so alike. It's like we were sisters in a way. . ."

"And what's her last name?" A ripple of panic as I racked my memory.

"Johnson, Melinda Johnson."

"The friendship was new. But we connected, like we had been friends forever. It's hard to explain." I stared hard at him, my eyes welling up.

92

"Right, right." He wrote it all down, talked to me a bit longer, took my info and then let me out of the car. He'd offered to give me a ride home, but I couldn't trouble him with that. Instead, I hung out by the stairwell, chatting with the crowd. I talked all about my friend Melinda and her tragic end. I was hugged by drippy eyed strangers. A handsome man offered to buy me a drink, since he thought I shouldn't be alone after such a tragedy.

I heartily agreed, and we went someplace quiet and intimate. We had drinks and I took him home.

We fucked. He was on top, and the whole time I gazed over his shoulder at my purse on the bedside table, picturing her ID nestled in there next to mine, like best friends, or sisters.

We were that close.

✺ 8 ✺
RIG RASH

The way I see it, the day they found oil was the day the town of Sanctuary was both saved and ruined.

Black Gold.

They flocked in like vampires to an open wound. First, the prospectors to confirm whether or not it was true; then the money men in expensive suits and slick black cars with their schemes to profit, profit, profit. Then the laborers, going where the work was. Once the laborers hit, well, then it was an explosion. Fast food chains, hotels, motels, and flop houses sprung up like a rash along the southern corner of town. Fellas get lonely out in the oil fields, need some company. That's where I come into this story.

I'D BEEN HITCHING, MOVING FROM TOWN TO TOWN, WORKING truck stops and the occasional motel room gig. But since I refused to work for a pimp, I couldn't stay anywhere too long without it involving some kinda altercation or violence. There are reasons most places don't like free agents. And let's be honest, I was getting a little long in the tooth. I'm not old, but I'm no spring chicken or tween bride.

Anyway, I was a few hundred miles farther south than I'd ever been before, hooking for a ride and a meal when I caught the first whiff of Sanctuary.

He was a Big Burly Man; red beard and red nose, stinking of sweat and sour mash. He spoke low and in circles. Like drunks do. His faux whisper carried across the whole room and right to my ears.

"I told my boss I wasn't going back there, no matter how much he'd pay me. Not about the fucking money...I mean money, yeah. Sure. Great. But, there's something wrong up there, people are getting sick. You go on up if you want to, man, but if you're smart you'd steer clear. Some things are better than money."

I disagreed with him there; not much better than money as far I was concerned. I thought to myself, *if Sanctuary's a town with jobs and those jobs are hard dirty jobs, the kind that need hard, dirty men, then it's the kind of place that could probably use a few more women.*

You're probably wondering: what did I think of his warnings? I didn't think of them at all. Everything makes you sick these days. The air is poison, the sea is poison. The burger I ate as I eavesdropped—probably making me sick.

Plus, I figured, if something's making people sick, it'll be in the ground. I'm not going to go into the ground. I'm going into the wallets of the people who're in the ground. . . and, if I'm lucky, the people who hire the people in the ground. Everyone needs "love" right?

⚜

SO, I THUMBED MY WAY OUT THERE. IMAGINE ME, ON THE SIDE of the highway, dollar signs in my eyes. A duffel and a dream.

A guy named Steve drove me the last leg of the way. He was an oil worker himself, heading back to Sanctuary.

Steve didn't want sex. In fact, he was a real family man. Headed back to Sanctuary after seeing his wife and kid back in Indiana. When I asked why he didn't bring them to live in Sanctuary, his face twitched, pinched up, clenched.

"Sanctuary's no place for families. For decent people." He gave me a sidelong glance.

I thought: *Shit, Steve, you're headed the same place I am.* But I stayed silent. I bet old Decent Steve would be knocking on my door soon enough. It's hard to be alone and unloved, right?

He dropped me off on the corner of Main Street and drove off, no doubt thinking only decent thoughts.

🦋

THE TOWN OF SANCTUARY WAS ABOUT AS UGLY AS A SMALL town could be. "Quaint" taken to a horrific extreme. A dusty one-horse town with little more than a few storefronts, some sad townie pubs, and the mandatory little white church. The occasional houses were small and run down. Even the gazebo in town square was leaning to the side. The air smelled of sulfur and chemicals, the gentle breeze caused my eyes to water.

The road was old cracked pavement and the sidewalks were vacant, save for a few rats scrabbling in the shadows.

I walked a block or two, trying to decide which bar might hold the man lucky enough to welcome me to town, and provide me a place to sleep for the night. A lone woman in a town like this, even a smart one, had to be careful. Too many landfills are filled with women in my line of work. Women as disposable as the trash they end up buried in.

"You lost honey?" The voice startled me. It bounced off the buildings, and echoed in the empty streets. I spun around and a man came out of the alley and staggered toward me. As he got closer I could see his rashy red skin, like he had scabies or something. I stepped back.

"Aww don't be like that honey, just thought you might need a little company." He took another staggering step my way.

I took another step back, but I didn't want his attentions turning hostile either. "I'm fine buddy, you just startled me is all." I smiled at him pretty.

The man smelled strange. The closer he got, the stronger it got. Oil, solvents and. . . fish? But I kept smiling.

He stepped out beneath a streetlight and I saw that the rash was much worse than I had thought. Angry welts and deep black furrows covered his face. His eyes were yellow, boiled-looking. The stink of him was overpowering. I covered my nose with my sleeve.

"It's the smell innit?" he said, offended at my revulsion, "It's the oil pits you know. Gets in your gloves, in your boots. In your masks. Like it wants. . . to be in you. You can wash and wash, but it sticks." He rubbed his hands together as if he were washing them in an invisible sink. "Taste it in my food, in my drink." He glared at me, "You'll get there soon enough. Then you won't look at me like you do."

"There a problem out here?" The voice boomed like the voice of god. Stinky Man and I both turned

A big man with an unlit cigarette in his hand stood behind me. Bending his head, he cupped his hands around his cigarette and lit it. After a deep drag he said,

"Bill Higgins, get your ass home and take a shower. And stop scaring off tourists, we're lucky to have a lady in town." Stinky Man stumbled away, muttering to himself. Big Man offered me a drag off his cigarette, and we didn't think about old Bill anymore.

☙❧

THE BIG MAN'S NAME WAS PATRICK AND HE CAME TO Sanctuary after working for oil companies in Texas and Louisiana. He drove a nice black truck and owned a small trailer outside of town, on a square of land he'd filled with bikes and a big dog house and enclosed pen.

"You have a dog?" I asked as he opened the door and helped me out of his truck. I liked most dogs but didn't want to take a chance on getting bit by a doggy who didn't like company.

His face darkened and he shook his head.

Later, after our business was done and he was serving me up some dinner, he told me more. He'd had two dogs when he moved to Sanctuary. Big dogs: one a Rottweiler named Lucky, and the other a German Shepherd called Shep. Smart, sturdy dogs that lived all their lives on oil rigs, going where Patrick went. Patrick said guys who work on oil rigs like to have pets to keep them company on the road. "This work breeds lonely men. Lonely men like the company of dogs, and they're cheaper than you lot," he said. "But animals don't last long in Sanctuary. They go crazy, run off, get bitten up by vermin or just drop dead."

Sanctuary sure got to his dogs. They wouldn't sleep, paced all night, whining and whining. Started picking at hotspots on their fur, gnawing themselves red and raw. Rashes all over. They became skeletal, crazy, dangerous.

Then, he said, a pack of rats attacked the dogs. Managed to chew a hole to something vital in Shep. Left Lucky frothing and injured. He shot Lucky in the head and then burnt both their bodies. He didn't want the rats coming back around, looking for leftovers.

"Rats?" I raised an eyebrow. "Those must be some damn big rats," he shrugged, indifferent whether I believed or not.

"Something in the water," he joked humorlessly. I set the glass I was about to drink from back down and wiped my mouth with the back of my hand.

EVENTUALLY I DID DRINK THE WATER. THERE WAS A FAINT foul taste to it, though it could have been my imagination. Like when you smell the milk after its 'sell by' date—it always smells sour. It's hard to tell what's real or if your imagination is playing tricks.

Sanctuary was kinda like that. How much was just bad luck, bad health, bad water? How much was more than that? More importantly, knowing what we did about the place, what kept us all here? Well, it was the money of course.

I thought about leaving that first night after listening to Patrick's story. But I'm stubborn, always have been ever since I slammed the door in my mom's face back in my teens and never looked back. Maybe, I just lacked sense, maybe we all did, but money makes fools of everyone.

❦

THE STILL-RIVER MOTEL WAS LOCATED JUST OFF THE MAIN drag. Its reputation was unsavory, but it was cheap and local, just what I needed for my business.

Quentin was the night manager. He looked how you'd expect: pasty, soft, shiny head up on top, ponytail down the back, and dark-circled eyes. Repulsive looking, but nice enough. After some business discussion, he agreed to provide me with a room and turn a blind eye.

The room Quentin gave me was disgusting. No one would ever say I had fancy tastes, but I do like sheets that don't peel apart like a grilled cheese sandwich. So, I set about prettying up the room before I started welcoming customers.

While I was laying a plastic sheet under the hotel sheets, on the cheap bare mattress, I saw the stain.

Now, there are many kinds of motel room mattress stains. I won't go into all the types, colors, and causes. I'm sure you can figure them out. Well, *this* stain was black. Black like ink. Big as a man. And it stunk. I'd never seen a stain like that before.

I stared at it, then tried to get rid of it. Scrubbing with water and cleaner didn't help at all. I tried flipping the mattress over, double sheeting it, and then lying down. But like a tell-tale heart hammering beneath the floorboards, I could still smell the fishy-chemical stink of it. You may be shocked to know a two-bit hooker would know a Poe story like that, but what can I say? I've always had layers. I always liked school and loved reading. If my home life hadn't been utter shit, who knows, maybe I'd have gone off to college. Doesn't matter now. Point was, like that heart thumping guilt through the floorboards, that inky stain was getting to me. I couldn't relax knowing it was there. I could feel the stain was under me.

Did someone who was coated in oil lay down on the bed? Was it a Sanctuary fetish, some sort of black gold body massage thing? Had a fire caused it? Mold? What?

Then there was the smell. That stain stunk. Fish-like, chemi-cal, foul. It stunk so bad I cracked the windows open.

I eventually paid Quentin to give me a new mattress. Saw him drag the "new" mattress out of the room next door. The "new" one stunk too but it was just B.O. It was riddled with the familiar old stains: yellow, red, brown.

But mercifully, no black.

❧

A FEW DAYS IN, AND I WAS WORKING STEADY. THEN THERE was a knock on my door. It was the nervous rat-a-tat-tat of a john looking for action.

I peered through my peephole. Outside the door, a man stood with his face turned away.

"Yeah?" I said through the flimsy door. I didn't like the way he moved; shuffling foot to foot, head jerking as he looked up and down the hall.

He put his eye to the peephole, trying to see in. "Looking for a friend, a lady friend. This the right room?"

My gut told me to say no, but my head said, "money's money." So, I opened the door.

He burst into the room, radiating nervous energy. Wired. He wouldn't make eye contact; paced the room like a cat.

"My friend is coming," he said after circling the room, "don't lock the door."

"Your friend?" My mind went to the knife I kept hidden under my pillow. You have to be careful with a knife. Draw it when it's not necessary and pretty soon it will become necessary, but it was good to know that it was there.

He stopped and looked at me for the first time. "Yeah, my friend. My name's Owen." He broke off eye contact and paced again. So, Owen and I waited.

After a while there was another knock. Owen walked over to the door and let another man in. This guy was silent, hood up, face a mess of stubble. I glanced at the phone and wondered if I should be calling the night manager.

Owen followed my glance. "Nothing sketchy miss, we promise," he said in a flurry, eyes too wide. "This is my buddy Peter." The hood just nodded.

"You're prettier than the other girl who used to use this room," Owen said, then looked away, embarrassed. I noticed the way he scratched at his arms, like a dog with fleas.

"What other girl?" I asked, mouth going dry, finding Owen's endless movement and Peter's stillness freaky.

"Never mind. Doesn't matter."

Turns out that Owen was a watcher and Peter was a doer. I don't mind a little weird stuff as long as the price is right. The price was right that night.

At first, it was just bad sex. Peter kept all his clothes on, even the hood. He didn't so much mount me as he did crawl up on me. I caught the chemical smell of oil and saw the dirt under his fingernails, but I've had worse.

While Peter started getting his money's worth, Owen settled into the only chair in the room, already working at himself with efficiency.

Thank god it was all over fast. Peter came almost silently. His body went rigid for a moment, then he slid off of me.

As he pulled up his pants, I noticed the red irritated skin on his thighs. He saw me looking and averted his eyes. Was he ashamed? He dropped the rubber in the trash beside the bed and wiped his hands on his jeans.

Then, with a grunt, Owen came. A spurt of black on the carpet. Black like oil. The kind of black you don't want to see on the business end of someone's dick.

A pearlescent black puddle.

I stared at it. He stared at me staring at it.

"I didn't touch you. No harm, right?"

"Get the fuck out, and never come back," I screamed.

As the door slammed closed behind them, I was on my feet and heading to the trashcan. I breathed out a sigh of relief when I saw the condom. No black slick there, just plain old cum.

AFTER THE LONGEST, HOTTEST SHOWER ON THE PLANET, I tried and failed to get some sleep. Images of the black stain came back again and again unbidden. Under a washcloth I'd spread over it, the puddle of black jism glistening on the carpet haunted me.

I went to Quentin that night. Stomped down the hall to his greasy little booth in my nightgown with a scowl that could strip paint off a building.

"Tell me about the other girl, Quentin, the one who used to work my room."

Quentin hemmed and hawed, but finally caved, as weak-willed men always do. He told me what I wanted to know.

"She was crazy, a junkie. She started saying something was burning her inside, from the inside out. Then one day she came down to my office clawing at herself and wailing, wanted help, wanted me to call an ambulance." He pulled his ponytail over his shoulder and nervously stroked the end.

"And then?" I prodded him.

"Then nothing. I told her to sober up or she would end up in jail or rehab. Sent her back to her room." Quentin paused then, a ghost of something crossing his face, regret perhaps. He flicked his ponytail back, and opened his hands wide. "Then she killed herself or tried to cut it out of herself and died, or something like that. She was nuts. I dunno, I mean she was a dirty crackhead. It happens."

"On my mattress?" I asked, mouth dry. "'Cuz' that's not blood all over it."

He shrugged, "Not your mattress any more. Not your problem neither."

Nice guy, right?

⚜

AFTER THAT I DECIDED IT WAS BETTER TO SEVER MY BUSINESS ties with The Still-Water Motel and its clientele. Start over. Step it up a notch.

I found the perfect location between the main drag and the oil fields. A little apartment over an old widow's garage. She lived in the main house. Mostly deaf, she was just happy to see another woman in town. If she knew how I paid my rent, she seemed indifferent. I paid on time, and she asked no questions. Word on the street was she used to be a cat lady, and her house did have that faint pissy odor. But the kitties had either all run off or died, like all the pets in Sanctuary.

As for the working girl in the motel? I asked around and learned that yes, she was a crackhead, and yes, I was much prettier, and she killed herself. Details of the suicide were sketchy. Some people said she cut her wrists, others said she disemboweled herself, and a few said that she tried to cut out her own womb open because something was growing in there. It was because she was crazy and a tweaker, they said, not because there was anything inside to actually cut out.

I upped my rate. I became a lot more discerning in my clientele. Referrals only. Showers for the clients before business, and I would inspect the goods. I was greedy, but I wasn't suicidal.

❧

I STARTED HAVING A RECURRING DREAM: I'M SITTING IN A bathtub, staring at my toes as they peep out of the water. Outside the window, the sky churns, and green clouds streak past, faster and faster. A warm, sickly wind flutters the curtains, bringing with it the noxious stink of sulfur and the chemical burn of solvents.

I watch as black fluid seeps from between my legs. It spreads like ink in water, like smoke. Oil: sticky and thick. Foul smelling. I stand and a great gush empties from my womb, painting my legs black. I open my mouth to scream and it pours from my mouth, gurgling and gagging me.

❧

ONE NIGHT AS HE WASHED UP, I NOTICED A RASH ON PATRICK, who had become one of my regulars. It was on one shoulder blade, in that hard-to-reach spot.

"What's that?" I asked, voice trembling. I knew but asked all the same. Patrick was one of my favorite customers.

"Oh yeah, that. Just Rig Rash, or Pit Rash, whatever you want to call it." He slid his shirt on hiding his face for a moment.

"You ever get that rash working on other oil fields? Outside of Sanctuary?" I asked.

He pulled the shirt down and shook his head. "Only here."

A moment later he added, "All the guys here get it eventually."

He was right about that. More and more of my clients came

in with blotches of angry rash, reminding me of poison ivy on steroids. The worse it got, the more the sores and rash wept, blackish and streaked with pus. The smell made me gag.

I washed all my linens in bleach after every visitor and practically scoured myself raw after they touched me. I filled the apartment with potpourri and scented candles. Still, my small abode took to stinking like everything else in the town of Sanctuary.

You may be wondering why I didn't pack it in right then. Truth is, folks were sick but I'd never had so much cash in hand in my whole life.

But yeah. It was wearing on me. The long days of strange pea soup skies and stinking hot air, the longer nights of bad dreams and sheets that never got clean despite gallons of bleach, it was getting to be too much. I looked at my reflection in the mirror one morning, wondering how bad it would have to get for me to leave. If I even could leave. I dreaded the answer.

ONE NIGHT I WAS SITTING AT MERV'S, A BAR ON MAIN Street, nursing a whiskey and waiting for a "date." I was surprised to see another working girl come in the place. She came over and sat beside me. She ordered a vodka and soda and lit a cigarette, blowing out a plume of smoke before talking to me.

The woman, older than me, or just harder living than me, introduced herself as Cheryl. She came from a neighboring pissant town for the boom, like we all had. Moths to a flame.

There are very few secrets between working girls, and Cheryl's tale was something else.

It seems one night she agreed to go to a foreman's trailer out on a dig site for a little fun. His birthday entertainment.

When she got to the trailer, three men were waiting outside. With the one who drove her there that made four guys. But my girl was a pro. Cheryl went in and they all proceeded to drink, dance, and have a good time. She was bent over the desk, one of the gentlemen riding her from behind while the others cheered him on when she saw something move in the far corner of the room.

She screamed. "I'm real afraid of rats! One of you get that thing or this party's over." She pushed away from lover boy and scrambled, still naked, up on the desk.

She was sure whatever it was, was hiding behind the file cabinet in the corner. The men, drunk and half-dressed, started to move the cabinet while one held up a fire extinguisher as a weapon.

Beneath the cabinet was a pitch-black stain in the carpet. At the center of the stain, was a hole in the floor. Cheryl said it looked like the stain was eating its way through the floor, right through the fiberglass insulation. Like something was trying to get in. Got in.

The men knelt and stared into the strange stinking hole. The carpet squished and bubbled up black fluid when one poked it with a pen. Cheryl wanted none of it. She was ready to go. She got off of the desk, and began gathering her things, getting dressed as fast as she could.

Just then, a rat exploded from the hole, streaked across the room and scrambled up her body, attaching itself to her forearm.

"ITS BODY WAS SLICK WITH OIL. THE BASTARD WAS SOGGY AND it reeked and it. . . it. . . ." Her breath was coming fast, and I could feel how freaked out she still was. She pulled back her sleeve and showed me the wound. Her forearm was gnarled and red with infection. A purplish-black scab had formed over the bites and scratch marks. "It still bleeds sometimes," Cheryl said, voice shaking, "never heals." She took a long drink of her vodka and went back to her story.

One of the men finally pulled the rat off her and threw it in the middle of the room. Another guy bashed it into pulp with the extinguisher. Even though it was a mess, you could tell it was a rat. But none of them had ever seen a rat like that before, dead or alive. Its body appeared to be more oil than fur, its blood was black, its organs tinged with green. Cheryl couldn't get out of that trailer fast enough.

Later, Cheryl heard the men had ripped up the floor and found a rat's nest under that damned trailer. Hundreds and hundreds of rats down there: living in the oil, drinking it, swimming in it, fucking in it, multiplying in it, dying in it. She shuddered, picked her cigarette out of the ashtray, and took a long drag off of it.

"I been to the hospital. They gave me those tetanus and rabies shots, and stitches too. Doesn't matter." She stubbed out the cigarette, grinding it hard against the plastic ashtray. "I may lose my arm; they say the wound is necrotic. They don't know what's wrong with it." She lit another cigarette and fell silent, rubbing at her arm over and over.

My mind wandered, trying to find connections. "You happen to know of another girl? Worked out of The Still-Water—one that killed herself?"

"You mean Shelley. I used to think what everyone else thought: that she was drug addled and out of her mind." Cheryl stopped rubbing at her arm and looked at me. "Y'know what I think now?" I shook my head no, but I had a suspicion.

"Now I think there really *was* something in her. Just like she said there was."

We got quiet again. Then Cheryl took my arm. Squeezed it hard and she looked me straight in the eyes. "Something is wrong in this town, and that wrongness is under our damn feet. I'm getting out. Come with me or not, but you sure as hell better get while the getting's good." She let go of my arm, her hand going back to her wounded arm, rubbing and rubbing as if she could rub out her stupid bad luck.

We parted ways not long after. I stayed, stubborn as hell, ignoring yet another warning.

⚜

THAT NIGHT I GOT INTO THE TUB, TRYING TO FORGET CHERYL'S story, but the dreams, the smells, the rats—it was getting to me. It wasn't just the stories, it was the town itself. Sanctuary was a queer little place: there were no kids here, no pets, and I couldn't remember having seen the goddamn sun once since I got town.

Could it really be the oil field causing all this? How could that even be? I'm not a learned woman, but I took some biology and earth science in high school. I watched the news from time to time. If it was as bad here as everyone said, even greed couldn't keep the town going. Right?

Conveniently a john, named John if you can believe that coincidence, suggested driving out to the oil fields the very next night.

He was ok for a trick. Young, optimistic, and not yet poisoned by the water and the land. New. He wanted to take me for a hamburger, have a real date, then impress me with his VIP access to ground zero.

I learned from young John that oil was first found on the Withers farm. The farm itself was long gone, though. Far as the eye could see were large rotating pumps and drills, lazily spinning, reminding me of dinosaurs. Above, the sky churned, and a sick feeling settled in my gut. That wrongness everyone kept telling me about—I could sense it all around me.

"This site is different, right? From the other oil fields?" I asked John as we walked closer to the job site, the smell growing thicker with every step.

John chuckled. Like I'd made a joke. But of course, I hadn't made any damn joke.

"People do have some crazy theories."

"Humor me, sweetheart—" I tucked my arm in his and he smiled down at me.

"Well, one of the guys—he's up and gone now—said that this oil, this whole operation was like nothing he'd ever seen. The actual crude oil is different. I don't believe him necessarily, but he said that's because the oil isn't from traditional fossils and organisms."

"I don't follow." But I had a bad feeling.

"Well, oil's a fossil fuel, right? Made up of old stuff, plants, animals, that died long, long ago. After all the years of pressure from the rock and heat, they become oil. But this guy thought the oil here all came from *one* dead creature. Not hundreds of dead dinosaurs or whatever. Just a single dead something. Huge."

I looked down at my feet. Couldn't help it. I had the unsettling feeling that I wasn't standing on the ground. Instead I felt like I was on a boat, floating on an impossibly deep ocean.

"Something bigger than the whole town. That guy thinks it's down there underneath this place. A creature so big no one has ever heard of it. So big it can't be discovered. Can you imagine, all this oil from one animal? That's the craziest theory I've heard, about Sanctuary, or any other place." We stopped walking, and with the hard sounds of the machinery all around us, he kissed me. I tasted his clean mouth and knew it wouldn't last.

☙❧

THAT NIGHT I COULDN'T GET JOHN'S WORDS OUT OF MY HEAD; a skittish part of my mind kept returning to it, trying to conjure what a creature like that would look like. Once asleep, I dreamt of black fluid pouring from me, and slimy-slick rats scrabbling in through the walls, up from the floorboards. Then John's there and he kisses me and black death spills from my mouth, covering his chin and bubbling over his chest; it keeps coming until he's soaked in it and stinking. Patrick's watching, laughing. All of us, filled to the brim with corruption.

At 3 am I woke and went for a glass of water from the bathroom sink. It was nearly to my lips when I caught sight of my reflection. I dropped the glass. It shattered on the enamel of the sink, but I barely noticed, because there on my collar bone, above the old tank top I wore to sleep in, was a patch of red rash.

"Oh fuck no." I'd been careful, so fucking careful, but it hadn't made any difference. I was going to end up like Cheryl, like Shelley. I felt along the rash's edges. The skin was hot and itchy as I prodded it. A sheen of pus came off on my fingertips, sticky. Stinking. It looked iridescent black in the bathroom light. As I prodded it, that fucking Rig Rash, it moved. The rash, keeping its outline, slithered downward, and settled on my chest.

Now, I know how that sounds. That sounds insane. But I swear to God. A saner woman might have gotten dressed and headed to the ER, but by that point I'd been in Sanctuary for five months. I knew that a hospital couldn't do shit for me.

In a panic I stumbled into my kitchen, found my biggest damn knife, grabbed a jug of Clorox from beneath the pantry, went back in the bathroom, and got to work. With my reflection to guide me, I cut the rash off of me before it could move again.

Once I'd filleted myself, I flushed the tainted skin down the toilet. I didn't know what else to do with it. I prayed to God, Jesus, Mary, whoever the hell might be out there, that I had gotten the infection out. Then I dumped the bleach straight onto my bleeding, skinless chest. Bleach kills everything after all.

Ohmygodohmygodohmygod. Once I stopped screaming and the throbbing eased up, I packed my bags, "borrowed" my landlady's car, left her enough money to buy another with a brief note apologizing for leaving on such short notice. Then I bailed, my foot to the pedal all the way past town lines.

Real or imagined, I could still feel *it* inside me, leaking out, staining the wadded-up bandages taped to my chest like a trail of squid's ink.

❦

THAT'S WHY I'VE GOT THIS STINKING BANDAGE ON MY CHEST and a wound that won't fucking heal.

That's why when you tell me you're headed up to Sanctuary I say, "Oh hell no." There's something in that boomtown getting fat on our greed and our disbelief. Something big and dead. Or maybe not as dead as we'd like to think, and it's under our feet. Hell, it's in our cars, it's heating our fucking houses. It's in the air we breathe. I know how that sounds, believe me. But everything I told you is true. Cut my heart out and hope to die.

Listen, how about we go back to your room now. We transact a little business. I'll give you a good deal on account of the bandage. Then we head south. I hear there's oil work in Louisiana. That's where I'm headed. You could go to Mardi Gras and kiss dusky Creole girls. Stand on firm ground. Make the right kind of mattress stains.

TRUST ME HONEY. SANCTUARY AIN'T WORTH IT.

𖤍 9 𖤍

DARK INHERITANCE

Emeline watched the car arrive. It gleamed like a beetle's carapace. And when the driver stepped out, he was thin as a bone and dressed in a fine black suit. He didn't react to the strange sight of the newly orphaned girl as she jumped into the backseat of the car and Emeline didn't look back at her old home as they pulled away. In her mind, she was already gone.

As the miles fell away, Emeline felt lighter. She was separated from her old life. Her future as wide open as the gray sky overhead. She was as free as the blackbirds that circled above the car. She was free of *It*.

For as long as she could remember, *It* had followed her, dogged as her very own shadow. *It* was the feel of air moving on her skin when there was no wind. *It* was the whisper of breath on the back of her neck when she was alone.

As a child, *It* kept her awake at night. Branches at her window became claws; creaks of the old house became *Its* footsteps drawing near. Every night was a symphony of small tortures, tiny paper cuts of fear, slowly draining her.

THE WORST THING? EVERY NIGHT ENDED THE SAME. SHE would wake at dawn with the weight of *It* on her chest, its invisible mouth latched to her own. Not in a kiss–it was sucking up her breath.

By the time she entered her teens, she was unstable and perpetually exhausted. Her grades were poor, her attendance spotty, and her friendships nonexistent. She wandered the halls of her school, eyes wide and feverish, dark circles under them.

To her peers and to Mrs. Johnson, her grandmotherly looking homeroom teacher, her demeanor appeared an affectation. Mrs. Johnson derisively referred to her as an Edward Gorey drawing come to life. Poor Emeline, so dramatic, as if she wanted to look like a ghost made flesh. They laughed and thought she was *trying* to be haunted.

Then, when Emeline was fifteen, her parents died. Her mother went first, succumbing to a mysterious illness. "Chronic Withering Disease," is what the doctor called it. *It*. Emeline knew he had no idea what he was talking about. But she didn't press for more information; the medical community could not help her. Then her father, driven mad with grief, took his own life soon after. Leaving her all alone.

They were dead and *It* was still haunting her every night. Worse still, *Its* attentions doubled after her mother was gone.

Emeline was to be shipped north. She had a great aunt there, her only living relative. Her aunt's name was Bernadette. Emeline had never seen her, let alone spoken to her. Emeline hoped that *It* would not follow her North. That *It* would be content to have taken her parents. She thought, surely, *surely*, the spirit would stay tethered to her home. That was how hauntings worked, right?

The driver was silent, so in tune with his car as to seem an organic extension of it. He didn't tell her his name, or offer any condolences for her loss. Emeline didn't mind. The simple peace of being out of her house, and free of *It* was all she needed. She closed her eyes and slept.

Hours later, they arrived at an old manor house. Emeline gazed up at it as she exited the car. It was taller than it was wide. A flight of crumbling stone steps led up from the road to its ornate wooden doors. Though it embodied every gothic fantasy and nightmare, the sight of the house still made Emeline hopeful.

She started up the stone steps into her new life.

AUNT BERNADETTE SAT IN A WHEELCHAIR BY THE FIRE. THE light and heat from it tried to chase the chill and the gloom away but failed to catch either. Bernadette was a small, hunched woman, with large eyes and a pinched mouth. Her hair was piled, tall and elaborate, on top of her head, reminding Emeline of an exotic bird's nest.

Emeline sat down in a chair beside her, her suitcase by her feet. Her aunt appraised her slowly, cautiously. Finally, she nodded and sat back in her chair, arthritic hands interlaced on her blanketed lap.

"You've got it. When I heard about your parents, I thought you might," her voice croaked, somewhere between a whisper and a groan.

Emeline was instantly covered in gooseflesh. She leaned in closer, to be sure she heard her clearly. "Got what?"

"Mara."

"My name is Emeline, Aunt Bernadette. Not Mara."

Bernadette's mouth broke into a sardonic smile. Yellowed teeth caught the glint of the firelight. "I know your name. Emeline was my mother's name," the old lady fixed her rheumy eyes on her. "A *Mara* is what you've got. It's trailing you. I'm close enough to death that I can almost see it." She cocked her head. Sniffed the air. "It's not as pretty as I thought it'd be."

"I don't know what you mean, Aunt." But even as she said it, Emeline knew it wasn't true. She knew exactly what her aunt was talking about. *It.*

It was still with her, floating just above her.

The unseen was dancing in the shadows with the firelight. Whispering in words no one could hear or understand. She felt *It* stronger now that her parents were gone. If anything, *It* seemed happy to be in a new place. Emeline nearly sobbed.

Bernadette saw the emotions and the realization cross the girl's face. "Runs in our family, unfortunately. They attach themselves to babies in the womb. Cause a lot of miscarriages. Me and my brother, your grandfather, were the only two of ten children that lived to adulthood. Don't know why our mother kept at it, the silly cow, but she did."

Bernadette smiled ruefully, and Emeline could see the pain in her aunt's eyes as she continued. "She just kept popping out the cursed and the damned."

As her aunt spoke, Emeline could feel *It* more and more; the Mara, perched on her shoulder, playing with her hair, fluttering her skirts. *Its* mouth under her shirt, on her skin, the prick of its sucking. Taunting her. Making her feel ashamed that she'd ever dared to hope.

It had a name now. *It* was real. Mara.

"I was lucky, if you consider being alive lucky. My brother had one, your Grandfather, that is. It killed him, killed his wife, killed most of his children. 'Cept your mother. But it got her too, eventually."

Emeline had never considered this. Never considered that perhaps her mother had suffered as she suffered. Perhaps she should have tried speaking to her mother when she'd had the chance.

"What is it? The Mara?"

"Precisely? I'm not sure. Consider it a parasite; a leech. A sucking thing."

"Can I get rid of it?"

Her aunt pulled a chain from around her neck. At the end hung a cluster of pendants and satchels. She fingered through them like they were some strange alchemical rosary.

"We can burn some sage, get you some charms, even say some prayers. But honestly, it won't do a lick of good. Some families have cancer or diabetes. We have this. My father spent his life researching how to rid himself of his Mara, with no luck. He never found a cure for it." She was so emotionless and matter of fact. Emeline's face darkened, angry. Her whole life she thought she was insane. Now this old woman was telling her that wasn't the case, but it was still hopeless. She was slowly dying no matter what.

"What about you, then? Why not you?"

The old woman's smile turned sad. "I was sickly—all my life, really—and weak. I guess the Mara didn't want me. It saw what was on the menu and sent it back to the kitchen."

⚜

EMELINE'S NEW BEDROOM WAS A TINY SERVANT'S ROOM IN A drafty eave at the top of the house. She sat on the narrow cot and unpacked her things. All her worldly possessions lay on the mattress before her; a few outfits, a photo of her parents, and some old books.

She took stock of herself. Yes, she *was* cursed. But the Mara, now that it had a name, was almost a comfort. At least she wasn't crazy. At least she wasn't Aunt Bernadette, stuck in a drafty house surrounded by empty memories of those she'd lost. Not yet.

Emeline crawled into bed and tried to fall asleep. Of course, the Mara's attentions were on her instantly. The pressure on her chest. The sucking on her mouth. Stealing all her breaths.

She lay there, as she had every night of her life. But on this night, its attentions were more intense, taking more of her than ever before. But that made sense now, didn't it? She was the last of her family line. The last of those afflicted by the Mara's kiss. As it sucked her breath away, it filled her with something new: resolve.

She would not go the way of her family. She was going to beat this.

⊗⁊⊗

BY THE ANEMIC DAWN LIGHT, SHE EXPLORED THE MUSTY, elaborate old house.

The library was two stories high, almost as full of books as it was of dust. Her aunt was right: her great-great grandfather had been quite the scholar. His collection was full of texts that dealt with the fantastic, with possessions, with spirits and hauntings. She spent hours, obsessively looking for some clue as to the origins of the Mara. As she retraced his investigative steps, she felt a glimmer of hope that, with time, she could discover something he had missed. She would find the clue, the antidote, the ritual, the *anything* that would relieve her.

That first day passed in a blur. The sky darkened. She stumbled out of the library, her aunt nowhere in sight, and collapsed into bed. Her dust covered fingers gripped the pillow as the Mara lay atop her.

Days passed, and she spent her time in the library poring over the pages and pages of arcane law and folklore. She learned about every beast and ghoul that had tormented the earth at one point or another, but never more than a brief mention of the Mara. Every turn she took through the maze of books was a dead end.

One day, she looked up to see Bernadette watching her. She'd wheeled her chair into the doorway and was staring at Emeline.

"You ready to return to school?"

"I'm looking for an answer," Emeline said.

Bernadette nodded. "I admire your will to live, girl. My father had that will, too. I loved that about him. He spent his life in this library, searching and searching. But he still ended up dead."

Bernadette started to wheel herself away then stopped. Looked back at Emeline. "Give up your search, child. Do not fear death. It is sometimes better than the alternative."

Emeline continued her hunt. That night, the Mara was so voracious that she woke with a bloody mouth from its incessant sucking.

⬧

"BUT HOW DID WE GET TO BE THIS WAY?" EMELINE WAS sitting at the dinner table, a bowl of steamy brown broth in front of her. She had no appetite and even lifting the spoon tired her. Bernadette stared at her from across the table.

"Surely there must have been a source. An originator of this. . . affliction."

Bernadette narrowed her eyes and sighed.

"It's just a story, one that my father used to tell me about his own father. He was an important man, a landowner and a businessman. I'm sure he had some good traits, but generosity wasn't among them." Bernadette stopped to slurp her soup.

"There was a drought. Nature's not known for its generosity either. Many of the farmers were unable to pay their rent. There was one family, an old and respected family, that allegedly practiced magicks. . ." she trailed off for a moment as if not sure what to say about them.

"My grandfather was a modern man. He was a skeptical man, not a church goer, and fancied himself a man of science. A great lover of Darwin and reason. He was warned, but he didn't listen. He evicted the family."

Emeline listened to all of this, rapt. "They cursed him?"

"If that's the word you feel most comfortable with, yes. I don't know what process they used, what god they invoked, what favor they called in. But that was the moment when the Mara became our family's burden. Our punishment. Since then, we've all withered. We've all wasted. And so, it will be. . . well, until we die. You are the last, after all."

Bernadette stopped speaking then. Again, it seemed to Emeline like the old woman was holding back a piece of information. Emeline watched her face, waiting for some final word, some clue to aid her search, some signpost to lead her out from under the Mara's shadow.

"How's your soup?" was the next thing out of Bernadette's mouth.

⚜

ANOTHER WEEK OF SCOURING THE LIBRARY, ANOTHER WEEK OF no answers. She started to get the impression that the Mara was laughing at her. Her dresses hung off her shoulders as the weight melted from her body. Each night, the three-story hike to her attic room became more and more of a challenge. She decided she needed to expand her search. Her grandfather had failed to find an answer in these books. She needed new ones.

She found the driver, still bone thin, still dressed in black, sitting in the kitchen, eating a sandwich.

"I need to go out," she said. He turned and looked at her. He appeared shocked by how wan she looked. "Can you take me to some place that sells old, rare books? Like the ones in the library here?"

He swallowed his bite of food and nodded.

⚜

IT BECAME CLEAR RATHER QUICKLY THAT THE DRIVER HAD A specific place in mind. He drove her away from the house, through a hilly countryside and finally into a quaint village. He drove her down small, nameless roads. Then he stopped the car in front of a rundown shop with a sign that simply read: "Books." She got out of the car. The driver waited.

Emeline was so weak from the Mara's nightly feasting that it took her two tries to push in the store's old door.

The room inside was narrow and long, crammed floor to ceiling, wall to wall, every inch, with books. There was no organization system whatsoever. Cookbooks and children's books, maps and ledgers, pulp ghost stories and field guides mingled together. Not even alphabetized.

A sickly ray of daylight struggled its way through the windows and Emeline had to squint to make out the spines on the old, faded books. She was halfway through the first shelf when someone cleared his throat behind her.

She turned, surprised. It was an old man, half her height, his bald pate shining, glasses so thick they obscured his eyes.

"I was looking for something, maybe you could help me?" she said timidly. The old man said nothing, watchful behind his foggy lenses. "I can't seem to navigate your. . . system."

"What are you looking for?" He said finally.

"Occult books. Specifically," she hesitated, not sure exactly how to say it, "for banishments. How to banish malevolent spirits."

The old man scratched his chin and looked down the line of the shop. "What kind of spirits?" he asked.

"A Mara," she said.

He nodded, like maybe he'd expected this. "We've got a book on that topic—only one. Highly specific, it is. Been here for a number of years. You'll find it in the back. You'll have to look yourself though—" He took his glasses off revealing two eyes clouded with cataracts, milky white. "I never find what I'm looking for anymore."

She went to the back. Shelf by shelf she searched, the hours passed, her eyes throbbing. She was going through the last shelf in the last row, when she accidentally shoved the book on mysticism she was holding with more force than was necessary. The entire case shook and a smaller book fell to the floor. With a sigh, she knelt, the movement making her dizzy, and noticed a book tucked underneath the massive bottom shelf. She reached for it, prying it free.

What she pulled out was an old book, older than the United States itself. As she opened its worn cover, she could feel the Mara's intake of breath next to her ear. She must be close to something.

It was an old grimoire, written in sprawling, ornate English. The ancient book was full of rituals, spells, incantations, and, yes, even banishments.

Her heart fluttered. There was an entire chapter of spells devoted to Maras.

She brought the book to the old man, fearing its cost, knowing she would have to steal it if the price was too steep. "How much is this?" she asked as the Mara scratched at her neck. She ignored it. The Mara then tugged on the book with invisible hands.

The old man said "I believe it already belongs to you. Just take it and go."

৩৵৩

AT HOME, EMELINE WENT RIGHT UP TO HER ROOM WITH THE book, ignoring dinner, ignoring her aunt. By the time she reached her bed, she was so weak and exhausted by the Mara's constant assault that she could barely read the book, even by the brightest light.

It was hard work to parse the meaning of the archaic text, but by deep night, she had finally uncovered something she doubted even her Grandfather knew about the Mara.

The more she read, the more vicious the Mara became. Its movements fluttered the curtains, her wardrobe door opened and closed, and the floorboards sporadically moaned. When Emeline saw the indentation of weight on the quilt beside her, she knew she must be close to something. She had never seen it so animated while she was fully awake before.

Her entire body crawled with excitement when she found the passage that she sought. The language was ornate, but it boiled down to one simple truth: *The Mara cannot be banished. It can only be absorbed.*

Absorbed. Into herself. As hard as she looked, she could find no information on what that actually meant. What happened when one absorbed a spirit?

That next morning at breakfast, Emeline could barely contain herself.

"Did your father ever talk about the Ritual of Absorption?" Emeline asked.

Aunt Bernadette gave her an odd look. She sniffed, and said "No. Why? What nonsense do you have in your head now?" Her tone was so clipped that Emeline thought she was lying.

"Nothing. . .just found a mention of it in one of his texts." Emeline didn't tell her aunt about the book. Perhaps the old woman was not an ally after all.

"Nonsense," Bernadette said, then went on forcefully. "There's no mention of absorption in any book in that library. Ritual magick is messy business. It is powerful and extremely dangerous."

⚜

WHAT DOES DANGER MEAN TO SOMEONE WHO IS ALREADY DOOMED? This thought pounded through Emeline's head that night as the Mara laid atop her, mouth to mouth. She felt her muscles dwindling, and she yearned for sleep: any sleep at all. What she wouldn't give for a single moment of unmolested rest. She hated the feeling of it clinging to her. Hated how fat the Mara must be getting off her life force. She thought it must look like a swollen gray tick, riding along on her back.

No. She would not allow the Mara to slowly drain her of life. She would not follow in her parents' footsteps. She would not die as three generations of her family had died. She was stronger. She would live.

She spent the entire next day gathering the materials needed for the spell. They were not as obscure as she expected: simple herbs, a cup of salt, three links of silver chain. The bird feather was the hardest, in the end, she pulled a pheasant feather off an old hat in her aunt's closet.

The blood was the easiest—she'd use her own.

That night, she set about drawing the sigils in salt and herbs on the floor. When it came time to gather the blood for the internal sigils and binding circle, she paused: hand poised above her wrist, razor touching the pale skin there. Could she do this?

Yes.

Yes, she could. And with a hiss, she cut, the sharp razor tracing over her flesh, parting it with ease. She filled the cup and bound the wound.

All the while, the Mara tried to stop her. Her skin bruised where *Its* invisible fists beat her. *It* ripped a chunk of her hair out and tossed it to the floor.

She ignored it as best she could and stayed strong, but her hands shook as she glanced from the book to the floor. Her fear of botching the ritual grew stronger as she checked each symbol, making sure she had followed the instructions exactly. She would get only one chance to do this. She knew the Mara would never let her try again.

Emeline trembled as she started to drip her blood into the shape of a circle. Her eyes welled with tears as she got closer and closer to completing it. Once the circle was complete, the ritual would begin.

The blood *dripped, dripped, dripped* onto the floor. The Mara screamed in her ear, she felt its mouth open in front of her, felt it trying to consume her, to end her. But she did not flinch. A lifetime of its nightly attacks had hardened her more than she'd even realized.

Finally, the lines of the circle met.

And the attacks just. . . stopped. As if a door had slammed shut. Inside the circle, the Mara could not touch her. Laughter burst out of Emeline. It was so quiet in the circle. A moment of peace after ages of endless torture.

But of course, the ritual wasn't finished. It had only just begun. She pulled the book to her lap and began to chant the words written there.

At first, she said them timidly. Soon the chant began to take on a life of its own. She said the words over and over, louder and louder. The words opened her up, pushing through her, inflating her.

She started to scream the words. Her body felt like it was being torn apart at the seams.

The candles went out. The only sound was her voice.

The darkness began to undulate. There was something out there, in the dark. Still she chanted.

The salt circle burst into flame.

She lost herself in the fire and the words. She felt like she was being filled with hot sand. She was going to explode, she was too full, she was stretched too thin.

The fire circle dimmed to a low flickering and she saw something on the other side of the flame. Something watching her.

It was more insect than human. Its eyes glistened blackly, looking in all directions at once. Mandibles clicked above a strangely human mouth. It smiled and revealed rows of sharp, needle-like teeth. Its neck was long, like a praying mantis. Its chest was lined with breasts, its legs covered with sharp quills. It circled the ring, hunched on all fours, trying to find a way in. Upright it was huge. Tall, with long lethal limbs, utterly inhuman, and strangely feminine. It breathed loudly in the silence. This was the thing that had slept on top of her, the terrible mouth that had been pressed to hers, the breath she had felt on her skin a thousand times. It was horrible. It was beautiful.

It was The Mara. Her Mara.

Time to finish the ritual, now that the creature has been made flesh.

Emeline's hand moved of its own accord, reached out and broke the circle of salt and fire.

The Mara charged in.

⚜

WHEN SHE WOKE, THE SKY WAS ORANGE AND PURPLE WITH dawn.

She stretched and stood, noting that the blood boundary was gone and the salt circle was now a black ring, burnt into the floor.

Emeline timidly crossed the line and waited. She could not sense the Mara anywhere. It had worked! She was finally alone. Truly alone.

It was on her second step outside of the circle that she felt it. Her insides were *off* somehow. The movement in her limbs, the air in her lungs, the taste in her mouth: all foreign and strange.

She rushed to the vanity mirror, brought herself nose to nose with her own reflection.

Her eyes had changed color. No longer pale brown, they were black as ink. She pulled back her lips and saw her teeth, blunt, regular, as was her tongue. All looked normal.

But those eyes. Those were NOT her eyes. As she stared into them, her skin tingled. Then itched. A sound began, inside her head, like a swarm of insects. Inside and out, her body revolted against her.

Emeline fled the horror of the mirror. Raced down the twisting stairs. Burst into her aunt's bedroom. The old woman was awake, propped up in bed. Emeline didn't have to say anything; Bernadette saw her eyes.

"What have you done?" she whispered, fearful, unsympathetic.

"I thought it would vanish. I thought the ritual was supposed to make it go away—"

"What ritual?"

Emeline's breath was short, her insides twisted into knots of pain and fear. "The Ritual of Absorption. I found a rare book, one from a bookshop—and I used it."

Bernadette frowned, her face falling. "*A bookshop*? You fool. You poor, young fool. I told you there was no cure. That book was nothing but false hope and evil. That is why I got rid of it all those years ago. To stop my damned father from doing that ritual. And you found it. I should have burnt it, it's no cure."

Emeline's dark eyes stretched wide. "What have I done?"

Bernadette laughed humorlessly. "The Mara is pure spiritual emptiness. That can't be destroyed. You can't smother a black hole, nor fill it in." The old woman spat the words, her voice caught between anger and sadness. "The void remains, girl. The hole always hungers. You didn't defeat it, you absorbed it into yourself."

"What does that mean?" Emeline's question was whispered in a voice that she no longer recognized as her own. Her head swarmed, her skin crawled, her heart thumped fast and hard.

Emeline fell into her aunt's arms, squeezing the fragile old body tight. She sobbed.

Whatever it meant, it was happening.

Awareness bloomed inside of Emeline. And with it, an appetite stirred. An indescribable emptiness awoke in her. The black hole, the hunger that was never sated. The Mara, now inside her, now a part of her, flared to life. It pushed her. She could sense the life force inside her aunt. She began to salivate.

Her aunt was old. She was weak. She could not fight.

Emeline pressed her mouth to her struggling aunt's. Sucking, starving, desperate. The old woman's fists beat feebly against her embrace.

Frustrated, her jaw opened impossibly wide, rows and rows of razor-sharp needles pushed out of her gums. Emeline took her aunt's whole head into her mouth. The old woman was too frail to fight back. But she did scream.

Emeline bit down. The skin and tendons parted below the chin, the skull bones cracked like thin ice, and a fount of hot blood erupted, spraying her face, soaking her nightgown.

Emeline moaned as she gorged herself on the meager life force. But it wasn't enough.

The old woman tasted sour. Her myriad cancers and ailments provided little nourishment. The Mara had been right to ignore the old woman all these years.

Emeline was now the Mara and the Mara was now Emeline. They were intertwined into one mind. They were very hungry.

She went to the driver's room next. He opened his mouth to beg, but he did not get the chance. His screams, like his blood, sated her. The Mara was no longer a creature of spirit, but one of flesh, and its hunger had changed accordingly.

Emeline/Mara crawled up the stairs to the attic bed and curled up, full and content. At least, for the time being. For the first time in years, Emeline slept.

Peacefully.

10

THE DROWNED SIREN

Hold your breath.

Keep holding it. Hold it until your chest is on fire, until you see spots, until your ears pop. Hold it even while your body bucks and begins to fight you, hold it.

And when you can fight no longer, and your body takes over your mind, forces you to take that breath, let the water in.

Let it fill you until you sink, let it fill you until you are dead.

And then you'll be with me.

"What?" I said, startled as I realized I'd been dozing on the bench, facing the sea, the spring day just on the side of too cold. Disoriented, I shivered and yanked my coat close.

I was alone. Dense wood at my back, and the sea in front, but I'd sworn there had been a voice at my ear. As if someone had been whispering so close that their lips nearly touched the side of my face. My fingertips traced the spot, skin crawling.

It was definitely a young woman's voice, breathy and high. What a strange dream: a woman whispering, telling me to hold my breath, to ultimately drown. Spooky. Remembering it motivated me to gather up my things and to stop milling around near the water, my lunch break was nearly over anyway.

Heavy bag across my shoulder, I was about to leave when an old man emerged from a thick copse of trees. I clapped a hand over my mouth to stop my scream. He was stooped, stout, and looked to be someone who'd been sleeping roughly for some time. Everything about him, from his hat to his shoes, was threadbare and a little grungy. His rheumy eyes watched me.

"She talking to you?" His said, his voice phlegmy.

"She? What?"

"There's a girl lives in the water there. Sad girl. Always trying to get people to jump in. So, it's best not to linger too long. There're some nice benches down at the west side of the park, those are better. Safer." He stuck his hands in ratty pockets, staring out at the glistening midday water. A few swans, surprisingly large up close, glided past.

"You telling me a ghost hangs out around here, trying to drown people?" I'm sure my voice positively dripped with doubt, but truth be told, I felt a thrill of fear as he spoke. Something *had* whispered in my ear, something feminine, and a little too close for comfort.

The old man glanced at me, squinting, before shrugging, "Whatever lady, believe what you want, I was just looking out for you. But you want to mess around and go swimming with ghosts, it's not my problem." He turned to go, back into the brush, like some woodland sprite.

"How do you know so much about her?" I called out, stopping him in his tracks. My curiosity winning out over my desire to move away from the beach and the man and the ghost.

The old man sighed, running a dirty hand over his face, "I've been coming to this park as long as I can remember, and she's always been here, waiting along the path, near this bench here. It's got an 'in memory of' on it. You see?"

I glanced down and was able to see the plaque from where I stood,

In Memory of Mabel Gray
beloved daughter
of Ernest and Geraldine Gray
1820-1843

"THAT'S HER, MABEL GRAY. THINK THAT SHE'S THE GHOST girl and this is her bench, and it's why she's always milling around, haunting it, trying to get others to drown like she did."

❦

LATER THAT NIGHT, I SAT IN MY SMALL ATTIC APARTMENT, A claustrophobic space with a peaked roof and tall skinny windows, and I conducted some cursory internet research on Mabel Gray and her patch of park.

The Willows was a small seaside park, established in 1800, that hugged a line of craggy cliffs and rocky beaches on the outskirts of town. In the past it had a boardwalk and a massive gazebo, and a large ornate carousel. All of that was gone now, destroyed after a terrible hurricane swept through in the '20s, and then again in the '40s. After that, the park was left to grow out more naturally, with snaking paths and small signs put in to educate tourists on the local flora and fauna.

In 1843, a year before the second terrible hurricane, a wealthy young woman named Mabel Gray took her own life by filling her pockets with rocks and walking right into the sea to drown. Her parents erected a bench at the spot, and her mother spent the rest of her life sitting on it, watching the sea and trying to understand her daughter's death.

There existed a semi-famous poem called, "The Drowned Siren" by C. Lowell Thomas, himself a semi-famous poet of that time and a suitor of Mabel Gray. In his biography, there was apparently an entire chapter that focused on his love of Mabel which grew into an unhealthy infatuation, and eventually, after she died, caused him to take his own life at the same spot. The very spot I had been sitting, and dozing, when something whispered in my ear.

It would be easy to say this was all just a fanciful coincidence, that I'd had a strange dream, and the old man perhaps even overheard me talking to myself, and was trying to scare me with a local legend. But something about the way it all lined up left me staring at my computer screen late into the evening.

In total, from what I could find, there had been at least three more drownings in the park. Two suicides and one body washed up on shore which authorities thought may have been foul play.

Three people, including Mabel and then C. Lowell Thomas, made five. Five was a lot for a sleepy little park in my opinion, though I had no comparable data on other parks. It was well after 2 am by this point and blearily I ordered an out of print copy of the C. Lowell Thomas biography as well as a small press book on local ghosts and legends of the Northeast that made mention of "The Siren of Willow Park."

My sleep, when it came, was strange. I floated in total blackness: the water warm as a bath. It was serene: the only sounds coming from inside my own body. The chug of my heart, the loud swallow of a throat. And as I bobbed in this warm, dark water, my eyes entirely useless in this dream, I felt the brush of something against the back of my legs, then something along my spine and outstretched arm.

Suddenly with that phantom touch, the dream went from relaxing to utterly terrifying. Every primitive part of my brain firing up in alarm all at once. There was something in the water, something underneath me. And even as I thought it, and tried to swim to shore or scream out, I found myself tangled, losing more and more mobility as something wrapped itself around my wrist, then my ankle, then my other ankle, it pulled me down, tightening as I struggled, the water splashing in my mouth, my panic making the salty brine taste like blood.

And out of the night-black water, a white face, skin smooth and almost rubbery, like the underside of an orca whale. Black, glassy eyes, a dainty pink mouth, a sad smile. And her long, long hair I realized with dawning horror, surrounded me, it unfurled like an oil slick, it was wrapped sentiently around my wrists and ankles, it was trying to drown me. She was. . .Mabel Gray.

I woke mid scream, bedsheets tangled around my flailing limbs as I choked and gasped for breath. A bad dream, that was all, a very vivid, very scary dream. I told myself it's what I got for staying up late reading about ghost girls and drownings. My imagination taking some spooky coincidence and making it into something more. The idea of laying back down and going back to sleep, of Mabel finding me in the depths of my own mind, got me up and about and ready to start my day while the sky still had a few stars in it.

"YOU DON'T REALLY BELIEVE IN GHOSTS, DO YOU?" BRIANNA raised an eyebrow as she sipped her coffee. I was sitting across from her at our regular table at the coffee shop where we usually spent our lunch breaks. While it was cute inside and had great coffee and sandwiches, it was always empty, and we both feared it would go out of business soon.

"I don't *not* believe. If that makes sense. But it is all weird right? I know you'll really think I've gone off the deep end with this next bit. . ." She waited, prodding me on.

"Turns out her family's house has been turned into a historical museum, and the lead historian there is also a paranormal hobbyist, and he wrote an article about ten years ago about the suicide phenomenon in The Willows and its connection with Mabel."

"And you are going to what? Talk to him?"

"Yes. I read his section on her in the local ghost tour book, but I think he knows more about all of it than what's in there. And I'm interested Brie, like really interested. I think I actually experienced the supernatural. And I want to follow it through. . . Crazy, huh?"

Brianna squinted at me, "You don't look crazy, just tired, you still not sleeping?"

I shook my head, wanting to change subject, "No, this recurring dream about her makes it hard to sleep."

"And you think talking to this 'expert' and researching her more will make the dreams about her go away? That seems kind of counterproductive."

"You don't think this is interesting at all? The mystery of it?" I asked, but Brianna's expression said all she needed to. She was worried for me.

❦

TERRY BRANCH WELCOMED ME INTO HIS SMALL, DUSTY office: a tiny room just off the main floor of the Gray House. It was stacked haphazardly with folders and books, and the sunlight illuminated the hordes of dust mites skating along on the breezes.

"So, Mabel Gray," he said as he settled in his squeaky old chair and regarded me, his comically bushy and vertically sloping eyebrows raised. "What do you want to know?"

I crossed and uncrossed my legs, trying to find the best way to explain without sounding crazy. I couldn't and finally said in a rush, "I want to know about her. I had something strange happen to me, at The Willows. Turns out I was sitting on her bench."

"Really?" he said with a smile, his prodigious eyebrows raised. "What happened?"

"Nothing much, definitely nothing interesting enough to put in a book or a supernatural account, but someone whispered in my ear. Told me to hold my breath underwater."

"Told you to kill yourself?" he said slyly. I nodded. "Yes, that's her style: our local ghost, she lures the lost and lonely into the sea to be with her. A classic lady ghost incarnation, ladies of lakes, or bodies of water, a siren who drowns the unwary."

"But if you know she exists, and I certainly do. . . I mean, isn't this proof of the supernatural? Or that there is something to these old stories? Who are these ghost women that drown people?" I was on the edge of my seat, palms sweaty, feeling like we were on to something. "Have you seen her?"

Terry squinted down into his lap, "A long time ago. I had just started here, as an assistant curator, and was cataloguing Mrs. Gray, Mabel's mother, her diaries. And I became totally enthralled by the historical period in which her daughter died. The woman was driven mad by her grief and spent her remaining days on that bench, begging her daughter to appear to her and angry that she lacked the courage to drown herself and join her. It was heavy, personal stuff."

"Mabel never appeared to her mother?" Terry shrugged.

"Hard to say. But I went out there, started having lunch at the spot, jogging in the mornings, strolling in the evening. Hoping to have a run-in with a real ghost."

"You said you did though."

"Sort of. It had been a few months of visiting Mabel's bench, and one day, no particular details of the day remain in my memory, I was jogging along and stepped into a puddle. I stopped, angry at my wet shoes, and noticed there were wet footprints along the path. I followed them to the edge, and without a thought in my head, very nearly walked right into the water. Like I was in a trance or something. It freaked me out and I fled the area, and honestly, I haven't been back there much since."

"But do you think something compelled you?"

"I do, and I think it was her. I think she is picky with her victims, that she likes to play games."

"But there are accounts of people seeing her, right? You said as much in your chapter."

"Oh yes, lots of people. To many, she looks like a lost young woman crying on a bench, in need of help. To others she was naked, a true siren or nymph, inviting them in for a swim. There have been many police reports of a naked woman in the park you know. Police don't even respond anymore, think it's just a prank. But this, this is where the story gets really interesting. . ." Terry met my eyes, excited. "One man I talked to said it wasn't a woman at *all*, but some sort of octopus thing floating in the water, with a woman's face."

I was suddenly covered in gooseflesh, remembering my dreams, that long serpentine hair, her bloodless face, her glassy eyes. "You alright Miss? You've gone white as a sheet?"

"Sorry, I'm fine, tell me more about the octopus sighting. Who was it?"

"Well, that's the issue with his account, first off, he's dead. He died not in the park, but in the hospital. He was a paranoid schizophrenic and he drowned himself in his own toilet, if you can believe it."

Terry opened a folder and slid it toward me across the desk, "But here is a corroboration of that sighting, this is an engraving from around 1905 by a local artist named Amelia Chabot. Called 'The Lady-Squid.'"

The picture showed a pastoral park scene, willow trees bending in the breeze, a low sun, and the sea reflecting it back, and in the gray water, a dark shape with long black tendrils reaching out. And the eye of the squid, when I looked close enough that my nose brushed the paper, was not an eye at all, but a woman's white face. A face I'd seen before. I sat back fast, my head spinning.

"You've seen her like that haven't you?" Terry said, watching me.

"In my dreams, a recurring dream, where she is all hair, no body, with a white face. I swear I knew nothing about that."

He nodded, "You'd best be careful then. I told you she likes games. Her boyfriend, C. Lowell Thomas, she infected him in this way after her death, he said she was constantly in his dreams, that she followed him endlessly, always at the corner of his eye, that he would find her hair in his bathwater. People thought him grief stricken and obsessed. Then he took his own life, joined her. Best watch yourself. No one will believe you, but I have folders of evidence here. But it's never enough to be more than a joke, or a local curiosity. You know I tried to even have that bench removed, and that area of the park restricted for safety."

"What happened?"

He frowned, "What do you think?"

THAT NIGHT, ALTHOUGH I WAS BONE TIRED, I COULDN'T SLEEP. I lay in bed staring at the ceiling, watching the shadows from the distorted branches scratch and claw along the peaked roof. The more I stared, the more the branches reminded me of tentacles, or reaching arms, or a hundred snakes. Or *Her*. I tried to ignore the shadows growing and swelling, leaving their branch shapes behind to become something more human shaped, more female shaped.

My breath hitched as I watched the shadows slither across my ceiling, deft and silent. The hair undulated, radiating from her head, I could see the delicate outline of a thin neck, shapely hips. No face, no eyes. Just a woman's outline. It crouched, above me, as if peering in through a skylight, hands and knees pressed to the cracked plaster.

I sobbed, frozen in place and staring up, my entire body soaked in sour sweat.

"What do you want from me?" I choked out, my pulse roared in my ears, my heart hammered like a bird in a felled cage.

At the sound of my voice she cocked her head as if she was listening and understood. "Why are you doing this? Mabel. Mabel Gray." Talking had given me back some sense of confidence, of self. As terrifying as the apparition stretched across my ceiling was, it was still only a shadow. And there wasn't an ocean to drown in tucked up in my tiny attic apartment.

I rose onto my knees, neck craned up. "Go pester someone else, Mabel. *Please*." The shadow ignored my request, watching me as I watched it. And only as the sky began to lighten and birds began to chirp, did she fade away, the shadows melting and reforming until only cracked plaster remained.

❧

"YOU LOOK REALLY BAD," BRIANNA said, "I THINK THIS GHOST stuff has gone far enough honestly."

I wiped at tears I hadn't realized were there and nodded. "If I sleep she is there, if I am awake she is there. No place to go."

"Maybe you should see someone, a doctor, someone. You can't keep not sleeping, it could kill you."

"I think that's what she wants—to kill me. She wants me dead and she is pushing me in that direction. Leaving me little other option."

"Now *you* are scaring me. You can't seriously be considering killing yourself? I will drive you to the hospital myself if that is what you are saying." Brianna watched me, frowning, and worried.

I put my hand up and sighed, "No, no I am not there yet. I am just saying that is what she wants. She likes to play her games. She likes to crawl around in my mind and on my ceilings,

I bet she would swim through this fucking coffee if I stared at it long enough."

"If you won't get medical help, what will you do? How do you stop a ghost?"

And that was really the question wasn't it. *How do you stop a ghost?*

"I have to go. Just tell Darryl I wasn't feeling well and went home early."

She snorted, "It's not a lie, he's worried about you too. We all are."

I left, catching a cab to the Gray Historical Mansion.

❦

"A BUNCH OF WEEDS?!" I YELLED, STANDING IN TEDDY'S office.

He shushed me, "Hear me out, I have been researching Mabel and your problem for years. And this is the best I can do. I believe if you wade in the water with these herbs in your hair and a wreath for her, she will leave you alone."

I laughed, but only because the other option was to openly weep. "That sounds like a death warrant for me."

"Hear me out. I think Mabel isn't just a ghost, I think she is something else. There are certain folk stories about creatures, water creatures who drown people. I think she is one them."

"And a fucking Christmas decoration isn't going to stop her! Teddy please. . ."

"That's the best I could find. There are tons of sources that praise sage as a ward against evil. Lavender, dill and rosemary, too. There is no murder to avenge, or body to find. Salt is often seen as a repellent for ghosts, but it's the ocean. This wreath is the best shot, you try to get the wreath around her neck or—"

"Or?"

"Move?" He chuckled, "Get away from the shore? Move to the Midwest far from the sea?"

I gave him a withering look and fought the urge to scream, instead opting to gather up my things. I thanked him for his research, took the books, and told him I would look over everything myself.

AT HOME, I TRIED TO READ, BUT THE WORDS SWAM ACROSS the page, exhaustion, a familiar companion at this point, perched on my shoulders and eyelids. Eventually, everyone must sleep, no matter how hard you fight it.

And she was there, I could feel her, swimming around me, her hair brushing my arms, featherlight, but no less terrifying for her gentleness. I was surrounded in darkness, entirely blind, no smell, no temperature even. Just the knowledge that she was near, and while I was blind in this dark dream world, she was not. I knew she could see me, and I knew she wanted me, that she grew impatient with me.

"I don't want to die," I said, or thought, as I wasn't entirely sure if I had a mouth in the dream.

She didn't answer, her hair sliding along, twisting around my wrists, my ankles, snaking up my legs. And out of the inky black, a glint of white, growing larger and larger, until her terrible, beautiful face was nose to nose with my own. Her skin glowed with a faint luminescence of a sea thing, or a fantasy thing, and her glassy eyes shimmered.

"You are out of time."

Her lips pressed to mine. Her cold tongue, like an eel, pried my mouth open, and a flood of water streamed in.

I woke sputtering and choking, the books I'd left open improbably soaked with salt water, as was the front of my shirt.

THAT'S HOW I FOUND MYSELF SITTING ON MABEL'S BENCH AT

dawn. If I wasn't there to meet a homicidal ghost, it would have been a gorgeous scene. The sun lit the water up in oranges and golds, the sea birds called out and circled above, and the air smelled of early summer: lush and verdant. Combined with the regular metronome of crashing waves, it was perfect and serene. This was probably the same scene Mabel's boyfriend looked at before drowning. And her sad mother watched over and over, spared and yet conversely tortured by the lack of her horrible haunting affections.

But I was out of time and I knew it, my sanity was dangling by the last frayed thread, and Mabel could get to me whether in or out of the water anyway. I'd been drowning in my dreams nightly for so long. And so, after leaving my things bundled up, with a letter addressed to Teddy, in case things went awry, I walked to the water's edge. I wore one wreath in my hair and carried the other. I lit my sage stick and tucked the lighter into my bikini top. It was only a few feet to drop in, though the water was misleadingly shallow and rocky. I gingerly scrambled over the coarse rocks and plants, careful not to drop my lit smudge stick of sage.

When the water reached my knees, the coldness had turned into a burning, but it was too late. I was in, and I knew she watched me from just below. I could sense her excitement, and her hunger. I prayed the wreath of herbs wasn't total bullshit as I squeezed the smudge stick, waving it around.

Hip height, my toes gone numb, then water at my ribs, then breasts, and soon my neck, the smudge stick gone out, I held it to my chest. My chin was insisting on keeping me above water. Fear a choking thing as the water splashed into my mouth, as the reality of what I was doing, and where I was, and more importantly who I was *with* became realer.

Head under.

I opened my eyes. It was murky, the early light doing little to help. The salt water irritated my eyes. I wondered how long I'd be forced to wait, or if my burning lungs would compel me up and out. I didn't need to wonder long though, for she appeared between one moment and the next, her hair unfurling like spilled ink, or smoke, and a young naked girl watched me, black eyes, small smile. And her voice filled my head:

"You came."

I responded in thought, always knowing, but only realizing now she could probably always read my mind. "I didn't have much choice."

"Are you scared?"

"Terrified."

"What's that in your hair? In your hand?" My hand fluttered up to the wreath. How would I get it over her head?

"Are you repelled?" She shook her head no, her smile growing.

"Old stories of the rusalka. To give people hope that they are in control."

"So, I am not in control?" She shook her head again.

My lungs were burning now and my vision had tunneled, I so badly wanted to breathe, to be above the water. She was closer now, and her two cold hands reached out and held my forearms.

"I'll be sad when you are gone," she said. In that moment, I tried to pull my arm free, to put the wreath over her head, get it around her neck. But her hold was like a vice and I could barely move.

I began to thrash, my legs kicking wildly, seeing the sky above, and wanting so badly to be out of it, but her grasp was intractable. As if we'd been fused. I was a fool, I realized: a fool to think I could reason with a creature like Mabel. Once she'd chosen me, shone her favor onto me, my fate had been sealed.

Teddy would receive my note, they'd find my body, the ridiculous herb crown, and Brianna would tell them how unbalanced I was, how I'd been haunted, delusional. And Teddy would argue that it was all real, bring out his manila folders of "proof," and then be laughed out of the police station as a kook.

"What a silly waste of a life." I thought to myself. What a fool to tempt fate and go to her with only a silly wreath of grocery store herbs in my hair.

"Shh," she said, and kissed my cheek with icy lips.

Just hold your breath.

Keep holding it. Hold it until your chest is on fire, until you see spots, until your ears pop. Hold it even while your body bucks and begins to fight you, hold it.

And when you can fight no longer, and your body takes over your mind, forces you to take that breath, let the water in.

Let it fill you until you sink, let it fill you until you are dead.

And then you'll be with me.

AND THEN, I WAS.

11

THE HORROR ON SYCAMORE LANE

I*t was such a shame.* The phrase was uttered reverently in beauty parlors and pharmacies, at the park, at the greengrocers. Telephone pole men up in cherry pickers hollered it down to old ladies on sidewalks. The entire town, it seemed, said it at least once. Head shaking, tongue clucking: *it was such a shame.*

Barbara, while quiet, was known all around town as a nice person. A kind woman who was generous around the holidays. She kept her house nice. Her yard was tidy, not flashy, not overgroomed, but tidy. Evenly trimmed grass, perennials mixed in with annuals. The garden was a reserved, orderly rainbow of color.

The black spot in her orderly life was her husband Bob. He was a salesman of some sort who traveled a lot. Not a very social fellow, his jaundiced skin and ruddy nose gave a clue of what his preferred hobby was. Bob was seldom seen on his days off, except when he trotted down the front path in his ratty old bathrobe, feet bare, to retrieve the newspaper.

Bob and Barbara moved to 220 Sycamore Lane as newlyweds. A spic-and-span housing development planted by the seeds of the GI Bill. Sycamore Lane blossomed into an unassuming street, filled with trim, middle-income homes. Bob and Barbara bought their house, with a small deposit provided by Barbara's widowed father. Bob's parents were dead. 220 Sycamore was a quaint Cape Cod style with yellow siding and white trim. It had a gray shingled roof and a stubby chimney, also painted white. As soon as they moved in they put a low chain-link fence around their postage-stamp sized yard. On Sycamore Lane the neighbors were not the type to clean up after their dogs. And there were enough dogs living on the lane to discolor and dig up a nice yard.

But the fence went beyond preserving their lawn. It was known around the neighborhood that Barbara was terrified of dogs. She had a small scar on her chin that she was good at covering up with makeup, but at the right angle you could see it. Everyone assumed it was from a dog bite. The scar marred an otherwise pretty face. Barbara was an average sized woman, curvy, with long auburn hair. She had hazel-colored eyes, the color of oxidized copper and fair skin with a dusting of freckles on her nose that made her look girlish. A pleasant looking woman with a shy smile and kind eyes.

When they moved into the house on 220 Sycamore, the neighborhood gossiped, as small close-knit streets are apt to. Barbara's widowed father was wealthy—at least by the standards of Sycamore Lane, and it seemed strange that a young rich man's daughter like Barbara would marry someone like Bob. He was considerably older than her, slovenly, and would barely wave if a neighbor called out. His clothes always appeared disheveled. Even when they were newlyweds, just moved to Sycamore Lane, his hair was thin, colorless, and not long for this world.

He also had, what Gloria Danforth of 200 Sycamore Lane, called, "dead eyes." Granted, Gloria Danforth had a spot of dementia, and rumors as to why Bob and Barbara had a chain-link fence put up also included a certain old woman—that looked like Gloria Danforth in a housecoat—who would pick flowers out of their garden at night. But Gloria was always very vocal about Bob and his dead eyes. "There's no soul in them," she said, "he stares right through you as if you were a ghost."

Barbara got pregnant a few years after they moved into the little yellow house. At that point Barbara had a few friends on the street, other women that waved and would occasionally chitchat on the other side of the fence while she gardened. She also made friends at the library where she volunteered once a week. With no mother or mother-in-law, the neighborhood, women worried about her. Alone while her husband travelled, keeping a house all by herself, taking care of a new baby all alone.

Mrs. Olivia Grady was as close as anyone to Barbara. She had even been inside their home. She and her husband Jason had been invited over occasionally for a meal or tea. Olivia had a small brood of children. She was a stout, kind-eyed woman with more heart than sense. She fussed over Barbara, helped her fix up a little nursery and prepare the diapers and bottles she would need. When Bob was in town, Olivia was not allowed to come over. It was through Olivia that the rumors of abuse came about.

Most of the neighbors could attest that Barbara occasionally had bruises, particularly around her wrists and neck, as if someone had grabbed her there, or choked her. She covered herself in makeup like old time movie stars, trying to hide the marks. But bruises were very hard to cover with makeup, they always seemed to show through the base.

It was a different time back then, and the sanctity of marriage was one of the few things respected by the residents of Sycamore Lane. If a brutish husband knocked his wife around once a month, what business was it of anyone's? Even Olivia Grady agreed. It was a terribly sad thing, she said, when the police came to her home for a statement, but what could you do? He was her husband.

When the baby came, Bob was away, on one of his many business trips. Olivia Grady drove Barbara to the hospital late at night when she went into labor. No one knew what number to call Bob at, and he didn't provide one. In the hospital gown, beneath the fluorescent lights, it was obvious that the dog attack Barbara suffered all those years earlier was more severe than first thought. Deep scars crisscrossed her chin and neck, down over the delicate skin of her chest. Her thighs were ravaged with deep grooves. Olivia Grady could only imagine the dog must have straddled her chest, biting at her throat, its hind legs clawing her thighs to find purchase.

Throughout her labor Barbara was a model patient, grunting and sweating, never swearing, barely speaking, and a few hours later, a tiny wet baby slid out. Olivia Grady gasped, looking from doctor to nurse, horrified. Barbara was exhausted, head leaning away, waiting for the sound of squeals and cries. Olivia could only stare, hand over her mouth.

The baby was covered with hair. A dark downy fur from tip to tail. At least there was no actual tail, just a regular baby bottom. Underneath the hair, the baby appeared ruddy, rubbery, and normal. After its air passages were cleared, it sobbed and roared with the angry vehemence of the healthiest newborn.

Despite this, the fur was a shock, even after the doctors assured both mother and mother's nosey friend that it was normal. The hair, called lanugo, would shed on its own. But Olivia was a mother three times over already, and was there for her sister, and the births of her sister-in-law's children. She had never seen a baby as hairy as this one. The baby was a girl; Barbara called her Isolde. Her choice of name for the baby was the talk of Sycamore Lane. What a strange name. Why not Sue, or Pamela or any normal name? And why so hairy? When they came home, new mother and baby received a lot of visits from the neighbors. They came with their arms laden with gifts and casseroles, but they all secretly wanted to catch a glimpse of the oddly named furry baby. True to the doctor's words, in a few weeks after coming home, the baby was as smooth, soft, and hairless as a normal baby. Bob returned, so no one else, beside Olivia Grady, dared come to their door anymore.

With a newborn in the house, Bob's behavior became even more curious. His absences were longer, leaving his young wife and new baby all alone for weeks at a time. When Bob was there, he never worked on the house, or even mowed the lawn. Even on the weekends when he was home, he would stay in that little house, the shades drawn. The only clue he was home at all was his big green Ford parked in the drive.

People gossiped at the grocery store when Barbara filled her basket with bottles of Rye and steak, so much steak, week in and week out. The talk about Bob the alcoholic, Bob the abusive layabout of a husband, continued with even more fervor. Barbara seemed happy as a new mother. Although she had puffiness under her eyes, and visible bruises on her wrists, she smiled and showed off her baby. Isolde was a lovely, chubby child. Her hair was redder than her mother's and her eyes were a pale sea-glass green. There was no mistaking the kinship: they were the spitting image of one another. Very little of Bob could be seen in the child, which the neighborhood unanimously agreed was a good thing.

Isolde was a charmer. She cooed and waved, smiling a toothless smile at all the fawning and attention. When Isolde was little, Barbara was seen around town more, proudly pushing her pram, bringing the baby to story hours at the library where she volunteered. She took the baby to the local nursing home to cheer up the seniors there. Isolde was a spark of light everywhere she went.

Bob, if it was possible, became more cloistered in their home. By the time Isolde was preschool age, no one even saw him emerge for the paper any longer. Only the green car, sometimes there, sometimes not, told the neighborhood he lived there any longer.

As Isolde got older, she grew into a shockingly beautiful child, the kind that takes your breath away. She looked like a perfect china doll come to life. Her red hair fell heavy and wavy down her back, her strangely pale green eyes were wreathed with thick dark lashes. She was shy though, painfully so. Her reticence to speak in class worried teachers. They wondered if she was able to speak at all. The bubbly infant had turned into a very serious little girl.

Mother and daughter were seen out and about less frequently, and when they were they were often whispering to one another. That was how Isolde communicated, whispering to her mother, and her mother speaking for her. Barbara seemed fine with the arrangement—which caused the rumor mill on Sycamore Lane to explode into a fury of gossiping. The stories grew: the child was simple, the child had been strangled by Bob and had damaged vocal cords, the child was crazy, Barbara was crazy and made the child afraid of outsiders...the list went on and on, growing more fantastical with every phone call and every teacup passed between neighbors.

Although shy and practically non-verbal, Isolde was a good student. She had no close friends—the few attempts to schedule play dates with Olivia Grady's children went decidedly unwell. Martha Plomp of 150 Sycamore Lane asked her young daughter, who was in the same class as Isolde, what she thought of the girl, and her child just shrugged. "She's spooky. But okay I guess."

Time passed on Sycamore Lane, and the green Ford was now more in the drive than not. Doris Heath, the aged head librarian, reported that Barbara told her that Bob had lost his job.

Barbara was seen out less and less now, and Isolde, a young lady, would run errands for her mother to the store and such. To buy the whiskey and meat that the family seemed to consume exclusively. What got the butcher and the cashiers talking again, were the bruises, just like the ones her mother had. At the young girl's wrists, at her neck. As if someone had grabbed her, or tied her down. They didn't see the bruises every time they saw her, but often enough. Barbara continued to volunteer at the library, until one day she sent a resignation letter. The letter said her family needed her too much for her to continue at the library, but thanked them for all the wonderful times. Doris Heath was worried, she talked to Olivia Grady about it. The handwriting was sloppier than Barbara's normal script, and Doris even wondered if Barbara had even written the letter. Isolde continued to attend school. She was now tall and willowy, her hair a shock of copper, coiling down her back. Her eyes were still that same strange green. She was beautiful, intimidatingly so, and although her nickname at school was still 'Spooky' the young boys started to take notice of her.

Derek Grady, one of Olivia's children, asked her to the homecoming dance. He told police later that she seemed surprised to be asked and blushed. She said yes and it was the talk of the entire school. Maybe Spooky was actually just a shy girl who had a drunk for a dad. Olivia was supportive of her son's impending date. She knew Barbara as well as anyone did, Barbara was a nice person. A good woman. Surely her daughter was the same.

When the night of the dance arrived, Derek nervously hurried up the walk, passing the chain-link fence, rusty with neglect. He heard neighborhood dogs barking, causing a terrible racket down the way. This was not surprising since those damned dogs, Old Man Walker of 68 Sycamore Lane's dogs to be precise, would arbitrarily pick a few days a month to bark and bark and bark. As soon as the barking would start, it would stop. It had been happening for as long as Derek could remember.

He got to the door, sweat soaked, knees knocking and reached out to ring the bell. He was scared Bob would open the door, and then he would have to make small talk with the intimidating, mystery man. His finger poised above the buzzer, a dreadful racket came from inside the house. A scream, genderless in its fear, tore through the home, rattling the glass panes. Derek panicked, unsure if he should run for help or stay, frozen in place by indecision. Something slammed against the door, and he heard the wood splintering. He fell backwards down the few cement steps. Another scream, angry and bestial as the door frame shook.

Derek scrambled away down the pathway, calling for help. Before he reached the chain-link fence, the front door exploded outwards, a shotgun blast splintering the wood and sending it raining down onto the steps. Derek dropped to his belly on the lawn. Timidly, he lifted his head an inch and saw movement through the hole. It was Bob, wearing a soiled undershirt, shotgun raised. While Bob's back was to him, the boy ran to the rusted gate, trying to loosen the latch. He nearly had it open when Bob slammed against the remains of the front door. His fleshy back was forced through the shattered wood, brought down by something furry and massive. Derek's first thought was a bear, his second a jaguar. Neither option made sense, but his brain was frozen. He stood on the lawn, corsage wilting in its plastic cube, while a dark mass of fury ripped Bob apart, savaging his throat and chest. Derek screamed. The thing froze, its head raised, its eyes a glassy strange green. Its black lips pulled back, revealing pink, blood-stained teeth, lethally long. The beast let out a growl. Derek vaulted the fence, dropping the corsage as he ran screaming down the sidewalk, police sirens already wailing in the background.

When the police arrived, the creature was long gone, a few reports had it running west toward the industrial part of town. The scene at the house raised more questions than answers. Derek sat in one of the cars with his mother, a scratchy wool blanket over his shoulders. Bob's body lay sprawled outside on the front steps. His throat was torn out. His yellowed eyes stared, filmed over, dead. Inside, the walls were scratched up and the furniture broken. In the basement, they found Barbara: nude, bound at the wrist and throat to the concrete wall with a rusty chain. Her chest was torn open, her torso traced with old scars and new wounds. Blood surrounded her like a lily pad. Barbara's heart was missing.

They couldn't find Isolde. Her room was untouched: a pink

dress laid out on the bed, pink shoes below on the floor, ready for the dance.

Sycamore Lane's gossip mills ran at full capacity. Had their neighbors been sex fiends? Perhaps they kept exotic pets inhumanely in their basement. A ferocious wildcat that finally escaped. And where was Isolde? They had seemed like such a nice family. Barbara was so loved down at the library, Doris said. Olivia clicked her tongue and remembered taking Barbara to the hospital the night she gave birth. "I guess you never really know anyone," she said, shaking her head.

From that night on, Derek Grady would often close his eyes, and see the beast's strange sea-glass green eyes staring back at him. He never told anyone who those eyes reminded him of. Needless to say, Derek didn't sleep very well after that.

It was all such a shame. Everyone in the neighborhood agreed.

12

THE RANCH

The thing darted from one tangle of brush and desert scrub to another. It was hunched over but fast. Its eyes shone red in the reflection of the lantern light. Heart in his throat, James held the light higher, painfully aware of how low the oil in it was. His other hand reached towards his belt where a revolver—and comfort—hung.

"Who's there?"

"You're trespassing."

James nearly leapt from his skin, he hadn't expected the thing to respond, especially not in a woman's voice.

"Show yourself!" He called out. "I am *armed*."

The voice, from the woman crouched in the bushes, concealed in shadow, simply laughed. "You're trespassing, and this land is not kind to those that do not belong."

He raised the lantern again, trying to see more than just an outline of the woman, "This Gerard Holbrook's land?" He asked.

"It may be that."

"My name is James Ashton. Mr. Holbrook sent for me, we've been corresponding through letters. I'm expected, if only you ask him. I've had a heck of time getting out here. My guide never met me at the train station, so I tried to make my way on my own, but my horse twisted its foot in a snake hole."

"You were expected yesterday." The woman said, and James felt a shiver run up his spine. If she knew who he was, why the hiding?

His patience grew short as anger burned away his fear, "I told you, lots of things got in the way of my being here on time. Please, I'm dead tired, walked all day and night with little food or water trying to make my way. I'm asleep on my feet ma'am— whoever you are. Can't you please come out and tell me who you are?"

"You don't need to know who I am just yet, Mr. Ashton. All you need to know is that I have been sent out to look for you."

"It's a miracle you found me, out here in this. . ." He wanted to say *wasteland:* miles and miles of sand and scrub, but he didn't want to offend her. "What should I call you?"

The woman sighed, the bush shook with her movement, but he could only see her outline on the other side of the spindly branches. "You may call me Louise, if you insist upon it."

"Thank you, Louise."

"Come on, it's still a long way to the main house." She set off at a brisk pace, and James had to jog to keep up with her. Her strange form always stayed just outside the light of the lantern. They traveled across the barren landscape for what felt like hours. He couldn't guess how she navigated in the dark, in all the sameness out here. James, silently trudging behind her, admitted to himself that this whole unpleasant adventure left a bad taste in his mouth.

He wished he could go back to when he first got the cordial letter from Mr. Holbrook. James had declined Mr. Holbrook's repeated loan applications, so it was a surprise when he got the letter inviting him out to the "Wild West" to see Mr. Holbrook's cattle ranch operation for himself. Holbrook felt that first-hand knowledge would change James' mind. James, for reasons that he could hardly recall now while trudging along in the desert, had agreed. His boss, old man Stimpson, praised him for his gumption, said he liked his drive. Stimpson told James that if he were ten years younger he'd jump at the chance to venture out to Holbrook's Ranch. It was in part to impress the old man that he accepted the invitation.

He traveled by rail for two weeks only to be dropped off in a dusty one-horse town. No guide awaited him as had been arranged, and the equally dusty townsfolk ogled him as if they'd never seen a stranger. No one could be persuaded to lead him into Holbrook's God forsaken land, hundreds of miles from anyone and anything. For an outlandish fee, he got a horse, some food, a lantern and a finger pointing west into the open plains.

He would have told Louise all of this, if she wasn't twenty paces or more ahead of him the whole time, never glancing back. Even when the last of his lamp oil ran out, and they were both submerged into darkness, she never came closer.

At nearly dawn, Holbrook Ranch, or what he hoped was the Ranch, came into view on the horizon. A dark scattering of buildings floating in acres of nothingness. He could have wept.

Louise opened the main gates, and then led him through a series of sub-gates. Each had to be unlocked and then relocked. James found the barriers strange considering there was nothing for miles and miles.

The main house was a handsome whitewashed building with a wraparound porch and a shining metal roof. There were patches of scrubby golden grasses and cacti planted along the porch, adding a homey feel to the harsh landscape. A few paces from the porch, feet aching and swollen, his satchel straining his arm, he turned to Louise to thank her. James was startled to see how far behind him she already was, already on the other side of the last gate they'd passed through.

With little more than a wave she vanished back into the night. James thought about how peculiar she was. It was impossible to describe her at all. Tallish, long dark hair, dark clothes that allowed her to move quite freely, and even, he shivered remembering, the ability to run on all fours.

He went up the front steps, noting the property appeared to be tidy. A lantern hung on a hook by the door. He knocked, relieved to be there, but worried about disturbing his host at such an hour. He squinted at his watch, but he'd forgotten to wind it. His neck prickled, and he spun back to face the open range. He saw nothing but heavy night. The wind rustled the few spindly trees and he heard the sand and dust being picked up and spread over everything.

Finally, the door opened, and a small man peered out, squinting into the dark. The man was fantastically old and wrinkled: his skin papery and white.

"Mr. Holbrook?" James said warily. He was fearful that startling the man would cause his heart to give out.

The old man frowned at James, "Oh no, I'm not Mr. Holbrook, I'm Archie, his butler."

Archie looked a bit frail for butlering, but James just wanted this terrible ordeal to end; he wanted to sleep, have a stiff drink, and to take off his boots. In any order.

"I'm James—"

"—You're late, you were due in yesterday." The old man moved away into the house. "Follow me."

The inside of the house was dark and smelled of lemon oil, and underneath that was the scent of animals. It reminded him of his senile aunt who lived in a tenement on Boston's south side, her apartment stuffed with clutter and cats.

James followed the ancient butler along the main hallway. The walls were bare, but beneath his feet were luxurious carpets. They made their slow way up a flight of stairs, Archie limping and James following. He led the way down another narrow wooden hallway to the last door on the right. James saw a wooden chair next to it, angled so the person sitting in it could look out the window and see down the length of hall at the same time. Its placement summoned images of prison guards, or gunmen guarding all entrances.

"I suppose you're hungry and thirsty?" Archie asked. "I'll bring you up some provisions. The room's outfitted with everything you need, but take a look around and let me know if anything's missing. Dirty gear can be left out here on the chair."

James thanked the old man, watching as he made his way down the hallway, slow as a turtle, back bent with age. It was only now, while he stood at the top of the stairs, his outline in perfect relief, that James noticed his legs. One leg was nearly twice the size of the other. His pants were altered to accommodate this oddity, and James forced himself to look away and not stare at the poor man.

The simple room was furnished with a brass bed and a dresser with a bowl and pitcher for washing. Along one wall was an armoire, and there was a rocking chair in the corner. The room was scrubbed clean. It had bare walls and floor. There were wooden shutters over the windows. He opened the shutters and peered out.

James could see or hear very few cattle, let alone smell them. Which he found strange. But then again, Holbrook Ranch was one of the largest ranches in the west. Bigger than Rhode Island, or so he'd been told. The cows could easily be a few miles away from the main house. He tried to imagine owning this much land, this *type* of land: low, flat, dusty, and hard to grow anything on. An endless sea of lizards and tumbleweeds, scoured by sand storms and tornadoes. James couldn't help but think of the Great Ozymandias. Who wants to own a desert?

ARCHIE CAME BACK IN, LOOKING EVEN OLDER AND STRANGER in the well-lit room. The butler's skin was practically colorless, and the asymmetry of his legs obvious. The oversized lumpy leg did not affect his gait as much as one would assume. He put a tray down on the table next to the rocking chair.

"Here's some beef stew and some fresh bread. Glass of water and a little whiskey for you. I'll have your things cleaned up and set out for you in the same spot come morning. Mr. Holbrook apologizes for being unavailable to receive you."

"Thank you, it is dreadfully late. I am just happy I survived the ordeal and that Louise found me when she did! If she hadn't I'd still be wandering out there, probably straight to my grave." He chuckled, but his heart wasn't in it. The old man watched him closely, especially when he mentioned Louise.

"Get some rest now," Archie said, leaving quietly, the drag of his odd leg slowing him just a little.

⌘

THE NEXT MORNING JAMES' FEET WERE SWOLLEN WITH blisters and his face was sunburnt. As Archie promised, folded neatly on the chair in the hall were his clean clothes. His shoes, freshly shined, sat on the floor beside it. He washed up and dressed and made his way downstairs alone.

The house was less ominous by day. Sunlight brightened the warm wood and the colors in the Persian rugs. It was extremely clean, just like his room. Yet there was still the smell of animals. James wondered if Mr. Holbrook owned dogs. He hadn't heard any, but James kept his guard up, as he did not like dogs. As a child he had been bitten by a dog; it had left a nasty scar on his forearm. He could not help looking around him now with a little touch of fear that some four-legged beast would trot by at any moment.

"Hope you slept well sir." It was old Archie, standing by his elbow. James hadn't heard him come in. "Let me show you to the drawing room where Mr. Holbrook is taking his breakfast. He will be very pleased to see you!" The old man ushered him towards a closed door, his hand on James' back, forceful.

The drawing room was at the front of the house; a bright room with many windows and a long table that filled the center of the room. In one corner, a handsome desk and leather chair. James did not come from a wealthy family, but had worked hard and clamored up a rung or two socially. The fine furniture in this room reminded him he still had a-ways to go.

"Mr. James Ashton sir," Archie announced to an apparently empty room.

Gerard Holbrook was angled in such a way that the bulk of the leather wing chair had hidden him from view. Now the man rose and rose. He was huge, easily six and a half feet, possibly over. He was not only tall, but wide. A wall of flesh. The trim, well-tailored jacket and shirt emphasized his muscular physique. Holbrook had a bushy red mustache which was trimmed so that it curved from under his nose to around his square jaw and connected to his wild mop of flame colored hair which was pulled back in a ponytail at the nape of his neck. His eyes were a hazel green that was nearly gold. He moved smoothly and silently for a big man, crossing the room with a delicate weightlessness. Holbrook smiled, displaying long white teeth, his hand outstretched. "Yes, yes. Mr. Ashton we finally meet! I heard you have had quite the ordeal getting here."

James' hand was engulfed by the big man's own. He was surprised by how rough Holbrook's palm was. This was not a gentleman of leisure. The rough hands and huge build said he was a man who, while rich, worked.

"It was an ordeal sir, but I made it." James felt weak and bookish as he pulled back his hand. It was smarting under the pressure of Holbrook's grip.

"Well, please sit, Archie will bring us breakfast and we'll talk, you and I, yes?"

"That would be nice, Mr. Holbrook."

"Oh please, you're in my house now son, and I am a plain-spoken man. Call me Gerard. And I shall call you James." He sat down in one of the chairs along the table in the center of the room and motioned for James to do the same. James sat, his hand still sore.

Breakfast was brought in on trays. A large platter of beef, very rare, a whole roasted chicken, a bowl of scrambled eggs, a rasher of bacon, and a loaf of freshly baked bread. A silver coffee service was rolled in, no doubt costing more than James' yearly wage. All brought in by Archie. James looked over the food, the quantity could easily feed triple their number.

Gerard watched him from across the long table, "Hope you brought your appetite."

James thought that something in the way he said it sounded like a threat.

AFTER BREAKFAST, GERARD SUGGESTED THAT THEY GO OUT riding so that James could have a tour of the ranch. James agreed reluctantly; he was still stiff from the night before, but he didn't want to offend his host.

When the two men reached the barn, the horses were saddled and waiting, placidly shaking their heads to send flies away. James found it odd there were no staff here, no groom held the horses, no stable boy waited to help them mount.

Gerard saw him looking. "I don't like my staff buzzing around like gnats. It's why I hate the city, hate the rat race. Too many people. Everyone dashing around. Spend your whole life toiling, never appreciating anything besides the almighty coin."

James bit his tongue, it seemed a strange sentiment considering he was there to approve a loan. Instead he said, "It does seem very tidy and orderly around here."

"Doesn't it? Good. Good." He scanned the land, reminding James of a feudal lord, or a king. He'd never met someone with such presence before as Gerard Holbrook.

"I settled here for two reasons James, the first was space. I wanted as much land as money could buy. End to end," He pointed with a large finger at the expanse before them. "The second reason was solitude. I wanted to continue my work in peace. If I don't want to see another human, I shouldn't have to."

"When you say work, do you mean your ranching?"

For a beat, Gerard turned and watched him with hard-golden green eyes then smiled. "Ranching is not my work, ranching is something I do to sustain my work, you understand? But to run a ranch as large as mine, a staff as large as mine, and to pay for my *true* work, I need more capital. I need that loan approved. By you."

James was silent, reminded that he'd come all this way to assess Holbrook's operation and report back if he felt it was a good or poor investment for his bank. Old Man Stimpson leaned toward the latter. James, at that moment, agreed. Gerard was a fanatic of some sort, James was sure.

The men rode across the unfriendly terrain for what seemed to James like hours. The sun was scorching hot, blinding. The sky a cloudless, endless blue, save the periodic circle of carrion birds. The land stretched out, golds and tans, yellows, and browns. The world was reduced to a single line that divided land and sky.

They crested a hill, horses hot, riders hot, and looked down upon a large body of water, rolling fields, and hundreds of shiny, brown-backed cows. He also saw a cluster of buildings, and farther out, barely more than specks, were a few figures working. James couldn't ignore their odd movements and asymmetry even from such a great distance. One stooped almost in half, another was on all fours dragging something. When Gerard let out a loud whistle, they both looked up and straightened themselves, continuing their work on two legs, upright. James couldn't help but think of Louise's strange gait, or of hobbling Archie. He looked back at his giant ginger host, curious about the staff cripples on his ranch.

"It was a godsend that Louise found me. How did she manage that, out there in the dark, no horse, no lantern?" He watched Gerard's face.

Gerard chuckled and scratched at his wide mutton chops. "She's a good tracker, strong nose, persistent. I had no doubt she'd find you. Let's go and look at the outbuildings."

☙❦❧

OVER THE NEXT HOUR THE MEN WALKED AROUND, GERARD showing off crops, irrigation systems, and residence halls. They never went into any of the buildings, and James never saw a soul up close. He felt as if the entire ranch population consisted only of Gerard and Archie. Even Louise seemed more like an apparition than a real person to James, the more time passed in this strange place.

James and Gerard stood in front of a large building, the outside looking like a common enough barn. Red paint, white trim, metal roof. He hadn't been in a lot of barns: his father was a clerk, his mother a teacher. He'd grown up in a city tenement. But after the tour today, he knew enough to know that this barn was not common when Gerard pulled open the vast sliding door.

"This portion of the ranch is for research. It's the most important. It's where my work is. Now that you've seen acres of cows and barns, of silos, you see we are a real ranch. You see the things that *cost* money to run a ranch as big as mine. Now you need to see what makes my ranch special."

Gerard strode into the large room, arms wide, smiling proudly, beckoning for James to follow. Long wooden tables with gleaming soapstone tops stretched the length of the wooden floors. On them were hundreds of tubes and beakers, bottles, and jars. Microscopes, Bunsen burners. The tables looked as if they could fit a hundred scientists in lab coats. And for all he knew, they did.

"What is this place?" James asked, noting again the strange combination of chemical and animal smells. It was even stronger in here then it had been up at the house.

"I am remaking the world James, and to do that, I need the

best scientists, I need the best everything. When you see how far we've come, I think you'll be happy to provide us with the loan to continue." Gerard's eyes were wide and bright, and again the word fanatic came to James' mind.

James lifted an empty glass beaker, the glass itself so light and paper thin he feared it would shatter in his hands.

"I am not a rancher," Gerard continued, "I'll be honest with you. The cows are mostly for show and food only, I have a large, hungry staff here. The money I need is for my work."

"Wait, Gerard, do you mean the cows we financed for you to start your ranch? How is one ranch eating that much beef? Even if you had a thousand ranch hands . . ." James looked around. Past the long tables and rolling chalkboards with what could easily be hieroglyphics on them to him, was a wall lined with doors, each with a number painted on it.

Gerard followed James' gaze, "Ah, the operating rooms."

"Operating rooms? What are you doing here, Gerard?"

The big man regarded him, sizing him up. He was too close for comfort, reminding James he was alone with this odd man, no one around for miles and miles. That Holbrook's business was a front. That the few staff he'd seen were deformed. James swallowed and looked down at his shoes.

"Follow me," Gerard said as he pushed past James. Behind one of the numbered doors the wood walls were whitewashed, a metal table sat in the center. Beside it sat a tray of surgical tools. Large toothy saws gleamed in the light, which was provided by a high set of barred windows. The air smelled of antiseptic and he could not ignore the stains on the rough wood floors.

"Why are men and nature so opposed? When did man's laws start overriding nature's laws?" Gerard's voice boomed in the smaller room. He ran his hand along the metal operating table. "Science is a lot like this wild land, don't you think, James? Harsh and mysterious, she guards her secrets. But if you can get them. . . pry her open, you could remake the world."

"Lofty goals, this world remaking," James said.

Gerard leaned over the operating table, rubbing his face along it, breathing in through his nose loudly. James stepped back, hip jostling the instruments on the tray there, reminding him weapons were near if it came to that. "We're getting close, James. Every inch of flesh that is parted here, restitched, remade, heads toward *my* new world." There was something almost sexual, almost animal in the way the larger man regarded James, head cocked oddly, looking up at him. When Gerard righted himself, he was smiling ear to ear. James avoided his eyes, rubbing the gooseflesh along his arms that had little to do with the temperature.

Gerard briskly strode out of the operating room and led James to the final door. He hesitated, hand above the knob, turning back to James, "I need money James. I need more cows and supplies to feed my people. I need to be able to lure the best scientists to my ranch. I *need* you to believe in my cause." James was struck by the desperation in the big man's eyes. Gerard suddenly looked vulnerable for the first time. "I'm not insane, like you think."

"No, just creating a new world order," James replied sarcastically.

"This is not a joke!" The big man yelled, his voice echoing through the rafters, sending a few nesting birds into the air. His nostrils flared, eyes bright with anger, or possibly zealotry.

Gerard pushed the door open. The dark, humid room reeked of animal, with no attempts made to cover the stench. The scent of wet fur and acrid urine instantly coated James' nostrils, the ammonia burned his eyes and he put his sleeve to his face. Gerard smirked. "This is my work James, come see." He walked backwards, arms extended like some sort of circus showman.

On both sides, the low-ceilinged room was lined with cages that had iron bars; like a zoo, or jail. The floors of the cages were covered with straw, it added a dusty sweet scent to the overpowering stink. James walked cautiously along the row, pulse hammering, as he squinted into cages. The cages weren't empty, but the residents clung to the deep shadows in the depths and were hard to make out. James peered in, breathless.

"Come into the light, let the man see you!" Gerard roared, and suddenly in a flurry of movement, grunts, growls, the creatures came close to the bars. James was not a religious man, had he been, he would have crossed himself.

These creatures were like nothing he'd seen at any zoo or in any book. Or in nature itself. The closest was female, its body covered in a pale golden down. It stood upright, hands holding the bars. Her torso was abnormally long, and running down it were pendulous, human sized breasts. Horrifically bowlegged legs trembled, as if standing upright was unnatural. The face, to his horror, was human, the only oddity a sharp underbite and protruding teeth. Her eyes, soft and nut brown, when James met them, were strikingly intelligent. The creature beseeched him with those eyes. He gasped and backed all the way to hit the opposite cage's bars, close enough that he felt the meaty breath of the thing in it. Screaming, he fell on all fours and scrambled to the center...as far from both cages as he could manage. The opposite cage held a male thing, with pointed ears, and swollen swinging genitals encased in a fur pouch. Its build was massive, with spotted fur, a long nose, whiskers, and again, eerily human eyes.

"What are these things?"

"These are not *things*, these are my children, my creations." Gerard's voice had a scolding tone. "They aren't perfect yet, but we are getting somewhere."

James looked around, noting the beasts seemed tame and watchful. His vision blurred as he counted them. Ten creatures total, five on each side. All watching him, listening closely, and he realized with a woozy sort of dread, understanding what he and Gerard were seeing.

"What are you trying to achieve here, Gerard?" James voice came out shrill with fear.

"Look at them as steps in the right direction. We are so close to the perfect balance."

James rose unsteadily and peered into each cage, observing the strange mutant things within. Knowing that they were somehow people, victims, compelled him to look upon them and respect that. "What is the perfect balance you are trying to achieve?"

"A perfect creature, halfway between animal and man. A lost tribe," Gerard replied. Some of the caged were more animal— quadrupeds with twitching tails. Others were upright and hunched, with only a hint of animal in the face or body. One was a small child, *a child*. James nearly wept looking at it. It had glossy black fur, and a completely human face. It smiled a sweet sad smile that caused James to cover his face with his hands.

"Monsters, Gerard! Monsters, you are playing god and making monsters!" He took his hands away from his face and stared at Gerard in horror.

Gerard frowned, scratching at his face and regarding the man. "It saddens me that you see them as such, they are my mission laid out in flesh. This is science, there is no morality here."

"I have to get out of here, now," James said, bile rising in his throat. He ran away from the cages and was halfway across the laboratory when a figure stepped into the doorway to the outside. Hunched and catlike, the silhouette was all he could see, but the posture looked threatening. It reminded James of the jackal-headed creatures of Ancient Egypt he'd once seen in a book.

He spun back toward Gerard, his curiosity overtaking his fear for a moment. "How? How are you making these things?!"

"Old world magic mixed with new science my boy, and the fantastic art of vivisection. Joining elements, joining creatures. Man has strayed too far from the jungle. I need to take him back."

"You are insane. This whole enterprise is grotesque! I will

not be a party to this monstrosity, and I certainly won't sign off to finance such things. It's just wrong."

"Do you not see the wonder? Aren't you even a little impressed at what we have achieved here? When you remove the rules of what you should and shouldn't do, miracles can happen."

"Blasphemy can happen!" James hollered back, looking between the door guard and Gerard. There didn't seem to be another way out. He thought of grabbing a beaker. If he broke it, he could use the glass as a weapon. But he abandoned the idea as fast as it came, because both Gerard and the monster at the door were easily twice his size.

Gerard smiled indulgently. "Blasphemy? The only god here is the Wild. You'll learn that in time." With that, a heavy figure dropped from the ceiling and strong arms encircled James. He screamed and struggled in its grasp, but the creature only held him tighter.

"Gorgo, take him to the Rancher's Cabin. I will be there shortly," Gerard ordered.

The thing holding James, *Gorgo*, dragged him out of the building and into the blinding sun. James tried again to fight but found it was like struggling with a statue. He could feel the taut muscle beneath hot fur, feel the creature's breath on his shoulder. A tawny forearm, ended in a hand that was half paw and tipped with vicious looking retractable claws.

The Rancher's Cabin wasn't far from the laboratory. The cat man hollered when they reached it, his voice garbled and barely human. James felt Gorgo's grip loosen a little as the front door opened. James fought his captor, stomping his foot and flailing, but froze when he felt the press of sharp teeth at the back of his neck.

"Do you want me to kill you?" The deep voice said, barely above a whisper, at his ear. He trembled at the terrifying intimacy. He shook his head no, and the cat man dragged him into the cabin.

Once they were inside, the door was shut and was locked.

The room was dark and all its windows shuttered. It smelled of old sweat, woodsmoke and dust. The cat man released him with a push and James pinwheeled into the space, crashing into a table and knocking over a chair. Another figure stood in the corner. Whoever had opened the door from inside.

"What is this?' James said frantically regaining his balance. "Am I a prisoner now?"

"Calm down, James." He recognized the voice instantly: Louise. "You are safe here, have a seat and I will get you some water."

She stayed mostly in shadow, "So you are like them then? Like him?" He pointed at the cat man, who in the dark room, was even taller and more terrifying. He was a perfect meld of cat and man, his head that of a feline, body that of a man, with a thick tail thumping and swishing along the floor.

"That's Gorgo and you should be kind to him. He is a gentle soul, unlike some here." She stepped from the shadow now, glass in hand, and he gasped despite himself.

Louise regarded him with pale green cat eyes in a Native woman's face. She smiled revealing pinpoint sharp fangs. Her black hair hung to mid waist, mixing with the black glistening fur that covered the bulk of her body, save her breasts, which were exposed and perfectly human. He averted his eyes, finding himself both deeply repulsed and somewhat aroused by her alien form, as she set the glass of water before him.

"How did he do this to you? Why?" James whispered, holding the water with a trembling hand.

"I had nothing, I *was* nothing. Just an Indian whore, bought and sold, bandied about, little more than a slave. Gerard gave me a new life. Now I am strong, powerful, unafraid. I may look like a monster to you, but I am free. Gorgo, he was a farm hand, simple-minded, underestimated. Now he's a god." She smiled at the big man, and he nodded in return.

James felt like he was losing his mind, that he was trapped in a bad dream. None of this could be real, all of this was impossible. You can't cut something up and sew it onto something else. He was no scientist, but even he knew that much. And even if you could, why? Why create a ranch filled with monsters?

"He's lonely," she said pulling the thought from James' head. She eased, boneless and felinely, into the opposite chair. Gorgo remained a silent sentinel at the door. "He's the last of his tribe."

"Tribe?" But as James asked the door opened, blinding him as the sun poured in, and Gerard entered, closing the door behind him.

The big man's face was hard to read. Something transpired between Gerard and Louise, unspoken, and she nodded. "Have a seat, father," she said aloud.

The wood creaked as it struggled to support his weight, "I need that loan, James. I need supplies, cattle, money to get the best scientists, the best magicians. You do not want my children to have to go hunt for their food out here. They are not all as civilized as Louise here. Or my new children in their cells." He smiled fondly. "I am getting closer all the time."

"This tribe of half men? It's madness," James said weakly, glancing between the two monsters.

Gerard sighed and looked up, once again scratching that bushy red beard. "I want a family. The old ones are gone, long dead, hunted to extinction. Only I remain."

With that, the large man stood and started unbuttoning his shirt, and then his trousers. James protested, made to rise, but Gorgo was behind him, claws holding his shoulders down. Louise leaned close to him on the side, practically purring in his ear. "Calm yourself James, this is something you'll want to see." He looked down to see her hand covering his hand on the table. Hers, furred to the knuckle and with human fingers. The pads of her hands were rough as sandpaper where they touched his.

Gerard was naked, broad chest, red thicket of chest hair, trailing down to an impressive manhood and two tree trunk legs. His whole body was covered with a sheen of sweat, and with a grunt and oath, he knelt double, his whole body rippling and stretching. Bones snapping, contorting, skin stretched. James tried to stand but Louise's hand pinioned him to the table.

A few moments of horror and Gerard was no longer Gerard. In his place, was a massive rust and black colored tiger. It stretched and straightened, opened its mouth and revealed yellowed canines longer than James' fingers. He felt his bladder contract and feared wetting himself.

"Isn't he beautiful?" Louise said, voice ecstatic. "To be able to change forms so perfectly, so seamlessly? That is what he hopes to one day achieve here. For us."

The tiger watched him, tail swaying. James imagined this massive creature running out in the fields, stalking and pouncing on cattle, ripping it to shreds. He could easily picture the creatures creeping out from wherever they hid all day. They would eat the remains, picking them over till they were little more than bones for the vultures and crows. Day after day. No wonder he needed such large orders of cattle.

James was at a loss, looking at his inhuman host, at his inhuman children. Their eyes burning with the fervor of true believers. Which they were, in their own ways; worshipping science and nearly extinct monsters.

He knew, looking at them in that dark room, that they would never let him leave now. He wondered what Gerard's motivation in telling him the truth truly was.

※※※

WHEN IT WAS CLEAR HE WASN'T A DANGER OR A FLIGHT RISK — after all, where would he go in the middle of nowhere? And how would he escape natural trackers and predators, him with no supplies, across the desert? They allowed James to explore the Ranch without permanent guard. Louise often joined him. Although he was sure she was assigned to keep an eye on him, he also got the impression she was lonely for conversation.

As the days passed, he saw more and more of the Ranch's

denizens. A strange lot, some more balanced between animal and man than others. They lounged the days away in the few trees big enough to hold them, or in the shade, their tails snaking about them. They romped in the fields, they hunted in groups, they coupled with little shame. Then they put on their lab coats, or shoveled the stalls, while others gardened. Deformed beast men rode nervous horses and herded cattle. Archie, the butler, removed his trousers revealing a feline lower half and a thick striped tail. All told, a hundred creatures lived on that ranch.

Occasionally he would see his host, *the tiger*, hear its roar echo out into the plains, watch the great beast running full force, leaving a trail of dust behind him.

"So, you are happy like this? Really?" he finally asked Louise, one day when he was sipping whiskey and sitting in a rocker on the porch, watching some kittens/cubs/children chase after a snake they'd found. Louise lay at his feet, in a position that was undignified for a woman, but acceptable for a cat-woman. He liked the warm weight of her pressing against his shins.

"If I wasn't like this, I would probably be dead. Either from syphilis or murder, no doubt. The human world was cruel to me, James. I can't blame you for not understanding, you are a man with a good job, good standing, you have value in their world. I may be ugly to you—"

"I don't think you're ugly," he said quickly, too quickly. He blushed and looked away.

"You don't?" She was kneeling now before him, and he again felt that discomforting duality of lust and disgust. "It's nice to leave the mortal world aside, to live as an animal. To smell the flowers, to appreciate the kill, to sleep soundly. No debts, no johns, just the moment."

And with that she leaned forward and nuzzled his face and neck. James went still, as her tongue darted out, and licked the skin along his throat. It was rough. He cleared his throat and she pulled back, her strange cat eyes meeting his. "Do you not like me?" she asked. "You smell like you like me." She breathed in and out, "You smell of desire."

"I'm just not sure this is right, or proper."

She laughed then, her sharp teeth on display. "James, there is no right or wrong, or proper. I'm a female, you're a male, and we want one another." She pressed her body against his, he could feel the heat coming off of her, and he petted the soft fur along her flank. She smiled and sighed. "Kiss me, James."

He did, the kiss growing deeper as she straddled him on the rocker. Her tongue was long and dexterous as it slid along the inside of his mouth. He enjoyed the feeling of fur turning into the smooth heft of her perfect breasts. As she unbuckled his belt, he froze, looking around.

"It's too public here," he said, voice hoarse. She took his hand, leading him into the cool shade of the house, up the stairs, and into his room. The door was barely closed when she was upon him, pushing him onto the bed, tearing off his trousers, her mouth all over his body. He groaned audibly, fighting his rational mind, fighting the impropriety of coupling with an animal. A lot of her was animal. He could not ignore that as she backed up to him, tail swishing, and stared at her sex, between two black furred haunches. But there was woman there too, in her beautiful face, her delicate fingers, and the gasp as he entered her. And the moans that followed.

When it was over, and they lay intertwined and breathless, he could admit to himself that her strange hybrid form may have ruined him for ordinary human women. That against all sane explanation he was falling in love with her.

WEEKS PASSED, AND AS JAMES LIVED WITH THE CAT PEOPLE, the more he ate with them, the more he walked the property, the more he saw the appeal of the world without humans. Of the simple life of animals: to survive, to hunt, and multiply.

So, James wasn't entirely surprised one night when while the two men ate dinner, a rare sirloin with potatoes and corn, that Gerard brought it up. "I need you to write to your employers and approve the loan. Double the interest if that is what it takes. Winter will be coming soon and we need the livestock. I have also found a group of amazing scientists in France and a warlock in Russia. I would love to send for them. Will you do this for us?"

James paused. He knew the answer would have to be yes, either of his own free will or under duress, or he'd be killed. Gerard was being polite in asking. "Tell me Gerard, what was it like when there were more like you?"

Gerard sighed, looking back into the past. Louise entered with brandy for them all and sat beside James, her furred body pressed up against his. Gerard told tales of his family. Of wild shapeshifters that lived deep in forests. There were whole societies, and families, and they had their own folk tales and songs. "But every year humans moved closer, covered more territory, built more roads. They became better hunters and we were little match for their guns. When I was a boy, my mother sent me away, told me to hide amongst them if I had to, that we would reunite. But we didn't." He sipped his drink, expression grim. "I went looking for them, but any evidence my people ever existed was gone. So, I took my mother's advice and blended into the human world, learned how it operated, and eventually made my fortune, since that is the real way to succeed alongside men. Enough wealth and you can do anything you want; you can buy anyone you want, including scientists, magicians and bankers. You understand, James?"

"I do." Louise was a warm presence beside him, her animal eyes flashing red in the firelight. James pictured the droves of farm hands, world scientists renowned in vivisection, old world witches and the like, all making their way here and then coerced into going under the knife, with a promise of a better life. To be remade in his image. For no humans were allowed at Holbrook Ranch.

Gerard continued, "You know I cannot let you return to the city, knowing what you know of us. I must protect my tribe, I owe them that much. I see how you look at Louise, and how she looks at you. Do this for us and you could truly be together. And your children will be a closer step still."

James looked at Louise. Would it be so terrible to become a creature like her, running through the desert plains, hunting and rutting like animals, fur against fur. Shamefully, he tried to remember his life in Boston. His small apartment, his meager savings. His few good suits. If he worked hard for a few more years, perhaps he would be allowed to oversee the larger accounts, or maybe even start his own business. Perhaps he would meet a woman and marry, have a family. Isn't that why he took the assignment out here in the first place? An adventure. To explore and see what the world held beyond his modest life.

How strange to be asked to transcend human life itself, to be led past the veil into the world of animals. To hunt. To love in a way unknown to ordinary men. To be of that tribe. In the end, he didn't have much choice, if he said no they would kill him and forge his name.

"Yes, yes to all of it," James said, and the tiger man smiled.

James was one of the converted.

❦ 13 ❦

THE WIFE

She pressed her forehead against the glass, savoring the feel of it, enjoying the way her eyelashes brushed against its near perfect sheen. Beyond she could see the street: gray concrete, wrought iron, vibrant greens of new growth. It was a rainy spring day. Although she could not smell it, if she squeezed her eyes shut she could imagine it. She adored the smell of rain.

"What are you doing, Vivian?"

His voice startled her, broke her reverie. She quickly turned her head towards the doorway. The sudden movement caused the bandage at her throat to throb, absentmindedly, her hand fluttered up to it. She knew there would be a face print on the glass, advertising her guilt. He took only a step or two into the room, but already his height and girth filled the space, stole the air, redefined the geometry to accommodate his mass. Even ten feet away standing up, she felt small. He did not move further, just crossed his arms over his massive barrel chest and waited. Obediently, she stepped away from the window. As soon as she did, she missed it, missed the freedom of the window. Every face that passed by had a story. Every closed door she saw out there held mystery. Every shuttered window encapsulated another life.

"You can't just spend all afternoon daydreaming out that damn window. Now come fix lunch, I have work to get back to." His voice boomed in the small space. She hurriedly stepped away from the window. He blocked the doorway, and when he did not step away, she tried to brush past him out the door. His arm shot out and stopped her. His massive hand encircled her entire bicep. She was aware of his strength, without him having to squeeze. Even now, when he tried to be gentle, his hand was a vice. He simply wasn't built to be tender, his every movement was a threat, purposeful or not. "No kiss?"

She shuddered, avoided his eyes, and turned back to look out the window. He waited, his fingers tensing on her arm. Finally, she nodded. Turning her gaze back to him, she stared at his bulbous nose, ruddy and pitted, and his fleshy lips. Those lips would be womanish if they were on a softer face. She puckered and pecked, trying to be as efficient as possible. But he pulled her in, pinned her with his arms. His mouth opened, tongue darting out past his lips and into hers. His stubble scraped her cheeks raw, his mouth tasted sour.

When he was done, he released her, and she nearly fell. He mistook it for a swoon and smiled wolfishly.

Moments later, he stood in the doorway to the kitchen, arms folded again, and stared at her as she set out the bread. Leered at her as she stacked meat and cheese. Grinned at her as she ladled soup into a small bowl and placed it on the table for him. He settled in, smacking his lips, and tucked a napkin into the collar of his dress shirt. She stood in the furthest corner of the kitchen, her back nearly touching the hot radiator.

He ate, making lots of noise, and grumbled when he realized she hadn't given him anything to drink. Two large glasses of milk later, he was up, burping and patting his stomach, then rubbing his entire face with the napkin like a towel.

"That was lovely. Never thought I'd like having a wife at all. But I'm so glad I found you, Viv."

She dropped her gaze and nodded. He kissed her on the head and strode out, the pots and pans jangling as his great weight passed by. When she heard the front door close and his footsteps on the sidewalk, she released the breath she was holding in.

🙵

THAT NIGHT SHE TOSSED AND TURNED. NIGHTS WERE ALWAYS the hardest for her. Every night, he forced her to go to bed with him early. She was a night owl so she spent most nights lying there next to him, staring at the ceiling. She knew he feared her being alone and awake in the house while he slept. He did not trust her. He would not admit it, but she could tell. If she so much as wanted a glass of water, he would gripe and come along. Something in her knew he shouldn't trust her, but the thoughts skittered away like shadows meeting light. A small persistent thought circled her head: he knew enough stories to be wary.

She tossed and turned. She tugged at her bandage and tried to find a comfortable spot. Too hot, too cold, entangled in bed sheets, and always his great weight—like a fallen log—pressing her into the mattress. She could hear night sounds outside the window: fire trucks tearing through the silence, cats in heat yowling, the soft footsteps of stalking predators and fearful prey. She longed to be out in it, she wanted to feel the caress of moonlight on her skin, the wind in her hair, the vastness of the sky. She had forgotten how long it was since she was outside at all.

In her dreams she flew. She soared through indigo skies, streaking above the sea. She raced her reflection in the dark water below. Close enough to run her fingertips through the waves and feel its inky spray. She luxuriated in the wildness and the freedom. She was weightless and unfettered. Then she would wake; tears on her cheeks, an ache in her heart, the phantom salt air dissipating in her nostrils as the dreams faded.

It wasn't always this way. She remembered only fragments,

but there was a life before this one. A life where she was free and laughed often. She had faint creases at her eyes, laugh lines, so surely there must have been a time when she was filled with laughter. There must have been laughter enough to etch it into her face. But her memories were fireflies, blinking in and out, eluding her capture. The more she tried to remember, the more the pain at her throat forced her to forget.

And the pain at her throat kept her from sleeping. Tonight, the pain was more intense than usual She knew it was because she had tried to remember. The dressings irritated her skin and there was a rash where the bandages wouldn't allow it to breathe. She wanted to scratch at it, but that only made it worse. Often, she would wake at night, her hands frantically tugging at the bandaged wound, her fingers operating without her mind's consent. He would be cross with her, if he noticed the bandages loose. He hated the look of the wound; he found it repulsive, and always forced her to keep it tightly covered.

She was uncomfortable: hot, in pain, frustrated. His snoring body half over her, sweaty arms and hairy legs pressing her down. Instead of feeling endless despair, as she often did, staring up at the ceiling, she felt anger. What had he said earlier that day? *I'm so glad I found you.* Found. Something was missing from her life and while she could not remember what it was, she knew it was gone forever. It angered her—this absence. And she knew he was to blame: a gross, cruel man who had somehow entrapped her.

Trapped. Not Found. Trapped. Once the word had tickled her mind, she could not let go of it. She did not know other wives, forbidden as she was to leave the house, but from what she could glean, they were allowed to go outside. They had jobs like her husband; each day they left their homes to go to work, or to the store, or to the park. They were not trapped like animals that took the bait and fell into a trap. They were not prisoners locked in their homes. Oh, he assured her that everyone has a secret wife at home—that stays home—that no one knows about. He promised her that. Behind every door there was a wife, bandaged up and hidden away. When she asked about the women she could sometimes see on the street in front of their home? Prostitutes, was his answer. They're tragic, unmarried woman who must have sex with strange men for money, in order to survive.

But what was the difference between those women and her? She was forced to pleasure this porcine man, willing or not, and cook for him, and care for him so that she would have a place to live. She had no job, nothing besides him and taking care of his home. Wasn't she a prostitute as well? He beat her savagely whenever she attempted to go outside. Once he loosened a tooth, another time blackened an eye, and two of her delicate ribs had been snapped beneath his boot. He thought she was escaping, but she just wanted to smell the air, to feel it on her skin.

So, she sat at her window day in and out. She envied those women on the streets, "prostitutes," some with small children in strollers. Walking outside so freely. They might have to lay with many men, but maybe some of those men were attractive? Or kind? At least there was some variety. She glared at her husband in the darkness, trying to remember why she married him, or if she even had. Her neck throbbed. She could not remember specifics. She couldn't even remember *how* she ended up inside his house. *Found*, he said. She knew she would have never chosen him over all others. His small eyes were cruel and he smelled, even after a bath. No, she would never have been duped into agreeing to marry him. Would a parent have allowed it? Did she have parents? How did she get there? All the while, she scratched absently beneath the bandage and it burned.

Yet, somehow, here she was. He cleared his throat, deep in sleep, his lips smacking together, and finally he rolled off of her. His weight lifted, allowing a breeze of cool air to dry her sweaty skin.

You must remember, Vivian.

Vivian? Was that really her name? He called her that. But she felt very little connection to the name, she could not remember anyone besides him even calling her by it. She could not remember anyone else ever speaking to her.

Her entire body was suddenly covered with gooseflesh and she *knew*. Vivian was not her name. She could not recall her real name, but she knew, at her core, that Vivian was only a name he called her. She was tugging at her neck, desperate for more air. The anger was fighting with panic. What had he done? How had he done it? Erased her memory. Renamed her. Trapped her in this house where she cooked and spread her legs and cleaned. Were all the women outside prostitutes after all? Or was she a fool? He was not a smart man, she knew that, so how had he imprisoned her here? Complacently believing all he told her.

She found it hard to think, the burning, the itching at her neck distracting her. Clawing at the red, raw skin beneath the bandage relieved some of the discomfort. But what she really wanted to do was pull off the damn dressing and let the wound get some air.

Why not? He was deep asleep beside her. Carefully, with wet eyes and shaking fingers, she pulled the sodden wrappings away, inch by inch, her breath coming short, until finally it was off. The yellow-stained gauze was a pale bundle on the floor.

She breathed a sigh of relief. Her delicate throat filled with joy at the feel of fresh air running over it. The wound ached, its sickly-sweet odor tickling her nose, turning her stomach. Oh, how it throbbed, in tune with her pulse. With careful fingers she explored the injury. She could not recall how she got it, just that it had always been. Trembling she felt the puffy damaged skin and the feverish heat it threw off. The cavity in her throat was large, the skin so tender she could not turn her neck too far in any direction. Her fingertips hovering an inch above could feel it pulsating and hot, the hole.

Just feeling it in the darkness was not enough, not tonight, when her blood was boiling, and her mind was so close to discovering something. The indignation and pain forced her up and out of bed, creeping on silent feet, cautiously listening for his steady breathing. It went unchanged. She closed the bathroom door as slowly as possible, and only once she was locked in, with a towel along the floor, did she turn on the light.

Although she looked in the mirror daily, on this night it felt illicit. Her eyes were large, almond shaped and golden. Her face ghastly pale and sickly—shiny with sweat. Around the bandages, her skin was discolored, and yellows and purples orbited the hideous wound. A hole, bigger around than her fist. Out of it sprouted yards and yards of her dark hair, shiny as a wet seal, as if it grew from the gaping hole in her throat. She leaned into her reflection, studying that hair, a thick rope, thicker than an anaconda, coiled up and buried deep in her ruined neck. Why?

Ugly. Horrible.

Surely, she had not put all her hair—longer than she was tall—a ghost memory whispered—into a hollow in her neck? Did her husband? Obviously, the skin was infected. It stank of gangrene and showed myriad colors that should never seen on healthy flesh. She whimpered as she fingered the mouth of the wound, her fingertips coming away damp with the greenish leaking pus and watery red blood. Even the gentlest touch caused shocks of electrical pain up and down her spine. Her eyes streamed and she bit the inside of her mouth to keep herself from screaming.

Staring at the strange and grievous injury, her rage blossomed into something darker. This had been done to her. Of that she was sure. She had a strange epiphany, like a whisper in her ear. This wound kept her complacent; weak, full of infection and corruption, kept her waiting on that man like a servant. A servant he could splay wide and pump full of his seed whenever he wanted. His slave, who was forbidden to go outside or even to speak with another person. She had no memory, but what she had now was the knowledge that something was missing. There was a void inside of her that did not exist a day before. Something was stolen from her: her name, her identity, her life. This gray-faced imposter in the mirror was substituted for her real self. She knew he had orchestrated it all.

With a will of steel, she wrapped her hands around her hair where it met the flesh of her throat. It was crusted with the wet and dried blood of months. She breathed deep, meeting her eyes in the mirror. *You are brave. You are taking yourself back. Do it.* And with a resolve she never knew she had, she gripped the hair in her two fists and pulled.

It hurt like she was being flayed alive, each nerve on every inch of her body lit up in small searing flames. Her blood ignited like gasoline rivers touched with a match. Her heart tripped, her bladder released, and her lungs squeezed and seized. She fell, consciousness ghosting her away, her head striking the sink as she went down. Finally, darkness swallowed her up—formless, mindless, and peaceful.

SHE GASPED AWAKE, HER SENSES FLOODING IN NOISILY, fighting for dominance. The overhead light blinded her, the sound of her heart chugging and blood rushing through her veins deafening her. Every inch of her skin tingled. Her hair was free: long, longer than her memory, longer than she was tall. It was damp and heavy, streaking the floor with a stinking slug's trail of her fluids. She could barely lift her head the weight of it was so great.

She rested, squeezing her eyes shut to block it all out. Only then, in the quiet of her own head, did she realize what was no longer missing. Her memories. Her. *Em. Her name was Em.* It was like a deluge pushing and vying for her focus. Rushing in from all sides: her life, her sisters, her. . . freedom. She could hear laughter, and feel the caress of familiar hands, a thousand days of sunshine and rain, of moonlit nights.

Em gasped and sat up, ignoring the weight of her hair. She barely felt the throbbing hole in her neck. He took her and renamed her, kept her sick and hurt. Envisioning that sleeping hunk of meat on the other side, she glared at the bathroom door. Anger pulling her off the floor and onto her feet. She remembered it *all*.

IT WAS A BEAUTIFUL CLEAR NIGHT, THE SKY LIT UP BY thousands and thousands of stars. Em dozed on a long, strong tree branch, enjoying the dark. Alone. Although her sisters warned that it was not safe to venture into this forest, she went anyway. She was the youngest of them, and often defied her older, bossier, siblings.

Then He came. He and others. With their snares and traps. She tried to flee, but they were prepared, too prepared, she realized. They were hunting her. It was as if they knew everything about her. She tried to fight. But they shot her with a dart, tangled her in a net, and when she tumbled from the tree, before she lost consciousness, they trussed her up and bound her mouth. She moaned, fighting wildly even as the drugs swarmed through her system and pulled her under.

"She's a strong one." He chuckled, "A fighter. Guess she'll be mine eh?"

They laughed, all the men, standing above her in a circle, too dark to see their faces. Her heart raced, and she looked for her sisters, hoping they would sense she was missing—that they would know she was in distress. But no one came to her aid. Consciousness vanished like a candle blown out.

Now she was back.

EM RUBBED AT HER EYES, TEARS STREAKED HER FACE AND HER bloody hands. She reached for the doorknob, feeling more alive than she had in months. Movement caught her eye and she turned to her reflection.

She no longer saw Vivian in the mirror, the scared, scarred thing all wrapped up in bandages. She looked down at the frilly nightgown, soaked in her juices and clinging to her body like a second skin. She pulled at the thin fabric, shredding it with her claws. Wanting nothing of Vivian to ever touch her. It fell away in sticky tatters and she breathed out in relief.

Free.

As she stood tall, her hair fell down her back to the floor, dragging and wet, but slowly untangling itself as if sentient. Her golden eyes were wide and aware. Em walked close to the mirror, nose to nose with her reflection. Already her skin was dewy, her eyes brighter, and she could feel the infection leaving her body. She had missed herself so much. The two of them smiled now, revealing two rows of dainty needle-sharp teeth.

Em opened the door, letting the light fall onto the bed. He snorted, rolled over, and then sat straight up, his sweaty face paling as he looked at her.

She was on him in two long strides, moving faster than he could see, gliding through the space like a blade. She bowled him back with her weight, her hair rising around her, writhing like a thousand snakes. He whimpered. Em laughed. This mountain of a man was afraid and his fear nourished her. She breathed in the stink and let her tongue rake along his pockmarked cheek, savoring the sour taste of his primal animal fear.

Em's clawed hands dug into the flesh of his shoulders, her toenails lacerating his thighs. He screamed, his mouth wide, and she took the opportunity to press her mouth to his, pulling his tongue out between her sharp teeth, severing it. He keened as they were both soaked in the fount of blood that erupted from his injury. She bathed in it, luxuriated in its warmth. He choked and gurgled, reduced to a sheep at the slaughter, eyes rolling mindlessly.

She pressed her nails deeper, digging through muscle and sinew, using the pain to force his mind to clear and focus on her. Wanting him to understand that she was strong and powerful and dangerous. He should fear her and marvel at her. Em spat the hunk of his tongue to the floor and took one hand off his shoulder to wipe at her mouth. She could do this for hours, and while tempted, the night beckoned. She could feel the moon pulsing past the curtains on the window.

She ran her bloodied hand across the coarse hair of his chest. He shook and shuddered, vainly trying to rock her off, but she rode him like a cowboy rides a bull, squeezing his fat gut between her thighs. When she gnashed her teeth at him, he blubbered, the blood spilling out the sides of his mouth, like an over-filled wine glass.

Em slid her palm over his ribs to the soft space just beneath, she felt his heart chugging—at a rodent's breakneck speed—and she wanted it. Pulling her arm back, flexing, with a roar she punched down, through his soft belly skin and the insulating layers of greasy white fat, past the strong abdominal muscles and then inside, wriggling through ropes of intestines, and slippery organs. Hot gasses belched out as she pushed her arm in further. His eyes were wide, showing all white, as they rolled back in his skull. He wheezed trying to get breath. Em found her prize, searing hot and moving like a lizard in a sack. She squeezed, enjoying the force needed to get her hand around it, and the teeth-gritting strength it took to pull it out. He screamed, more animal than man, before his head dropped to the side, eyes open, mouth slack.

She pulled the heart out. Big as a cow heart. Em looked at it in the darkness. It beat once, twice, the last of the blood pumping out through the torn ventricles down her arm and body. Turning the heart side to side, she admired the thick muscles, and imagined the strength that such an organ would need to animate a body as big as his.

Laughing, she bit down into it, gnawing at it like a dog. She ate it all. It sat heavy and hot in her stomach and she savored the closure it gave her.

Em was free. Stepping off him daintily, she stretched, luxuriating in the feel of air on her skin and neck. The hole in her throat now only gave an occasional pang of discomfort, the skin was healing. Her hair hung over her like a great cloak. Its weight was no longer a burden, but a comfort.

Barefoot, claws clicking on the parquet floor, she went to the window. Pulling back the curtains she saw acres and acres of rooftops clustered together. Further still, the glint of the ocean. Above it all was the moon, welcoming as a mother.

She pulled up the window and balanced on the sill. Glancing back, she stared at him. Her captor. Her *husband*. Em snorted. Now he was little more than a hunk of rotting meat spread eagled on the bed, with a perfectly round, fist sized hole in his chest. She absently ran her hand over her own gaping hole at her throat. It almost felt good.

A breeze passed by her. Carried on it were the smells of the city, and of the sea, of a thousand lives lived out in each window she could see. Her yearning for the night pulled her out of the window. Airborne, she dropped two stories fast, heavy as a stone. But she was not a stone, and the air was her mistress as much as the night sky was. Hair unfurling, catching the errant breeze, it pulled her along with it. Weightless, she flew above the rooftops and spindly chimneys, streaking across the sky, gaining speed, higher and higher. She could no longer tell his rooftop from any other and she was glad for it.

The city grew smaller and smaller. She spun, corkscrewing through the sky and clouds, luxuriating in her hair. Now twice as long as she was, it wrapped around her, hugging her in its warmth. Ahead, she saw the ocean. Em wanted to feel the surf on her skin, to clean Vivian off her body once and for all.

Near to the shore, the briny air was intoxicating. The moon was bright enough for her to see her shadow, a black blossom on the glowing sand.

She called out in joy, in exhilaration. Her call caused distant windows to rattle and dogs from miles around to howl. In the distance, Em heard a response, then another. Her sisters. Her heart doubled in size picturing each of their faces, hungering for their embraces.

AND SHE BECAME A TRICK OF THE MOON, A SHADOW, A mystery thing, once more.

⚘ 14 ⚘
MATER ANNELIDA

She ran it over her body. Its coolness, its smell, the feel of its grit on her sensitive skin—she loved it.

Pressing it to her face she breathed deep, intoxicated by the heady scent. It was vegetation, it was time-rendered to dust. It was that which had lived and that which wished to live again.

She knelt, naked, in a rounded clearing worn smooth by centuries of feet. The foliage grew in on all sides, dense and reaching, but the circle remained clear. It was as if an unseen force kept the forest at bay. Her eyes were shut; she was resting, preparing.

One cannot go into this sort of thing unprepared. And she had prepared for months and months. Nine whole months to be precise.

Now the time had come.

The moon was full and fat in the sky and it shone down upon her. Her fair skin was bleached by it. White flesh surrounded by dark night. Her hair hung down her back, nearly to her bottom. She imagined herself a reflection of the moon. It was pale and round in the sky, she was pale and round below. Her gritty hand rolled over the swell of her belly;

she marveled at the responsive movement on the other side of her taut, warm skin. Where her hand moved, flesh followed. They were in synch. They were mirrors. Like the moon and her.

She cleared her mind and purged all extraneous things from it. To be a vessel, an empty, transparent, focused vessel, was what she needed. Or she would fail. So, she breathed, and she scrubbed at her mind till it emptied and opened, till only a singular goal existed within.

Then the chanting began. Low in her throat, guttural, the lowest octaves she could reach. Her hands moved. Scooping and gathering. Piling up, packing down. Piling up, packing down. All in rhythm with her chant.

The moon, twin and mirror, shone clean and kind. Like it knew what she was doing. Sweat beaded on her forehead. She wiped it away, leaving a smear of dirt on her brow.

When the mound she had made was tall and smooth, she stood and looked upon it. It was a mud woman. Sculpted in her own likeness, it looked up at her without eyes, its hands over its distended brown belly. It was her and she was it. She mirrored her creation; it mirrored her.

When she knelt and straddled her effigy, her belly wriggled eagerly. She whispered and cooed, and eased her nakedness onto her earthen twin. Bulbous belly met bulbous belly; breasts met breasts. She kissed her dirt twin's mouth. As she did, she found her eyes had grown teary.

Amen, she whispered and opened her mouth.

First, she ate the face of the dirt woman. The dryness choked her, each swallow harder to get down. The grit and grain scraped along her insides. She yearned for water. Just a sip. But there was none. This was not about comfort. This was bigger than her thirst. She focused and continued devouring herself.

By the time she reached the clavicle and breasts she was sobbing, a slugs' trail of snot and drool stretched from her face to her avatar like a spider's webbing.

When she looked up at the moon, beseeching, it shone down, pure and bright. It gave her strength.

With new vigor, she resumed eating, and found her rhythm at the belly. Perhaps because its roundness reminded her of her own, and what this was all for. The pain became pleasure, the taste of earth a delicacy as her senses transformed.

When she reached mid-thigh, she could feel a warm wetness between her legs and the movement in her womb intensified. As her mouth grazed at the mud-woman's knees, she could feel pressure, the pressure of something wanting to get out.

She forced down another mouthful, silty and delicious. It landed heavily inside of her. The weight of her mud effigy now nearly matched her own. She pictured herself as the wolf from the fairy tale, its belly filled with stones.

By the time she ate her ankles, the pressure in her loins transformed into pain: a throbbing, gut carving pain. As the last toe on the last foot crumbled in her mouth, she cried out. The pain was explosive; tiny starbursts and electric rosettes blossomed behind her eyes.

Finally, the toe was swallowed. She lay back and let her eyes fasten on the watchful moon above. Only then did she push.

Time slowed and the forest was silent; silent as if in anticipation, as if nature were waiting to see what would happen. The night held its breath, watchful.

Her will was sharp as a needle and singular: push, push, PUSH.

Then she opened like a flower blooming. Shiny and wet, it unfurled out of her, and slid free to the ground.

HER WORK WAS DONE

Her skin cooled and her eyes glazed over. The last remnants of her life ebbed out, wetting the soil, softening it.

Her offspring writhed between her splayed legs, moving slowly away from her body. Steam rose from its brown glossy skin. Eyeless, its other senses exploded with stimuli. Finding the soft earth, damp with its mother's blood, it knew what to do.

It burrowed.

Mindless, save for hunger, it took its first huge bites of dirt. Inside of it, elaborate tubes of muscles coiled and uncoiled, not so much digesting the dirt as changing it, remaking it, then forcing it back out through its anus.

As it ate, it was propelled deeper into the Earth. Bite by bite it would go, remaking the entire world in its own image.

❧ 15 ❧

THE WOMAN OF THE WOODS

The jeep skidded to a dusty halt in front of the house and a woman exploded out of it.

She was screaming, her arms clutched around a small bundle wrapped in a blanket. She was nearly at the front door when Prim rounded the corner of the house, surprised, wet, and nude. The woman, eyes rolling and wild, came at her without slowing.

"I need your help, please, please." The woman was frantic, as she bore down on Prim. She gnashed at her lip and it began to bleed. She licked it away, but the blood bloomed again. Prim noted that another figure was stepping out of the jeep now. A man, youngish, and much more composed, than the driver. He approached slowly and unlike the hysterical woman, gaped at Prim's nudity.

Prim looked from the staring man to the hysterical woman and back again.

"Let me get dressed," Prim said.

ONCE INSIDE, PRIM FELT AN OVERWHELMING URGE TO CLOSE

up the shutters and lock her door, so tired was she of these desperate visits by the locals. But it was her job, so resignedly, she toweled off from her swim and dressed quickly. From the window, she could see the man: clean shaven, handsome in a generic way, and a mystery to her. An outsider at her door was a strange occurrence indeed. Without thinking, her hand had drifted to the large old candle on the windowsill. Heavy and greasy, stained by years of dust collecting in the wax, but comforting all the same. She ran her fingertips along it. She hated being a pawn of fate.

Because she knew nothing happened by chance.

PRIM EMERGED WRAPPING HER LONG HAIR INTO A DRIPPING coil at the nape of her neck. The woman was on her knees in the dirt, clinging to the bundle, her head rising when she saw Prim. The man stayed a little behind.

"Please help me. Help save him." With that, the woman opened the bundle, revealing a small child, still and pale, in her arms. Prim watched coolly and unsurprised as a tiny hand tumbled out.

Prim glanced at the man, whose hands were in his pockets as if to protect them. She knelt down next the woman.

"What happened?" Prim asked as clinically as she could.

"He was playing. By the pond. He. . .he. . ." The woman broke into wracking sobs, her grief contagious. Prim delicately pulled back the blanket revealing a tiny, cherubic face, and pale violet lips. There was no life in the child that she could glean.

"Why would you come here to me with a dead boy?" She said, finally touching the silken arm, noting its coolness. While she asked the mother the question, her eyes strayed to the outsider.

"I heard stories. We all know the stories. Of what you can do. Please, please I beg of you. I will give you anything you want."

Prim let her hands fall away from the child. "You have nothing I *want*." She looked to the man, standing impotently near them.

"And you're not the father?" she asked him, though she already knew the answer.

"Me? No. No. I'm not from around here."

Prim's eyes narrowed, curious and wary.

The man held up his hands, defensive. "She needed a ride. Jesus! I was driving along and she came running down the street screaming. I thought we were rushing to the hospital but. . . instead we're here."

Prim released a long breath. It was suddenly too loud in her head, the pressure squeezed like a vice behind her eyes. She pinched at her nose. "What do possibly you think I could do for a drowned boy?" She said harshly to the mother. The woman blubbered, nonsensically, hysterically, before finally saying, "Save him, you could save him."

"Do you think I can bring back the dead?"

The mother clutched her child, her lip quivering wetly. "Can't you?"

Prim felt a thousand years old. The woman believed in her magic and was a local of New Durham. It had already begun. Prim shot her eyes to the man, better dressed than a local, curious but not hysterical. That in itself was strange. Nothing happened by chance.

Prim sighed, "If you ask me. . ."

"What is your price? What do you need me to do?" The mother was squeezing the dead boy so tight her knuckles were white.

"What you're asking me to do is *unnatural*. It goes against that which has occurred. To buck fate. To ride back to this world. . .he will not be alone. And the cost is high. Too high for what you get frankly."

"I don't care. Anything to get my baby back."

"I think you should bury him and grieve. Forget you came here. It was an accident after all, it was not your fault."

"*What do I need to do?!*" the woman screamed. The man stepped back, looking back and forth between the two of them, his cheeks gone pink.

"Are you telling me that you seriously believe she can bring your child back from the dead?" The man finally said.

"Yes! She can. She can. Please, please. . ."

Prim knew her opinion would fall on deaf ears. This woman would agree to any terms, would walk into Hell itself. She knew this, and the Devil knew this. He was always waiting at cross-roads for the desperate. She could almost feel him looking out of her own eyes. She liked to think she wasn't evil, but doing this sort of work made that impossible.

"Come on then. If this is what you want," she said and walked away knowing they would follow. The mother was close on her heels, the man trailing behind loudly questioning the situation but curiously not threatening to call the police or leave.

Prim led them down a narrow path. The ground was worn, and nearly smooth, the boundaries of the path were outlined by small evenly spaced stones. With each footfall she could imagine her mother, and her mother's mother, walking this same path, each of them leading the desperate of their own era into the woods.

If Prim were being honest with herself, it rankled her to be just one in a line, following the path that had been taken because it was always taken. What choice was there? She felt the ripple of power as she stepped over a boundary of smooth stones and fleshy white mushrooms. The locals called this a fairy circle. It was silent in the circle, eerily so, as if all the wind and sounds of nature had been muted.

In the center of the circle was a stone altar. The stone was weather worn, its surface scoured and stained by hundreds of years and hundreds of rituals.

"Lay the child here, please."

The man took in the scene. Prim could see him trying to process what he was seeing. Wondering what he was about to see.

He opened his mouth to speak, thought better of it, closed it again. "Stand there," she said and pointed to the outside of the circle. He did. Prim returned to the mother who had the child laid out on the cold stone. It was still bundled in the blanket.

Prim assessed the small boy, trying to embody the professional remove her mother had always cultivated. As had her grandmother. Cool and clinical. She would never have the icy poise of her mother though, just a pale shadow, she ran too hot. If it were up to her, she would happily send this woman home to order a small coffin. Just because she could do what the locals asked, didn't mean she wanted to. But there were rules for her, as there had been for all the women of her bloodline. The man shifted his weight and a twig snapped, and Prim frowned at him in her periphery. Tempted to shush him.

The little boy had damp brown hair, and a delicate fan of thick eyelashes. He could not be older than three or four. His chest was bare, sodden shorts and nothing on his feet. Such a lovely and perfect child. He *had been* at least. She covered his eyes with her hand and looked at the mother.

"Give me your hand."

Prim took the woman's hand. It was a coarse working hand, reminding her of her own mother's. Though this one was clammy and trembled fiercely. Prim turned it palm up and said the words. The same words her mother had said. . . and her mother's mother...the words that thinned realities, the words that cut a slice in the ether.

When it was done, Prim reached with her free hand and pulled out the needle from her bun. Her wet hair untwisted, hitting her back with a slap. With a practiced movement she guided the woman's hand over the boy's heart.

"The cost will be your life, shortened by half. And once dead, your soul. Do you agree to these terms?"

The woman nodded, her eyes entirely round and glassy.

"Say it."

"I do. I do, oh god I do. Please." Fat tears streaked her lined face. Prim nodded.

Pressing the woman's hand firmly over the still heart, she raised the needle high and struck down into her hand, pushing the spike all the way through. The silver needle was wickedly sharp, but she still had to use force to clear the boy's breastplate. The needle had to pierce his heart. That's how it worked. How it had always worked.

The mother screamed. They always screamed. She tried to move, instinct forcing her struggle to free her hand, but she was trapped, pinioned to her dead boy by a foot-long knitting needle.

The color drained from her face, her breath coming in pants.

The man called out, running toward them.

"What the hell are you doing?!"

Prim turned, meeting his eyes and letting any facade she kept in place fall away. She could imagine what it would look like to an outsider, her otherness on the surface. She had watched her own mother, and her grandmother when she was a child. They had in them power, real power that was so much bigger and *more* than a single human life. Beneath her ordinary skin and bones, was an elemental thing, brighter and stranger, utterly inhuman, and able to remake and reimagine reality itself. Prim was no more human than the trees around them, or the rivers, or a bolt of scorching lightning. Her power was awesome and terrifying. It was why the Woman of the Woods *had* to live apart. Whether she wanted to or not.

The man witnessed and was frightened by the truth. He backed away so fast that he fell. Prim turned back to the mother.

"Say his name and call him back to you."

The frantic woman nodded, chanting the name over and over.

"Jacob Ian Black, Jacob Ian Black, Jacob Ian Black..." Prim matched her chant to the mother's: the power of the two voices echoing through the space. The mother had her eyes squeezed shut, tears streaming. It could have been hours, days, or seconds. Even the man had joined in the chant, at a far border of the clearing. Jacob Ian Black, Jacob Ian Black.

"JACOB IAN BLACK come back to us!" Prim screamed, her voice cracking.

The boy gasped, chest filling with air, a stream of blood spilling over his pale, tiny, rib cage. The mother screamed out, embracing the boy as much as she could with her hand attached to him.

Prim took the needle, gripping it firmly and pulled. It slid out of the woman's hand and from the boy. He sat up ramrod straight with a great gasp and burped a fount of filthy water from his mouth.

The small hole in his chest bled.

He was panting, choking. Prim set her hand on his back. Helping him clear his lungs. When he turned to her, his eyes were dark. The sclera swallowed by black. He regarded Prim curiously, inhuman eyes gleaming like a shark.

"Welcome back Jacob Ian Black," she said softly. The boy smiled, a quirk to the lip, and a small nod of his head. A gesture utterly foreign and almost gentlemanly on a body so small, still chubby with baby fat. The mother was near hysterical, praying and praising, her bloody hand smearing the boy's skin wherever she touched and fawned over him.

Prim stepped aside, allowing the boy to slide from the altar, his mother falling upon him with kisses and embraces. He tolerated them, but his eyes stayed locked on Prim. She hid any discomfort as she looked down upon him.

The man had not risen, instead opting to stay sprawled on the ground, his mouth opening and closing like a fish. He kept looking from the boy to Prim and back. No one noticed or cared that he was still there at all.

They walked back to the cottage. Prim in the lead, although if she was honest, she did not like the boy at her back. The mother was cooing and coddling as she carried him. The man stayed a ways behind, looking shell-shocked.

When they reached her door, she leaned against it, desperately wanting them gone. She was exhausted from spinning a spell so complex and her whole body felt empty and nearly transparent.

"Do you want money? Is there anything I can do for you? Anything at all?" The mother said, coming almost up to the same step as Prim. The boy watched from his mother's arms, eyes locked on her.

"No, no nothing. Just take your boy and go."

"Yes, yes." The woman looked away, realizing suddenly, almost dreamily, that she had made a deal essentially with the Devil.

"A piece of advice: Love him, but also always remind him who he is. And watch him. . .closely."

The mother nodded, snuggling the boy and kissing his face and neck.

The man said nothing. Then they drove away, leaving Prim with a headache and a feeling of unease.

☙❧

A FEW DAYS LATER, THE WARM SNAP ENDED, AND COLD miserable rain poured down in sheets. Prim sat at her table, staring out the gray window at the dark, damp forest. Her fat cat lay at her feet, purring quietly.

She felt restless. The rain had kept her cooped up for days. She had her fill of knitting and reading. She cooked, she cleaned, she slept. Three days of the same had left her feeling bored. And, strangely, lonely. That was not an emotion she was used to feeling.

Later she heard commotion coming from up the road, went to her front window and saw the yellow glow of headlights. The same jeep from the other day pulled up, and the same man jumped out.

Coat over his head, he came running toward her door. Prim thought about blowing out the candles and locking the door. Loneliness was perhaps preferable to trouble.

But then again, nothing ever happened by chance.

She yanked the blue door open just as he reached the step. His jacket was soaked and he brought in with him the damp and cold. She tried to imagine what her home must look like to an outsider. She stared at the peaked roof, the books lining every wall, floor to ceiling, thousands of them, a world of knowledge, and handy insulation for the long winters. The soft wood floors swept clean, the stone hearth and small cook stove roaring to scare off the chill. Her work table, laden with herbs and bottles. Her knittings, her small bed built right into the wall, the books surrounding it like a cave.

"It sure looks like a witch lives here," he said, looking at every inch of the room. His face was stubbly, obviously he'd gone days without a shave, and his brown hair was plastered wet to his forehead. He was tall, not so tall as to have issues standing inside, but tall.

"What do you want?" she snapped. When he turned to her she pulled her shawl closer, feeling strange having a man inside her home, having a man so close to her body.

"I want to talk about what happened. That kid doesn't seem right. . ."

Prim ignored the question. Pushed by him and reached for the kettle on the stove for some tea. She could feel his eyes on her back as she worked. "What's your name?" she finally asked him.

"What? Dan, not that it matters."

"Dan. I'm Prim. And it does matter, because you came to my home, unannounced, *twice*, and are questioning things that are very much not your business. You are not from the village."

"You're joking, right?"

She poured tea into two cups. She handed one cup to him and he stared at his suspiciously, not even attempting to be subtle as he sniffed it.

"Just tea. Drink it or don't." She sipped her own, "Now, I would like to ask you a question because I don't think you care about that kid at all. Why are you here, *really*?"

"I'm a reporter."

"What's a reporter doing here in this sleepy little hamlet, Dan?"

"Honestly? I was looking for *you*. Researching the history of the region for a story. I found accounts of a rural New Hampshire community that still uses a town witch. I combed old papers and historical records, cross referenced and discovered the town was New Durham. So, I came here. Talked to the historical society's president. He wouldn't give me an address, just told me to focus on the woods off Middleton Road. I went driving around the past few days, knocking on doors, not sure what I would find. Then this lady runs in front of my car. Really."

Prim sniffed, "Really? You try to find the local witch and you just happen to stumble across a woman who not only believes in her but wants to take you to her. That seem normal?"

"I know, believe me I know. But it's not a lie."

"I know it's not a lie. I'm tied to this land and this community. It was orchestrated that you would be driving by when Jacob Ian Black happened to be drowning. Things happen for reasons, Dan, the universe is a strange and complex mechanism. A butterfly wing causing a tornado a continent away and all that."

"Okay...let's say that's true. Why?"

Prim shrugged and poured herself more tea, it was now her time to buy time. She looked over the rim of her cup at Dan, who was sitting uncomfortably in her small home. The only man that she had ever allowed inside. She had never known her father, and her mother never spoke of him. Her eyes shifted to the large old candle on the windowsill. The rendered fat sweated so close to the fire. The flame danced and flickered, the wick thicker than her finger. It had been her mother's candle, made when she was pregnant with her. Every piece of the room had belonged to a woman of her bloodline—except that candle, that was hers.

The silence stretched. She had a feeling that her father, whoever he'd been, had come in and sat and looked at her mother, and that they had talked in a similar manner.

"That kid was dead. I want to know how you did it. Who taught you? What else can you do?"

"So, it's an interview you want. I don't think so."

"I will change your name, change the name of the town, change anything that could tie it to you. Please. 'Interview with the Witch', or something like that."

She sighed, staring out the window at the endless rain. It was lonely in the woods. She wondered if her mother and her mother's mother had felt the same way while they looked out the same damned window. Everyone who came to her wanted something, even this man, this outsider. She wondered if someone would ever come to *give* her something.

"I was born here, in that very bed, and raised here my whole life. As was my mother and her mother...passing on the knowledge of these woods."

"Who was the earliest descendant?"

"The story goes that we are not descended from people at all, but rather the Spirit of the Forest that took on the form of a woman when the first villagers settled here. We are bound and ageless, tethered to these trees and streams. Unable to survive outside of them." Prim rolled her eyes and leaned back.

"Do you believe that?"

Prim shrugged and petted the sleepy cat that had leapt up into her lap.

"Have you ever left the forest? Ever?"

She did not reply for a while.

Finally, she said, "Why leave when everything I want, or

don't want, is brought right to me?" She smirked, "Even pizza delivery."

"Are you teasing me?"

Silence filled the space between them, but a smile played on her lips. She wasn't too keen to follow through with this night, with what the fates had laid out for her.

"Tell me about yourself Dan. Help me to trust you."

He crossed his arms and stared up at the ceiling. "Let's see. . .I was a bad student and allergic to most of nature. The only thing I can do, or am good at, is being a reporter. I have a good instinct for stories. It's like I always know where to be, always at ground zero, first on the scene. Like the other day with the boy..."

"Most people are a little sensitive. Here give me your cup." He finished the dregs and handed it to her. She swished it, once clockwise, once counterclockwise, and then emptied its contents onto the saucer. Dan snorted, even after all he'd seen, the idea of her reading tea leaves felt absurd.

Her heart squeezed in her chest, she'd suspected why he was in her home, but now she knew. Prim stared at the leaves for some time, the truth of them weighing heavy on her. She wanted to chuckle, or cry, for Lady Fate had a strange sense of humor. It was not the first time, nor even the fiftieth time, she saw an omen in the leaves, or cards, or however she was divining. But it was the first she'd seen one for herself.

She had felt lonely, and it seemed fate wanted her to have some company.

"Well? Your pause is making me nervous Prim." Dan squirmed in his seat, eyes darting to the small dish, vainly trying to understand what a few leaves in a puddle could spell out. "Are you going to tell me what you see? You're starting to freak me out."

"It's nothing. Really." She smiled, forcing it to be genuine. "Just a silly parlor trick."

"I don't believe you, you can reanimate the fucking dead. How do you have that kind of power?"

"Let me say this: there are some, myself included, who understand the world and its parts on a deeper level. It's like a mechanic knowing how to repair a car. It may seem like magic to someone who does not understand the complexities, but to one who does, it's as easy as snip this and replace that."

"It's a little more complicated than replacing an engine don't you think. . . ah what are you doing?"

Prim stood while he spoke and began unfastening her dress.

"The cosmos is too complex for us to get but a glimpse, Dan." Prim crossed the room, blowing out candles as she did, all but the large one in the window.

"Okay fine, I get that, but what are you doing? Prim..."

She let her shift slide off her. She was naked beneath. He averted his eyes as she stepped nearer.

"It was in your leaves," Prim said, trying for confidence.

"My tea leaves said to take your clothes off?" He chuckled, shielding his eyes with his hand like an awkward boy. Prim stepped closer, close enough to him that she could feel the heat radiating off his skin.

"Something like that," she whispered, moving his hand away, and touching her lips to his. He wanted to fight her. She knew he was conflicted by what she was and what she could do. But he was a curious creature by nature, so he allowed her to lead him to the bed, to undress him, and lay him down on the ancient quilts, knitted by grandmothers and mothers long gone.

Prim crawled atop him, hoping to look skilled and confident. Inside she was frightened, and ill-experienced. She'd never held a man's hand, let alone gone to bed with one. But the leaves didn't lie. No outsider came to her home unbidden.

They kissed, and touched, and eventually she guided herself onto him, wincing as her hymen tore. She moved atop him, exploring the combination of pain and pleasure. She noted the tang of blood in the air. Prim could feel the magic on her bare skin.

When it was over and his seed trickled from within her, she lay beside him. Watchful. The fire flickered on his sweaty skin. Her long hair trailed down her body and she imagined herself a fire dappled Lady Godiva. She debated telling him the truth. She imagined her mother doing the same, and hers before that. It was the endless conflict of the Women of the Woods. The curse of knowing too much and never knowing how much to share.

"The tea leaves told me that I would become pregnant this night. That you would be the father of the next Woman of the Woods."

"What?!" He rose quickly, gathering his clothes. "You're crazy, this was a mistake."

As he continued dressing and cursing, she slid a robe on and went to the table pulling out a bottle and two glasses from a cupboard above.

"Please, have a drink. Sit. Let me explain."

"No, I think I'm good. This whole situation is too weird for me."

"Dan, please don't leave, you didn't even get your interview." Prim could see the fight in him, his hunger for a good story, his fear of her manipulating him. "Besides this weather is positively hostile. Much cozier in here. Here, have something a little stronger than tea." The fire popped and hissed. Prim tightened her robe, cinching the waist and feeling more comfortable covered up. Dan finally sat and she slid a glass of whiskey his way. She sat opposite, drink in hand.

"So, you think that the fates wanted us to get together?"

"Yes. How else would you have found me, why would you have returned?"

He sipped his drink and winced.

"Dan, you must understand. There is no clear path to my cottage. Only those that seek me *and* are deemed worthy can find me. The Woman of the Woods lives apart. In a fold of time and space." Prim walked across the room and lifted the large old candle, her candle, the only light, save the fire. It was big as a piece of kindling, a sickly yellow color and half burnt.

"See this?" she held it out to him. "My mother made this candle and burned it her whole pregnancy for me. Her mother had done the same, and the day my mother died, her candle was all but gone. Whenever I would fall ill or get hurt as a child, she would light this one and it protected me. It's a tallow candle you see. Made of rendered fat, my father's fat. *This is my father."*

Dan tried to rise. She almost pitied him, but he had meddled in things beyond his understanding, and fate sent him on this path. He swayed, vision blurring as she stepped nearer with the hideous old candle extended. The smoke from it was black and acrid, greasy. She'd always felt both comforted and put off by this candle. He coughed as the stink from it wafted his way.

"I feel weird. My drink—" he slurred, trying to focus on her face. Prim's heart pounded in her chest like a trapped bird. She set the candle down, wiping her sweat slick hands. "What was in that?" He looked at his glass and then crumpled to the floor, loose limbed and unconscious.

She knelt beside him, sweeping his dark hair from his face. Her other hand absently trailed to her stomach, and already she could feel the bloom of life there. She smiled. Once the rain let up she would get to making a new candle, for her daughter. She would render his fat and boil his bones. He would be buried with all the rest of the fathers.

She looked forward to meeting her daughter, to teaching her the path.

And Prim no longer felt lonely.

❧ 16 ❧

THE DARE

"**I** don't think this is a good idea." Belle chewed her lip nervously. She glanced at the tall wrought iron gate in front of her, and at Ingrid behind her. Ingrid sighed, a sound she'd been making more and more around her best friend lately.

"Come on Belle, it's no big deal. A stupid dare, and not even that hard of one. We go in, take something, and come out. It's fine."

Belle stepped closer to the gate, wrapping long fingers, with chipped blue polish on her short nails, around the rusty bars. "Are we sure no one lives there? Or that there will even be a way in?"

"No, and no. That's why it's a dare, Belle. Now open the gate, we're running out of daylight."

She did.

THE TOWN OF PIKE'S HOLLOW WAS NESTLED IN THE foothills of the Black Mountains with the mountains on one side and Black Lake on the other. The town was small, quaint, and could grow no larger unless it expanded over water, or up steep cliffs. Its enforced small size, and beautiful natural amenities like skiing, boating, and hiking, made the town a destination for tourists. The real estate market was very competitive, as were the B&B and motel industries. Ingrid knew all of this in part because her mother was the star realtor in Pike's Hollow.

All of this made the fact that Grange Manor had sat vacant, or nearly so, for two decades, all the more curious. It was a massive sprawling house on grand grounds, the whole property encircled by tall ornate stone fences. The house was positioned on a hill, allowing it the impressive view of both mountains and water, and the sleepy village in between.

Grange Manor had been built by Pierce and Millie Grange, owners of a very profitable boat building company at the turn of the century. The couple had taken a trip to England and were so inspired by the grand country houses of stone, surrounded by rolling fields of meticulously landscaped green, that they simply had to build one of their own.

The giant house was a grey stone box, with oxidized copper/green accents, and a hundred blank windows. It was a cold house: lovely, but unwelcoming. The residents of Pike's Hollow always regarded it as something of a curiosity, as it was such a contrast to the quaint colonial charm the rest of the village had carefully cultivated.

The boating business and the Grange family died out over time, leaving just one ancient Grange living in the mansion alone with a nurse. When Belle and Ingrid were born, the house was vacant. It had been left in a will to a distant relative who, it was rumored, had no resources to pay and keep up such a large and high maintenance home. There was an ancient groundskeeper, Charles Ernst, to mow the lawn and do minor repairs. For years, he was the only one who went in and out of the big old house.

When the girls were in elementary school, someone in town noticed they hadn't seen old Charles for a while. His body was found in the Grange Manor, pretty far decayed. It was the talk of the town. Rumor was that the groundskeeper had been killed by ghosts, though the police insisted no foul play had occurred. Just an old man, suffering a heart attack all alone, with no one left to report him missing.

"The real story is one of loneliness." Belle remembered her father saying over the supper table, pausing for effect as he looked over his family one by one. "That someone could be so alone in this world that no one cares if they go missing. I wouldn't wish that on anyone. That is what we should focus on, not ghosts and fantasy. We need to take care of each other." Belle's father was a sentimental sort, the local pastor, with a streak of something poetical.

After Charles' death, the house languished on the market, neglected. Ingrid knew this because her realtor mother called Grange Manor the "White Elephant of Pike's Hollow."

"The commission on that house," her mother often said whenever they drove past, "would be a year's salary."

"Why hasn't anyone bought it?" Ingrid asked, squinting up at the place that was practically a castle.

"It's a few million dollars, and it needs a ton of work: electrical, plumbing, roofing. The upkeep of the house and grounds is a major expense. It's just too much, even for people with cash to burn."

THE GATE WAS LOCKED, BUT RUST HAD WEAKENED THE HINGES, and with some pulling and pushing, they were able to open the gate wide enough to squeeze through. They'd chosen the back-yard garden gate because it was hidden from the road and they'd guessed correctly, neglected enough to get through.

The back garden sprawled before them, grasses hip high and swaying in the midsummer heat. Bugs buzzed and chirped, silencing when the girls passed by. The sky was darkening, purples and oranges, and the house stood watchful atop the hill, its windows reflecting the sunset.

Ingrid led the way, Belle trailing nervously behind. "I just don't want to get in trouble," Belle whispered, even though they were alone. Ingrid glanced back, her pale hair whipping in the wind.

"You never want to get in trouble. If it was up to you we'd be up in your room reading Bibles all summer."

Belle felt her cheeks get hot. "That's not true. I just don't think we need to break the law to impress those boys is all. I don't even like them."

"Not even Evan?" Ingrid shot back as she clamored over a low stone wall, like a daddy longlegs in tiny daisy duke shorts. Belle had to straddle the wall and, being a bit shorter and stouter than her friend, barely got over it.

Evan. Evan Cooper. A summer boy, with a summer home right on the lake, and rich parents, who were never around. Tall and golden skinned, hair highlighted by the sun. Flat abs and sunglasses, a big white grin. Probably going to be a governor or something someday. Belle hated that she liked him, hated that his generic handsomeness and obvious charms had caught her.

"I doubt he sees me as anything but a kid with a crush."

"Exactly. That's why you have to do it," Ingrid said, stopping to wait for Belle to catch up. Ingrid was tall, model tall, and lean. Her long white blonde hair and pale blue eyes gave her an elfin quality. Ingrid always turned heads and had grown comfortable over the years with the attention. It was her looks, more than anything, that caught Evan and the other summer boys' attention when the girls ate ice cream on the docks. The boys invited them boating. To a cookout. To play truth or dare, which put them at Grange Manor. "Belle, if you come back from the dare, *victorious* —a dare I doubt any of them would have the balls for— well...then he'll remember you, he'll be impressed by you."

Belle nodded and forced a smile, the whole thing felt stupid.

They reached the area of lawn closest to the house, and both girls couldn't help noticing how quiet it was. The immediate area around the big house was hushed, as if it was holding its breath and watching them through its dusty windows. The girls got quiet as they got closer, their footsteps loud on the stone veranda against the back of the house. They tested windows and doors, trying to stay as close to each other as possible, without letting on to the other that they were frightened.

Belle knelt, moving aside some vines, and found a basement window with no glass. She could smell the damp of the basement wafting out, the opening impossible to see into. She debated about covering it back up, lying to Ingrid, and just aborting the plan, when Ingrid rounded the corner and hooted in victory.

"Nicely done Belle! We have our way in."

⊗

"IT STINKS IN HERE," INGRID WHISPERED AS SHE WIPED HER grimy hands on her scant shorts. Belle flinched, even whispering felt loud in the silent gloom of the house. They both squinted, letting their eyes adjust after they'd left the bright sunny day behind.

"Looks like the washroom. Got an old timey laundry machine, slop sink, some indoor clothes racks." Ingrid pointed as she began walking. She sounded exactly like her realtor mother.

"Technically," Belle said fingering an antique clothespin, "This thing here would meet the terms of the dare." She held it up. Ingrid raised her eyebrow and snorted.

"A *clothespin*? Come on Belle. Try to have a little sense of adventure here. We could've found that anywhere. I did not come this far to bring back *that*." She plucked it from Belle's hand and tossed it. The sound of wood striking cement was unbearably loud to Belle.

"Fine," she hissed, gesturing for Ingrid to lead the way.

Ingrid stepped into the role of leader with pleasure, tossing her blonde hair over her shoulder, and continued on, tennis shoes muffling her steps.

THE BASEMENT WAS ENORMOUS, AS WAS THE HOUSE ABOVE IT, and it took them some time to find a way up and into the house proper. There was little of value or interest in the basement, but considering the overwhelming stink of damp, it probably wasn't wise to store anything good down there anyway.

The narrow creaky stairs opened up into a nearly vacant butler's pantry. The few dusty jars of preserves on the empty shelves looked like they would be more at home in a science lab than a kitchen. Ingrid picked one up and dusted it off. She read the label. "Cauliflower. I wonder how long pickled cauliflower actually lasts." She put the jar back on the shelf and they moved on.

The pantry opened up into the kitchen, which was small and modest considering the grandness of the house. Dusty copper pots hung above a big sink. Here the windows faced the back-yard. If someone watched from the kitchen window, they could see anybody walking the whole way up to the house. Belle shuddered at the thought.

"I was hoping there'd be more. . . stuff in here, didn't you? Like cool small stuff?" Ingrid said as she wandered down the main hall. Belle agreed there was little that they could carry out. Only very large wood furniture remained. But she could imagine the house at its finest. Candles burning in sconces along the hall-ways. The marble glinting underfoot and ornate ceilings soaring above. Murals along the walls. People laughing, the swish and rustle of fancy dresses.

"It must have been so beautiful. Like a fairy tale," Belle whispered, spinning in the main foyer, the large front doors, the grand main staircase, fit for a princess to descend.

"Let's go upstairs. Maybe a bedroom closet has something. Ooh, maybe jewelry?" Ingrid ran up the stairs quickly, Belle huffing behind. She glanced back from the top of the stair, noting the stained-glass ceiling for the first time. She also saw that their footprints had disturbed the dust on the floor, down the hall, and all the way up the stairs.

THE GIRLS WANDERED ROOM TO ROOM. MOST STILL HAD BEDS, which were stripped bare, and white sheets covered the few pieces of furniture. Belle's eyes stung from dust as Ingrid pulled open yet another set of heavy drapes to let the last of the day's light in.

"Are you going to close all those when you leave?" she said chidingly to Ingrid, who was frantically rifling through drawers in a vanity. Ingrid truly looked like a burglar now—dirty, hair wild, eyes bright.

"It's getting dark, we should go," Belle said when Ingrid didn't answer.

"We could just sleep here," Ingrid said over her shoulder.

Belle's mouth dropped open at the thought.

"I'm kidding, God, Belle, you really need a sense of humor."

Belle glowered and moved about the room, touching things absently as she went. It must have been a lady's room. The rose wallpaper, and pink brocade drapes were very feminine. Maybe the daughter? There was a delicate E carved onto an enormous wooden armoire. The daughter's name popped into her head, Esme.

She went to the armoire, noting the ornate keyhole was missing a key. She took the handles in her hand, turning back to Ingrid as she pulled them open.

"Wouldn't it be amazing to find a ballgown or—" Before Belle could finish the sentence something was on her, something man sized, plowed into her like a freight train from *inside* the armoire. It wasn't particularly heavy, felt like a bag of sticks, but it was strong and the more she tried to fight, the harder it held her. Before she could scream or call out, it covered her mouth with one dry hand and bit into her throat. Pain, immediate and electric. She thrashed, feet knocking against the floor. She felt the wet mouth, the rough tongue like a cat. The thing atop her rubbed its body into hers, grinding her into the floor with its sharp bones. She could barely breathe. The rough, cold hand was clamped seamlessly over her mouth and nose. She bit down, the withered skin flaking into her mouth and with it, a foul rush of blood. She gagged, the bile mixing with the blood, choking her. The hand never budged. She feared drowning then, and only through sheer willpower alone could she calm her panic enough to swallow it all down and focus on getting enough air through her nose to keep from passing out.

She heard Ingrid scream, call her name over and over, but it was miles away. Belle fought, but was growing weaker and weaker by the second, until her limbs felt leaden, her senses smothered, and then she was gone.

⚜️

SHE HEARD MOVEMENT. THE SCRAPE OF SHOES AGAINST THE floor. She felt fabric under her fingertips, softness under her body. A bed?

Belle tried to sit up, and the pain in her neck stopped her. Her whole body ached and she trembled. Her stomach churned and she turned her head, a hot spurt of burning vomit spraying out before she could stop it. She fell back. It must have all been a terrible fever dream. She was home, she was sick.

Then footsteps. She wasn't alone. "Mom?" she whispered, her voice sounding strange in her own ears, "I'm sick."

The steps drew nearer, a cool hand on her forehead, taking her temperature. Then a cup at her lips, she sipped, then gulped. Hadn't realized how thirsty she'd been.

⚜️

BELLE OPENED HER EYES, AND NOTED SHE WAS IN THE SAME room she'd been attacked in. That revelation filled her with fear and she sat up, fast. Her head was spinning, and she looked around in panic. She had no idea how long she'd been in that bed, but her last memory was being attacked, and now there was no sign of Ingrid. It was night, and the curtains were open revealing a wedge of moon and the glinting town and lake below.

She swung her legs over the bed, noting her shoes had been removed. They were lined up neatly at the foot of the bed. With shaky hands she reached for them. A movement in the corner of the room startled her.

Frozen, she scanned the room with her eyes. In the corner, a figure sat in a chair. Ice poured into her veins and a spike of adrenaline demanded she bolt for the door. The memory of the attack, of the thing knocking her down, biting into her skin, all flooded back. The licking and suckling, the press of something hard against her stomach. Her vision swam.

"How do you feel?" The voice was little more than a whisper. Male. Raspy. She squinted into the darkness, wanting to see more than a gray shape with a pale face. He rose, and she started, a foot moving toward the door before she even realized.

He repeated the question.

"I feel. . ." she said, her voice sounding painfully loud in the silence. "I feel scared and confused. I would just like to go home now. My mother will be worried."

"Belle," he said. There was something about the way he said her name. . . almost fondly.

"How do you know my name?" she whispered.

"Your friend screamed it over and over."

"Where's Ingrid?"

He ignored her question and stepped closer, passing through the square of moonlight beaming in from the window. She saw dingy clothes, a tattered old suit, long gray hair. But the face stayed in shadow.

"You can't go home Belle."

"GOD YOU ARE A PRUDE SOMETIMES! IT'S JUST A GAME AFTER all," Ingrid said, half laughing, half angry as she looked at Belle.

"It wasn't just a game, he deliberately dropped the card so he could kiss me and grope me. You didn't see."

Ingrid rolled her eyes and tossed her hands up. She was drunk, and alcohol always made her cruel. "Belle, *I saw*, you didn't get assaulted, he was just messing around. Maybe he likes you. Maybe he thought it was the only way you would kiss him."

"I think he was making fun of me."

Ingrid's look was withering. "These are cool *Summer Boys* with a boat and beer, and this amazing house. Don't ruin this for me."

"Ruin?" Belle's eyes burned, when had they stopped being a team? When had a bunch of rich boys mattered more than her feelings? Belle wanted to leave the party. Evan Cooper still didn't care who she was, his friends were all jerks, and she didn't like the version of Ingrid that they brought out.

As if on cue, Evan popped his head out, "You guys okay out here?" He smiled, rows of perfectly white teeth gleamed back, no doubt from expensive teenage orthodontia. Belle hated the traitorous trill in her chest when his gaze swept her way and tried to ignore the sensation of it curdling as he passed her by and his gaze lingered on Ingrid. "Chad can be a real jerk. Sorry if he was bothering you, Beth."

"Belle."

"What? Sorry. *Belle*, I mean."

"We're cool, Evan. We just needed some air. Right, Belle?" Ingrid's stare skewered Belle to the wall, the implication if she did anything but nod, clear on her face.

HE SAT AT THE LARGE DINING TABLE'S HEAD. HE'D PULLED THE dusty white cloth off beforehand, and now regarded Belle, sitting at his right. The girl stared at her hands, pooled in her lap.

She was petite, barely five feet, and curvy to the side of chunky. Her dusky skin and pale green eyes made him wonder about her heritage. Her hair was pulled back in a high ponytail, thick, black, and wildly curly.

"So, you won't let me leave," she said, voice barely a whisper.

"I'm sorry, no. I wish it were otherwise."

She raised her head, eyes narrowing as they met his.

"Why can't I go? And where is Ingrid?"

"It was all an accident."

She snorted and crossed her arms over pert breasts. The tank top she wore was soiled from crawling around the dusty old house. As were the cutoffs below. Her knees were dirty too.

"And now you're keeping me prisoner." Her lip trembled. She had full pouty lips. It had been a long time since Ellory had been around anyone, let alone someone as fresh and lovely as this girl. His attraction distracted him.

He sighed, "Prisoner is a strong word. Try to see this as an opportunity."

She swiped at her eyes. "No thanks. I just want to go home. Never even wanted to go on this stupid dare. Please tell me Ingrid is okay."

Ellory opened his hands wide, as if to say, what can you do? He was already tired by the barrage of questions. He debated if it would be better just to kill her and be done with it.

"Who are you anyways?" she asked.

"My name is Ellory Grange."

She huffed. "That's impossible, Ellory Grange disappeared like fifty years ago!"

He shrugged, "I did. Now here I am—reappeared."

"Did you kill Ingrid?" she asked, her eyes wet. "Please just tell me."

He smiled humorlessly, "Not yet."

Ellory Grange never fit in and always felt like something of a disappointment to his parents. As the youngest son, he would never inherit the title or the business. All of that would go to Milo, his too perfect, goody-two-shoes brother. Esme was always too busy wandering around with her nose in a book or running off with one of her young summer girls, to pay him much mind. For the times and their generation, his parents were shockingly indifferent to Esme's dalliances. Perhaps they didn't care because they had perfect-in-every-way Milo, so the other children were just backups anyway.

It didn't matter. Ellory was an afterthought in his household, and the town regarded his family as rich and tacky. He found it hard to socialize with Pike's Hollow locals or the summer elite. The former, too hardscrabble and redneck, and the latter, too snobby. Ellory, a fun-loving eccentric, found them all dull, and so it was with great eagerness that he left home for the city.

Or cities. Ellory travelled extensively, hungry for life and experience, hungry for adventure. He experienced loads of both. He took any odd job he could, and by the end of his twenties, he'd mucked stables, put up houses, shot pigeons in stadiums, worked as a doorman for a whorehouse, washed dishes, taken tickets at carnivals, was a nude model, and even a busker. And he had fun. It was a fun life filled with other vibrant, hungry people all trying to make their mark.

But there was still a little hole in him, something insatiable, that kept him moving around and unable to settle down or be satisfied. He'd hunted big game, visited the brothels of the world, eaten exotic fare, visited all the sacred sites. But it was never enough. . .

Then there was the party. This was the swinging flapper twenties and Ellory, and his worldly friends, were tucked away in a tiny back room speakeasy that by day was a kosher deli. It was there he got a lead that would change his life. He was flirting with a young blonde in a sparkly dress when he noticed his friend Charles talking to a strange man he'd never met. The man was artificially pale, as if wearing makeup, with a sharp suit and a shining cravat. He had a pencil mustache and wet eyes with long, feminine eyelashes. The man's voice had an accent, but one Ellory couldn't place.

"This party isn't for tourists. Red only entertains the cream of the crop, and the gift you bring, she must deem it worthy. If it isn't, she'll turn you away, or worse."

"Worse?" Charles snorted incredulous, "What, like she has you killed? Come on! I've heard of some elaborate entrances into gin halls and speakeasies but this takes the cake." The pale man shrugged and took a pull off his cigarette, indifferent.

Ellory was turning from the girl and listening to the men's conversation before he even realized what he was doing. "Are you talking about the Ruby Room?" he asked, mouth gone dry.

The pale man met Ellory's eyes, and he was first to look away. "I am," he said coolly.

"It's a racket Ellory, don't bother with it. You have to bring this red lady a special present. And if she don't like it," Charles dragged his thumb along his throat, miming a slashed throat, "apparently the broad kills you."

"And if you do bring her the right present?" Ellory asked, pulse speeding up. He had heard about The Ruby Room, but it was only talked about in the most hushed tones. A party to end all parties. One filled with the most decadent, deviant individuals. Where anything was allowed, any predilection, any impulse. Red Ruby herself. . . an actual goddess.

"If you do then you get the keys to the kingdom," the man said licking his lips with his very red tongue.

"What did you bring?" Ellory asked the man quietly, after Charles stomped off, tiring of the conversation.

The man looked right and left, then beckoned Ellory closer. He lifted his jacket and shirt, revealing a puckered scar on his milk white right side. The scar was thick, pink and raised like a slug, easily five or six inches long. Ellory met the man's eyes, eyebrows up.

"She cut it out of me herself," he whispered in answer to Ellory's unspoken question.

⚜

"How long have you been hiding here?" Belle said, finding her courage the longer she was forced to be around this strange man. If he even was a man. He looked like a monster. He was little more than skin and bone and had honest to goodness talons at the end of his fingers, reminding her of a hawk or eagle. Then there was his face. Sharp cheekbones, hollow cheeks, dried gray hair like straw. His sunken eyes were black, and shiny, like an insect's.

"Long enough to look like this," he muttered, gesturing at himself. "I've wasted away."

"Why? Why are you here?"

Ellory sighed. "You ask a lot of questions. Shouldn't you be more scared?" He scraped his nails along the old table. "I could disembowel you: leave your guts in your lap, in seconds."

"You haven't though," Belle replied, chin high. She refused to cower, he might be a monster, but he had been hiding in a wardrobe, and he did attack two young girls—not particularly impressive. She was terrified, but held onto her anger, it kept her thinking.

"I needed a place to hide out for a while, so I could figure out my next move," he sniffed, the petulant tone highlighting the spoiled brat he once was. *Little more than another Summer Boy*, she thought.

"So, you're hiding from someone? On the run?" Belle was intrigued. Who or what could a shambling monster be afraid of? And she knew the more he was talking, the less he was doing anything to her. "Did you kill the old groundskeeper?"

"Not on purpose, it was an accident. As with you two. . . I'm trying not to hurt anyone, but everything I touch turns to shit. She made me like this. Poison." He stared at his hands, then his eyes slid to her, "you'll know soon enough what that's like, if I let you live."

Belle shivered, her fear thick in the back of her throat.

THE RUBY ROOM WAS IN A ROWHOUSE THAT LOOKED LIKE every other house on the street—the only difference was its red door. After the night with the pale man, Ellory planned for weeks to figure out his "gift" and after exhausting all thoughts of jewelry or priceless antiques, he turned inward. But how many livers or kidneys can a girl want? Then late one night, drunk, lying next to some girl he felt nothing for, he figured it out. His gift.

He was at the red door, then he was in the vestibule. A thin dark-skinned man with eerily light colored eyes opened the door, and the two stood in the tight space together. "This is a private club," the man said. "With a steep cover charge."

"I've got it. Let me see her."

The man sized him up before nodding and opening the next door, leading him down a dim hallway and into a small drawing room. The room was very dark, and there was only one chair. In the chair was a woman. The doorman closed the door and suddenly Ellory was alone with her.

The room was warm, uncomfortably so, and smelled. Musky, meaty, and a trace of perfume, he found it both cloying and nauseating.

A match was lit, and he followed the light to a candelabra. The light flickered, revealing a woman both beautiful and terrible. She was shapely in a fitted dress. Her skin fair, her eyes gleaming, a perfect bow mouth, and a tumble of red curls neatly pinned on her head. She watched him closely. He did the same, and noted her mouth was cruel. Although she was outwardly lovely, there was something loathsome about her. A wrongness.

Ellory dropped his eyes from hers, unable to hold the connection and his skin was pebbled in goosebumps.

He felt the room spin and wondered if he would faint. She almost smiled. "You brought me a present?" she said, and her voice was deep, husky, and caused his body to stir, the arousal near immediate.

He closed his eyes. Breathing in and out, fearful he may just pass out, he nodded.

"What have you brought me?" she purred, her lips so close to his ear he felt the air move from her breath. He'd never seen her move from the chair. The pressure in his head squeezed like a vice.

"Myself. I'll give you myself. To use as you see fit. Body and soul."

"That's a generous offer," she said, and he risked opening his eyes and meeting hers. "I wonder if you understand *what* you are offering?"

"I've seen it all, done it all, and I want more. I want to see behind the veil. I hear you can show me that."

"I can. You haven't seen it all, not by half. But the once seen cannot be unseen, and once I receive a gift, I do not return it. Are you ready for those consequences?"

Was he? Ellory was terrified, and aroused, and dizzy, and sweating. He knew he straddled worlds, and if he went with her he could never return. He knew she was not human. But he saw little to keep him in his life. As he'd said, he'd already seen it all. "I am ready to accept the consequences."

"You are reckless and you have a big mouth." She pulled him to her, and she kissed him. And then he was hers.

She was a terrible thing. He worshipped at her altar, supped at her table, and was forced into every humiliating and degrading shape she decided, because he'd given himself to her.

She thought it funny, for she was a cruel mistress, to make him her *mouth*. Everything he ate filled *her*, every lover he kissed, *she* received the pleasure. He was cursed to be hungry forever.

To want forever. She wanted more than food and kisses, she wanted blood, and flesh, she wanted everything. And even worse, he was contagious.

ELLORY DEBATED WHAT TO DO WITH BELLE, WISHING SHE WAS still unconscious so he could move about the house without having to worry about her escaping or attacking him. She was the type of girl that used to be called a 'spitfire.'

"Do they still call people spitfires?" he asked her idly.

"What?" Her face crinkled, confused, "I guess so."

"I must go see your friend now," he said rising from his chair. Belle stood up in a snap, her eyes wide. "You may come, but I will not hesitate to kill you if you try anything foolish." They started to walk out of the room when Ellory paused and spun back to the girl, "And I decide what is foolish."

He was very weak after subduing Belle. She had fought with the tenacity of someone who wanted to live, and it had taken every ounce of strength to stay on her and get his fill, enough to detach and grab the other girl. She had less vigor, and when he bit her she lost consciousness instantly. He managed to drag the blonde to the next bedroom over, his brother Milo's old room when they were children. He tied and gagged the girl there with old curtain tiebacks. That was where she'd lain ever since.

Belle gasped when she saw her friend trussed up. Dirty and bloody. Belle rushed to her. "What's wrong with her, why is she asleep still? Did you drug her?" She was shaking her friend's arm. Belle, dark and small, fleshy and alive. Her friend gaunt and thin, her blonde hair limp and almost colorless against the white pillowcase.

"She's dying."

"Dying!" Belle said tears streaking her cheeks. "Ellory, please just let us go. I won't tell anyone, hell, no one would believe me anyways. Let me go and take her to get help. Please? She's my best friend."

Ellory stepped toward the girls, and Belle stepped back, bumping into the night table. It fell over releasing an enormous cloud of dust and an overly loud bang in the quiet. Ingrid opened her eyes and squinted in the gloom. "Belle?" Her voice was barely a whisper.

Ellory leaned over the bed and opened the prone girl's legs. He wanted the vein at the inner thigh and her shorts were so short he needn't do much to reach it.

"What are you doing?!" Belle screamed. Ellory ignored her and bit down. The blonde's skin parted easy, and although it was a hot summer night, her flesh was almost as cold as his. Ingrid barely flinched as he drank deeply, nearly emptying her. He was lost in the pleasure of that moment, he could almost feel his flesh reknitting, his muscles plumping, when a sharp pain cracked across his back. He detached from the girl, falling onto the floor as another blow came, this time to his skull, then another, then another. Something cracked in his head, and a sheet of wet covered his eyes. His blood.

"Belle," he gasped as he put his hands up defensively, the blows stopped when he spoke.

"I'm getting us out of here," she said, panting. He was able to make out her outline. Belle held the now shattered, marble-topped nightstand in her hands. The marble, no doubt, the reason for his head injury.

"Belle you can't go anywhere, you don't understand. . . how long do you think you were asleep?" Ellory was on the floor, curled in the fetal position, a hand out in a vain attempt to stop her blows.

The girl raised the table up to strike again and he flinched. "What do you mean? Why does it matter?" She asked.

"Three nights. You were unconscious for *three nights*. I nursed you to health you remember?" She lowered the stool a few inches, confused. He could see her trying to remember. "I gave you something to drink. Remember? It was *her* blood."

⚜

"YOU'RE A LIAR!" SHE SCREAMED AND SWUNG THE TABLE again, the marble corner hitting Ellory in the wet mess of his damaged skull, splitting it open. The blood flowed freely now, filling the air with an iron smell. He fell back, mouth opening and closing, taloned fingers scratching at the floor.

In all the madness, Ingrid was trying to sit up, weak and bleary eyed, but still tied to the bed. "Belle?" she said.

"It's all right, I'll untie you and we will get out of here," Belle said and hit Ellory again with a satisfying wet crunch. He was still, his face little more than pulp and hair. Belle went to Ingrid and untied her bindings with trembling fingers.

Ingrid was so weak that Belle had to shoulder her entire weight. They were nearly out of the room, standing in the doorway when Ellory whispered, "There's no escape. You'll feel her inside your head soon enough. Your new goddess. She's like having lice on the *inside* of your body."

Belle ignored him. Instead she focused on the one step, then another, getting Ingrid down the grand staircase. Stairs that only a few days ago she'd imagined a princess descending. Then they were out the front door, and down the driveway. It took quite a lot of effort to get Ingrid over the stone wall, but she did. The two girls walked down the road, heading toward home.

It was terribly late, or very early, just before dawn and there were no cars in sight. Ingrid couldn't walk any longer, her head lolling, feet dragging. Belle was too short and too tired to keep dragging her along the road. In exhaustion, she eased her down on the shoulder, hopefully someone would stop to help.

Ingrid came in and out of unconsciousness, and she bled from many bites. Belle found the smell of the blood not altogether unpleasant. The longer she sat, silent, picking at the stray threads of her grimy cutoffs, the more she wondered about Ellory. About what he'd done to her.

She was hungry. Before she knew it, without really thinking at all, she dragged Ingrid into the ditch and past that into the thick overgrowth. There was a manic energy inside her, almost a giddiness that Belle found entirely foreign, as if she was someone else. Ingrid mumbled, her weak arms batting at Belle, but with little effect. When the two girls were safely hidden from sight in a dark patch of brambles and brush, Belle pulled Ingrid into her lap. She was so long and bony, hard to hold. She stroked her friend's skin, noting how soft it was. Then she was licking Ingrid's skin, and then she was biting it. Belle gnawed into Ingrid's forearm, all the way to bones and tendons. She sucked every drop of blood from the body.

As the sun crested the tree line, Belle found herself digging herself a hole in the ground, burrowing down, to be safe and to sleep. Once there, cocooned by the cool weight of earth, she couldn't ignore an itch in the back of her head. A niggling sensation like she'd forgotten something important. A *someone* important. A woman with red hair. Red. Throughout the day as she tried to rest and sleep, while Ingrid's body was found, while police combed the area, while Ellory burnt up in his childhood home, catching the old manor house on fire, the red woman picked at Belle's mind. Like lice on the inside of her body.

⚜ 17 ⚘

THOSE BENEATH, DEVOUR

I t happened.

"Holy shit," Greg whispered. His hand was up to his mouth. His eyes were wide and his face was unnaturally white.

I didn't need to say anything, his face said it for me, for all of us. My stomach flipped and I nearly barfed right there. I breathed as shallowly as I could. In through my nose, out through my mouth. Breathed in the stench of burning flesh. Breathed out panic. Breathed in the rotten egg stink of sulfur. Breathed out panic. Breathed in the cloying smell of decay. Breathed out panic.

"What happens now? I mean this was all Georgie's idea. What happens now, what was *supposed* to happen even?" This was Deena. Her voice was shrill. Her arms were wrapped tight around herself and she was trembling. Normally, Deena was nearly unflappable; she was clearly flapped by all this.

This is real and this is bad, was all I could think.

"Did it work though?" Greg, eyes red rimmed, stared at the scorched hole in the floor. "Did she get what she wanted?" None of us were brave enough to go to the edge and look down into it.

"It didn't work and she's fucking dead!" Deena shouted, and

I shushed her. Then felt like an idiot. Considering all the noise and goings on of the last hour, I don't know why Deena's yelling would make a difference. There was a good chance people were actually fleeing from the library—not running toward it.

"She's not dead. She can't be." Greg swiped at his cheeks. Greg loved Georgie. She had never reciprocated; too busy with her studies and her obsessions, and all the guys that were more handsome than Greg.

I asked her many times why she didn't just throw him a bone, go out for coffee or a glass of wine or something.

The last time I asked her, she sniffed and rolled her eyes. "C'mon Carmen, he's a geek. He's my friend sure, but that's as far as it will ever go. Tell him that. I've tried a thousand times, maybe you'll have luck getting it into that thick skull." Was it really only two days ago since she said that?

"I'm going to be in so much trouble over this. I can't believe I bought into Georgie's bullshit," Deena said. She sat heavily on a foldout chair, and stared into the hole, a hole in solid, or once solid cement, bored through from underneath.

I covered my eyes, not wanting to look at the hole, or my so-called friends, or think about Georgie's face in those last moments, the switch from excitement to. . . what had that emotion been? Utter, abject terror, probably.

Then. . . in that last second when her eyes went wide. . . and met mine.
. .

. . . I folded over and my puke splashed down between my knees into a stinking, steaming puddle. The regurgitated Chinese food a reminder that a few hours ago everything was normal. We were just a group of friends eating at MoonStar Cafe, as we did weekly ever since Georgie assembled us for her little side project. Georgie and I split the last dumpling. Now there it was: glistening, half-digested in a pile of bile.

I wiped my mouth on my sleeve and stood back up, knowing that there was no point bickering or standing around any longer. Deena would continue to bitch and worry about her scholarship, just like she had every single week since Georgie conned her into going out to eat with us. Greg would sob and defend Georgie till the end, like he always did. Right now, we had to clean things up, and we had to get out of there, because like Deena said, someone would be by eventually. Stepping over my barf and, with new resolve and a freshly empty stomach, I approached the hole.

The cement was scorched black and crumbling around the edges. The entire molecular surface seemed compromised and almost crackly as I stood on it. A memory ripped its way up and into my mind. Me at age twelve. Ice-skating on a lake not totally frozen, watching my best friend Teri plunge through it and into the water. One minute there, the next gone. I remembered dropping to my hands and knees, fighting the urge to flee to shore, to safety, to where the other kids were screaming in terror. Instead, carefully, carefully, I moved along the ever-thinning ice, trying to be lighter than a feather. Just get to the hole in the ice, reach in, try to find her, and pull her out. All the while, fissures in the surface spread out around me. You know what death sounds like? It sounds like ice cracking.

Back in the basement, back in the now, I reached the mouth of the hole, and cautiously peered inside. The stinking black pit was even blacker inside, and so deep we could probably drop a flare and it would fall for miles and miles. At the very edge of the hole, drifting on the foul breeze coming up from below, a hunk of blonde hair attached to a sizeable chunk of bloody scalp fluttered. Georgie's hair. Georgie's scalp.

I looked away fast, fist to my mouth. I could feel Deena and Greg watching me from the corners of the room. No one spoke. My eyes landed on the book where it had been dropped in all the madness. I wish Georgie never opened it, never got ideas about it, never talked Deena into sneaking it out of its case for her. Never pushed her tits up and flirted Greg into translating it for her. Never duped me because I believed in her, believed she could do what she claimed, because we were best friends and

roommates. Because I never had a friend as pretty and interesting as Georgie.

Without meaning to, my eyes drifted back to her hair,
clinging like scrub to a cliffside, still unable to process that her
spell had *worked*, and now she was dead and gone, and we were
left to clean it up. I knelt, keeping my eyes on the hole, and
picked up the old book. I hated the feel of its cover, knowing that
it was made from human skin, and I was tempted to toss it into
the hole. Words like vile and evil seemed dramatic and flowery,
but there was something truly evil about the stinky old text and
the sooner I could hand it off to Deena the better.

Was it really only a month since Georgie got us all together to
pitch her scheme? That day I got to the restaurant and saw
Georgie sitting with a girl I'd never met, but recognized, a girl
who worked in the library. On Georgie's other side sat the ever-
doting Greg, a nice enough guy but only a few degrees from a
stalker in my mind. I made it four. Her little team, assembled and
sworn to secrecy, so that Georgie could play magician.

Without express permission from the university, access to the
book was forbidden. Unlike Georgie, the rest of us were on some
sort of scholarship and didn't want to risk expulsion. We told her
all this when she explained her scheme to steal—"borrow"—the
book. Deena objected because she was employed by the college
as a library assistant, and was the only one with access to the
book, so she would clearly be the first person accused if the theft
was discovered. Greg and I tried to make her see how disastrous
it would be if either of us lost our scholarships. Georgie insisted
we were all paranoid, but promised that no one would get in
trouble. And for some reason we believed her.

The three of us looked at each other and the situation and
decided we wouldn't tell. I didn't love hiding what happened, or
the fact that Georgie's death would be our horrible secret, but it
was her plan, and her folly. It was unfair that we would all be
brought down because of it. She promised we'd be okay. It's
what she would have wanted. That's what we told ourselves.

Except I could already picture her haunted parents and imagine her little brother Brice crying. Never getting any closure. No one would ever know the truth, except for the three of us that remained.

The library's basement was a hoarder's paradise: boxes atop boxes, whole storerooms of furniture, and bric-a-brac. We laid a large piece of plywood we had found in the maintenance closet over the hole, and a moldy threadbare carpet over that. Carefully, we moved a banged-up reference desk and some chairs to sit on top of it. We even took the time to lay out books on the table, as if someone had been looking up something.

The ceiling was scorched, and we could do little about that: just hope no one looked up. Deena cracked open an ancient window a few inches to air out the singed smell.

When the space looked no more suspicious than any other space in the dusty old library, we packed up and cleaned our sooty selves up in the bathroom. Deena returned the book to its locked case. We snuck out, promising to check in with each other the next morning.

⊗⅍⅋

"YOU OKAY TO GO BACK TO YOUR ROOM ALONE?" GREG ASKED me once Deena was out of earshot. She lived across campus in one of the newer dormitories, Akeley. Georgie and I lived in Mason Hall. Greg lived off campus with his parents. "I could walk you, if you'd like." He was so pitiful looking that I almost took him up on it, but in the end told him no. I needed to be with my thoughts. Besides, I told him, he was parked in the visitor lot and would have to walk all the way back for his car. He reluctantly agreed and after an awkward and impulsive hug, he went on his way, leaving me standing alone in the quad.

It was late and utterly silent. The grass twinkled with early morning dew, and the air smelled of spring and rain. Just that morning, Georgie had opened our dorm windows and talked about getting some tulips for the room. "To celebrate spring finally coming after a long and horrible winter!"

Remembering, I fought the urge to cry and instead jammed my hands in my pockets and hastened my pace, not liking how vulnerable I felt out in the open all alone. The only sound was the echo of my boots on the sidewalk, the only company my extended, distorted shadow along the groomed lawns just starting to return to green. I kept glancing behind me, fighting the tickling sensation that someone was watching me, *something*. There could be, that was the crazy part. I was now part of a select group that knew without a doubt, that there were things out there, under the ground, anywhere they wanted, that were beyond the realm of what we knew.

You dumb bitch. My grief shaped itself into anger. Why did she always want everything? She was smart, brilliant even, beautiful, and rich. Everyone liked her: she charmed professors and students alike. Why couldn't that have been enough? Why did she want more, when so many would be happy with half of what she had? Hell, I'd have been happy with a quarter of her life.

The wind picked up out of nowhere, and every blade of grass and leaf fluttering under its onslaught, made me jump. I was running before I realized it, the staccato clack of my boots keeping time with my heartbeat.

When I finally, breathlessly, reached my dorm, it took a few tries to get my shaking hands and the key to cooperate. Inside I locked the door, my back pressed to it, dreading going into a room that Georgie would never again inhabit.

The old dorm's hallway was equal parts decay and charm, with cracked marble floors and elaborate moldings, little empty niches, and dusty rectangles on the walls where paintings once hung. My mother, practical to a fault, raised an eyebrow at the place when she helped me move in, thought it was a little rundown for the price of tuition. But I was charmed by the history, thinking of the hundreds of students who had come before me. Then I got to my dorm room, high on the third floor, a corner unit, larger than the others on the floor, with an old fireplace mantle and two big closets, tons of sun pouring in tall windows and a gorgeous blonde girl, who looked like a movie star. She smiled and hugged me, welcomed me, and I felt so excited. I felt like I was home.

Now, four years later, when the door swung in, it was to a dark messy room, colder and damper than the hall on account of the windows still being open. Georgie's bed was unmade, a few books left open on her desk, pages turning in the breeze.

Tears streamed down my face as I shut the heavy windows. I tried to ignore all her stuff, tried to ignore the entire day, and the sight I'd had of the thing that took her screaming.

Her last words, her eyes on mine, beseeching and terrified: *"Carmen, help me!"*

I REMEMBER HOW COLD THE WATER WAS, SO COLD THAT IT burned, and I remember my chin pressed to the craggy ice as my gloved hand searched as far as I could reach, trying to make contact. I worried that Teri had gone further down on a current and was trapped below the ice, trying to find a place to come up for air. It must be like being inside a looking glass, pounding on a mirror. I felt something, not a fish, something with hands and hair. I grabbed hold for dear life, and hollered. Help was coming, the people on the shore called back. Slowly, slowly I pulled her up. She was so heavy, soaked and cold, and my arm was screaming. I was just a scrawny little girl, but I was able to pull her up out of the water. I kept pulling my limp and unresponsive friend along the ice, and it was cracking and breaking off behind us, and finally, we reached the snowy shore, and with my lungs on fire, my body on fire, I rolled onto my back and stared at the flat gray sky. I could hear others talking to her, reviving her. I knew she would be okay, but I didn't bother to look, I was too tired.

But I couldn't save Georgie.

꧁꧂

I SHUCKED OFF MY CLOTHES, STINKING OF SMOKE AS THEY did, and jammed them in the trash. I'd never get the smell out. I wanted to shower to get the stink out of my hair, brush the sour vomit taste out of my mouth, but the bathroom was all the way down the hall, and the idea of even walking down the hall alone terrified me.

So instead I swished some tepid water from a glass by my nightstand and spit it into my trash can and crawled into bed, bundled up as tight as I could in the blankets, wishing I still had my old teddy bear which was packed up in an attic at my mom's house three states away.

I hunkered down, blanket over my head, and tried to sleep. Instead, all I could see was Georgie's face the moment when her victory turned to horror, her hands reaching for me. The force with which she was pulled down, her head striking the side. There one moment, gone the next. *Carmen, help me.*

I let the worm god eat her and I puked up my dumpling.

꧁꧂

"YOU MUST BE CURIOUS, CARMEN, BE HONEST." I HEARD Georgie's voice in my ear, "You wouldn't be helping me if you weren't."

"I'm helping because I want to see your stupid face when nothing happens." I huffed and she laughed until she snorted. "And I can't wait to see *your* face when you see the book I found."

"Georgie come on, this isn't a game. You know Deena could lose her job, hell her scholarship, if you mess with those rare books."

"Carmen, what if it's true what they say?"

"That magic and monsters are real? C'mon get your head out

of the clouds. You have everything anyone could want. If that scary stuff is real, why would you want to mess with it?"

"*Because*, God Carmen, you have no sense of adventure. Because it's there! Because this can't be all there is. There has to be more."

"I like the world as it is, thank you."

"You are boring Carmen. I love you and you are my best friend, but you are boring. You will never get anywhere with that attitude."

My pillow was wet with tears. *Look where you got with your attitude.*

Did she die instantly? Did its viscous body melt her and burn her on contact? Hell, it dissolved the concrete, so it must have, right? When she was pulled into its mouth did it chew on her? Or did she just travel down its length being slowly dissolved into soup? Was that even a mouth? Was she already worm poop smeared along some horrible tunnel deep below the ground further than anyone has ever gone before?

The questions keep coming and coming.

I doubted that ugly thing thought about much, probably dumb as a post, just a big stomach most likely. A big hungry monster, oblivious to time, humanity, the sun, living its days in the endless dark, surrounded by the perpetual press of earth, deaf and blind. Until some foolish girl summons it up to eat her in the basement of a fucking library.

Why that thing? was the question I would ask her if I could. She looked through hundreds of pages of that book, what was it about that particular one that caught her eye? I'd never asked her what she thought it would do, because I didn't believe. Maybe if I had, or even just humored her a little more, none of this would be like it is now, maybe I could have talked her out of it after all. I thought it was a lark, a goof, a stupid game. The only risk was Deena losing her job.

Outside my blanket cave, I could hear birds chirping and the wall opposite me grew brighter.

Morning.

With the light would come other people's questions. First of all, there'd be Dylan, the handsomer-than-Greg-sort-of-boyfriend. She had told him we were all going to study at the library till late.

There were her parents, doting and waspy, rich enough to hire private detectives when the police came up with nothing. There's no way I could lie effectively to them. I knew it. I've never been a good liar. But would they believe the truth? Subterranean monsters had eaten her. . . I made it just in time to the trash can and vomited again.

I remembered when the ambulance arrived, they put Teri on a breathing apparatus that made her look like a scuba diver, and wrapped her in a blanket that looked like tinfoil. They strapped her onto a gurney and lifted it, her skin was bluish and her eyes were closed as they passed me.

An EMT leaned over me, shining a light in my eyes. "You are a hero young lady, a real hero."

I don't believe in fate, or karmic balance, or any of that, but I couldn't help but wonder, as I looked at Georgie's empty bed, if I had used up my one chance to save a friend that snowy day in New Jersey.

Maybe Teri was fated to live, and maybe Georgie was fated to die.

Maybe I was fated to bear witness, watching the thing from beneath emerge and devour this friend, and know that they were down there. Always down there, waiting.

Big stomachs and big mouths.

TWO MONTHS LATER I SAT ON A BENCH, WATCHING A BUNCH OF fools playing ultimate frisbee. It was impossible not to feel a little thrill of fear watching their bare feet in the grass, tromping on the ground. . . daring whatever was down there to come up.

Nothing came of the police investigation, or the college's inquest. They asked questions, we answered, and everyone moved on. Georgie's sad eyed parents hugged me as they packed up her things. Greg found a girlfriend and stopped calling, and then Deena transferred far away. Georgie was just gone. It felt like a waste to me, she had been so vivacious, so inspiring, but still she could be snuffed out like a candle flame, forgotten with the passage of time. I was alone. Sitting in the sunny quad, happy idiots all around me. Sky overhead, the ground and its memories beneath. *Georgie* buried beneath.

And me? I was left to know things ordinary people just aren't meant to know.

❧ 18 ❧
THE NO PLACES

Beth never knew exactly why she was chosen that night.
Perhaps, being alone, fresh off a bad breakup, left her vulnerable to the universe. *Receptive*. Perhaps something in her was calling out, yearning for connection. Maybe her loneliness was a beacon, attracting anything that was listening.

She had planned to be with Eric forever, and they made it five years. Long enough to make plans, to have sleep positions. The big spoon, the little spoon. Long enough to know each other's quirks: cabbage made her comically gassy and he always cried when someone died of cancer in a movie. She knew that was in part because his father had died of cancer.

Five years was long enough for cancers to infect their relationship as well. Like *Sharon* from work. Sharon the perky coworker, who listened and was easy to talk to. Sharon, who shared myriad inside jokes with Eric and casually texted at all hours to "check in" and "see how things are."

It annoyed Beth how utterly common the whole thing was. As unremarkable a life-cycle as a couple could have from beginning to end. Even the woman he chose to have the affair with was absolutely forgettable and ordinary. Beth could barely get up the energy to hate her.

Instead she packed up what remained of their meticulously divided life (blender for her, sandwich grill to him, cat to him, energy bill in collection to her) and took her beige, banged up Toyota on the road heading for points further east.

The second day into the drive and she was already bored. The highways stretched and blurred and blended, one state resembling the next, but at the same time not. It reminded her of dreams in that way. *It was you, but it wasn't you. . .* She puttered along, her backside asleep, tired of singing loudly along to her MP3 soundtrack of loss and vindication. Yawning despite her audio book, a gripping thriller of love and betrayal that replaced the music, finally she decided to stop. She needed to wake up, stretch her legs and get a bite.

Outside the truck stop, the sky was clear and filled with stars. The only sound from the occasional car rumbling along the nearly empty highway. Beth stared up into the night and took in its vastness and in turn her smallness, breathing in the crisp air, and breathing out the kink in her neck. She ignored the hole in her gut where surety used to live.

"Are you, all right?" a voice said at her side, startlingly close for comfort. She stepped back, her hip hitting her closed car door as she turned.

It was a withered old man, or possibly woman, with a chin full of bristly whiskers, a huge mop of tangled white hair and wet feverish eyes. The old crone was barely four and a half feet tall, and was so bent she was reminded of a scrabbly tree that grew clinging to a mountain ledge. They had to look up at her, neck cocked at an odd angle, like a bird.

"Are you, all right?" the crone repeated the question, almost annoyed.

"Me? Oh yes, I was just stretching and getting some fresh air." Beth couldn't help but stare, this odd creature was mere feet from her, but she hadn't heard them draw near. They were wrapped in layers of stained cloth, but she could discern no odor.

The crone continued, "It's beautiful out here isn't it? You

wouldn't think a lonely truck stop could be a wonder of the world, possibly one of the most beautiful places in the world and then...well, here you are and you know it to be true."

"I don't know about it being the most beautiful place in the world. But, it is a pretty night. Well, I should be on my way into the store now. . ." Beth looked around, her car was the only one in the parking lot. Outside the neon glow of the store and gas pumps, there was nothing but darkness, copses of black trees, and open fields that stretched on and on. She wasn't entirely sure where this person had come from.

"I suppose you could jump back in your car, drive on and on," the crone said, smacking its lips in a way that made Beth think there weren't teeth inside. "Or you could take advantage of being someplace so beautiful, with me."

"Umm, not sure what you are looking for sir. . . ma'am. . .but. . ." Beth felt a surge of panic looking at this stooped old person. They must be homeless.

"No funny business. Just for company. I have this bottle of wine and just wanted to sit on that picnic table there and take in the stars and the sky and the endlessness of it all." Beth looked to where the gnarled finger was pointing, a sagging old picnic table, not too far away. "And I can think of no one better to share it with than a fellow traveler. One made small and awestruck by the night and its great size, just like me."

"I don't think so, I have a long way to drive."

The crone raised an eyebrow, "You and I both know you have no place to be. I saw the way you stared up at that sky and just breathed, absorbing it all, really savoring it. I saw you, what you really are."

The whole situation was strange and a bit unnerving, and yet, hadn't Beth just been lamenting how dull and ordinary her whole life was? Sitting with this strange old crone, sipping wine, and contemplating the universe was something utterly outside her norm. The old thing was tiny and frail, what could it possibly do to her?

"What's the harm? I'm old and lonely, and you have nothing but a long night of driving ahead of you. Indulge me, I insist."

Five minutes later the odd pair was settled onto the picnic table, its surface scarred with hundreds of initials. Beth ran her hands over them and could almost picture the scores of faces that had sat at this table, finishing a soda and plastic wrapped sandwich, stomping out a butt, spitting, and then carving their name as a kind of toll for the road-trip gods. The gods of motion, of here-to-there, the gods of the journey. She wanted to put her own initials into it before she left.

The wine was surprisingly good. Beth allowed the crone to pour some into an empty water bottle she found in her backseat. Sharing the bottle with the toothless old creature, mouth to mouth, was just too much. So, the two sat, taking in the large clear sky, the bright moon, and the mild weather. Beth caught herself sighing and hated to admit how relaxed she was. And maybe a little buzzed.

"It's the *no places* where the real wonder lives, did you know that?" the crone said after a long period of quiet.

"I didn't, no," Beth replied and sipped her wine, not sure what nonsense the old creature spouted, but enjoying herself.

"Everyone is always looking for the big moments, the big scares, the big joys, but they are wrong. It is here, the in-between spaces, it's the movement at the corner of the eyes. The moments that can be overlooked. That's where magic and wonder live. Most people are blind to those secret moments and the magic that lives in them."

Beth wondered if this person was actually crazy, or senile. Either way, she didn't feel unsafe, so she allowed the crone's musings to wash over her, like white noise. When they went silent for a few beats, Beth turned.

"Where did you come from?" Beth asked, her voice a little slurred. She knew she shouldn't drink anymore if she wanted to drive, but the wine was so good, and it soothed her parched throat and warmed her limbs.

The crone shrugged and gestured broadly with a small hand. "I come from here, there, everywhere. Does it matter? Do you really care? Where do *you* come from?"

Beth snorted, "Nowhere special, some town, some parents."

"Exactly. That's everyone's story at the end, or some variation of it. Can I show you something amazing?"

Beth was surprised by the enthusiasm in the crone's voice, and, for the first time since sitting down, felt wary.

The crone hurried on, "It's not far, just over that hill there, see those two tall trees crossed like an X? Right there, it marks the spot, X that is."

Although Beth's body and mind seemed in agreement that she would not go any further with this person, she rose and began to follow. She felt like there was a lasso about her waist. *This has gone too far.* Yet she continued on. The old crone was slow and careful. They made their way through hip high grass with unsure footing beneath. Night creatures chirped, then went silent until they passed, hidden from sight.

There was a slight wind and it caused the grasses to swish and sway, sounding like breath. As if they walked upon a sleeping giant, like they were little fleas on the back of a dog.

The sky was purple and soft like velvet, each star blinking and twinkling. A thick slice of yellow-white moon glowed high above, watchful.

The gas station was long gone now. How had they walked so very far? Beth looked behind and could no longer see the parking lot, or the highway, or even recall which direction they had come from. Not wanting to get even more lost, she followed the crone closely through the dark, seemingly endless field. They were barely taller than the grasses they swam through.

Finally, they reached a clearing. Standing beneath the tall spindly pines that leaned into one another making an X, just as the crone had said. The ground beneath was spongy and mossy, quite a relief after all the bushwhacking. Between the two trees was a stone that glowed pale in the darkness, flecks of mica sparked in the scant moonlight.

"Here we are," the crone said with a smile.

"Where is here?" Beth said, her voice small, almost reverent. Something about the tall trees, and the stone, which looked like an altar up close, made her feel like she was in church.

The crone reached into the folds of its clothes and pulled out a small white kitten. She patted the mewling thing and held it snug. Its other hand held a gleaming silver knife.

"*What are you doing?*" Beth squealed. She shouldn't have followed, she shouldn't have drunk that strange wine. Why had she done any of it?

"Lay down on the stone Beth. I want you to stare up at the stars and think about all that we discussed tonight. The places in between, the moments in between. The smallness. The finiteness. When you close your eyes, I will cut your throat." Beth wanted to run, but her feet, her whole body was still as a statue. The crone seemed taller, straighter in the darkness. "Then you will be both more and less. A quiet thing, up in the sky with all those stars. Isn't that what you want? A change? To be something more than ordinary?" Its eyes shone, inhumanly, in the faint light.

"No, no." Beth's voice was little more than a whisper.

"Tell me then, what is the point of your life? Better to give it up to me, for something useful, than live fruitlessly. I could use your time, your spirit. Better to give it to me than waste it."

"I'm not wasting it. I'm just in transition," Beth said.

The crone looked her up and down, assessing. "Do you want to survive this night?" She nodded, "You do?" They thrust the kitten at her. "Then make this creature your avatar. Free your spirit and stay here on this plane."

"You're crazy, all of this is crazy. I am so out of here." But even as she struggled, her feet stayed planted to the ground. She was twice the size of the old crone and certainly could run faster or fight away the knife. She could free the kitten, get the knife, escape. She could. . .

"You've come too far Beth. You can't go back, you can't go home, we're in this together. Now choose." The crone's face had changed subtly, the lines were smoothed out and its skin held a dewy luminescence. Their shiny eyes nearly glowed.

Beth imagined herself lying on the stone, staring up and letting go of it all. Free of the weight, floating like a feather on the breeze, forever. It was attractive. But for all the grayness her life had been, there was goodness too: being a little spoon and feeling the press of another body breathing and sleeping beside her, filling her mouth with a decadent dessert, laughing until tears streamed. The small things that mean so much and are so easily forgotten. A touch, a smell, a taste. The spaces in-between where the magic lived. Just as the crone had said.

She suddenly understood and reached out. "Give it to me."

The crone smiled and handed the shaking, mewling thing to her. The kitten was snow white, thin and bony, with a rattling wheeze. It was a sickly thing, and she tried to focus on that as she set it on the stone. The crone handed over the knife, warm and greasy from its grip. "It's dying, can't be helped. Better it dies in service to something greater and larger, than to waste away cold and alone, unknown by anyone."

"To the small things. To being more than all this," the crone whispered. Beth nodded and in one move stabbed the pitiful creature in the heart, or where she hoped the heart would be. The kitten cried out, once, and stiffened, and then went limp as the life and the hot blood fled its little body. Beth's hands were coated and trembling when she dropped the little deflated thing. She stared at its white fur, at the steam that rose from the blood staining it.

"*To the small things, to being more*. . ." the crone repeated, over and over. Beth joined in and whispered along, all the while staring at the kitten's body. The metallic scent of blood was thick in her nose. The tall trees swayed overhead on the breeze, the grasses all around whispering.

After a long time, she knelt and wiped her hands on the ground. They shook, her whole body shook. Still, she couldn't deny that she felt powerful and alive, she felt a lightness that was indescribable. Each star seemed to shine just for her. Her spirit was barely contained inside her skin, it threatened to explode out of her and just fly away. She was too large for her human shell, she'd become more.

Beth squeezed her eyes shut, and could still see the sky stretched out above her, burned into her memory. She could feel the sensation of alive/not alive in her own hands, by her own hands. She lay down on the moss and took it all in, breathing and listening to her heart, and to the night. She felt the moss, and smelled the rich earth, she sensed the burrowing things below the surface. She was both floating in the sky and sinking into the earth.

Time passed.

When she sat up it was near dawn and a band of orange could be seen on the eastern horizon. She was damp with dew.

The crone was gone.

She dug a shallow hole with her hands and placed the poor little kitten, now stiff, into it. Thanking it for its sacrifice.

She made her way back through the long grasses and was confused by how short the journey was, and how close the truck-stop and her own car were. She didn't understand how she'd become lost the night before.

She stopped at the picnic table and saw her initials, freshly carved, in the wood. They were the only ones. Weren't there hundreds and hundreds just hours before? She'd run her fingers over them.

Inside the truck stop, Beth started to wonder if the whole incident was just a strange dream. The blood crusted on her hands and the sour wine taste in her mouth told her otherwise.

The attendant gave her the once over as he handed her the bathroom key.

In the grimy yellow bathroom, she looked wan, her hair lank, but her eyes held a new fire, a wildness, a hunger, that hadn't been there before. As if lit from within.

She washed her face and scrubbed the blood and dirt from her nails. She bought herself a soda and a plastic wrapped sandwich.

Beth drove away, feeling more alive than she ever had been before.

ACKNOWLEDGMENTS

First, thanks must go to my husband, Philip Gelatt, for always believing in me. You are the best cheerleader, father, and husband one could ask for. Next, a big thanks to CLASH's Leza and Christoph for seeing something in this collection and for being amazing publishers. Thanks also to the whole CLASH team that worked on the book. I am honored and humbled to be a part of the CLASH family. The majority of tales in this collection are reprints so a big thank you goes out to all the original publishers who accepted the stories and got them out into the world. Writing is often a solitary road filled with bumps. There is something so wonderful about sending work out into the ether and getting a yes back in return. It's nice for these tales to live again. And finally, a thank you to the readers—it would be a lonely dance without you.

INDEX

ABOUT THE AUTHOR

Photo by Laurel Leaf Photography

Victoria Dalpe is an artist and writer based out of Providence, RI. Her dark short fiction has appeared in over thirty anthologies and her first novel, Parasite Life will be re-released in 2023 through Nightscape Press. She is a member of the HWA and the New England Horror Writers. Victoria also co-edited the Necronomicon 2019 Memento Book with Justin Steele.

WE PUT THE LIT IN LITERARY

CLASHBOOKS.COM

FOLLOW US

FB

TWITTER

IG

@clashbooks

EMAIL

clashmediabooks@gmail.com